ALSO BY MARK GREATHOUSE

The Frontier Chronicles

Perilous Trails: Jack's Adventure Begins

Wyoming Calls: Jack's Risky Quest

LONGHORNS NORTH: JACK'S GREAT TRAIL DRIVE

LONGHORNS NORTH: JACK'S GREAT TRAIL DRIVE

THE FRONTIER CHRONICLES

BOOK 3

MARK GREATHOUSE

WISE WOLF
BOOKS

WISE WOLF BOOKS
An Imprint of Wolfpack Publishing
wisewolfbooks.com
1707 E. Diana Street
Tampa, FL 33610

LONGHORNS NORTH: JACK'S GREAT TRAIL DRIVE. Text copyright
© 2024 Mark Greathouse

This book is a work of fiction. Any references to historical events, real
people or real places are used fictitiously. Other names, characters,
places and events are products of the author's imagination, and any
resemblance to actual events, places or persons, living or dead, is
entirely coincidental.

Paperback ISBN 978-1-957548-58-6
eBook ISBN 978-1-957548-57-9
LCCN 2024944725

Dedicated with love to my wife Carolyn, our two sons Mike and Matt, and the memory of my father John F. "Jack" Greathouse

Christ is my firm foundation (testify)
The Rock on which I stand.

CODY CARNES, "FIRM FOUNDATION"

THE CAST

Jack O'Toole – Seventeen-year-old son of Joseph and Kate O'Toole. He strives to carve a life from the Texas frontier on the easternmost reaches of the Comancheria.

Mukwooru (aka, Spirit Talker) – Seventeen-year-old son of a Penateka Comanche chief camped within the heart of the Comancheria. The warrior name bestowed upon teen Wild Horse in recognition of his apparent connection with Taa Narumi (the Comanche Great Father) whom they confused with God.

Blue Flower – Young sister to Spirit Talker and daughter to Buffalo Hump, she's married o Jack.

George Freeman – A Black cowboy driving cattle north; later an Army scout. He establishes a ranch on the North Platte River in Wyoming.

Running Waters – George Freeman's Pawnee wife.

Kate – Jack's twelve-year-old sister.

Buck – Jack's seven-year-old brother.

Mato (aka Bear) – An Oglala Lakota warrior.

Otaktay (aka Kills Many) – An Oglala Lakota war chief.

Isaac Fisher – An Amish farmer from Pennsylvania seeking new opportunity on the frontier.

Sarah Fisher – Isaac Fisher's wife and mother to baby son named for Jack.

Topsannah (aka, Prairie Flower) – Young Comanche girl captured and enslaved by Arapaho Tribe and living with George Freeman.

Hakan (aka Fire) – Comanche shaman or medicine man that visits Penateka Comanche village as a prophet.

Sam Collins – Owner of the Circle C Ranch located near Jack's spread.

Hank Johnson – Drover on Jack's cattle drive to Fort Laramie. He carries deep prejudice against Indians.

Juan Perez – Creative, hard-nosed Mexican cook on Jack's trail drive.

Shorty McBride – Drover on Jack's cattle drive who lives up to his nickname.

Preacher Leon Rollo – Itinerant preacher accompanying a wagon train that survived a Lakota attack.

John Kenny – Wagon train boss, leading a group of settlers westward on the Oregon Trail past Fort Laramie.

Lieutenant Cort Johnson – Army officer stationed at Fort Laramie.

Joseph Bissonette – Livestock trade working for the Indian agent Thomas Triss.

Bart Toliver – Ne'er-do-well traveler from a passing wagon train on the Oregon Trail.

HISTORICAL CHARACTERS

Buffalo Hump – War chief of the Penateka Comanche, the southernmost band of the Comanche people in the Comancheria. In the famous Council House Fight of 1840, he led roughly a thousand Comanche across Texas to the Gulf Coast where they ransacked Victoria and burned Linnville.

Captain Nathan Benton – Texas Ranger captain assigned to protect settlers from Indians in the Leona River region northwest of Fort Inge. (Benton eventually would serve as a lieutenant colonel in the Confederate Army, 36th Texas Cavalry.)

Makhpia-Luta (aka Red Cloud) – Chief of Oglala Lakota of the Sioux Nation.

Tasunke Witko (aka Crazy Horse) – Future chief of Oglala Lakota of the Sioux Nation. He is about 19 years old at the time of this story, but already gaining attention of tribal leaders. He will go on to lead the massacre of General Custer's troops at Little Big Horn (aka, Greasy Grass).

Tatanka Iyotake (aka Sitting Bull) – Chief and medicine man of Hunkpapa band of Lakota Sioux.

August Klappenbach – Early settler of Bandera, TX and owner of first general store and post office.

Thomas Twiss – Indian agent assigned to Fort Laramie region.

Major William Hoffman – Officer-in-Charge at Fort Laramie in 1857.

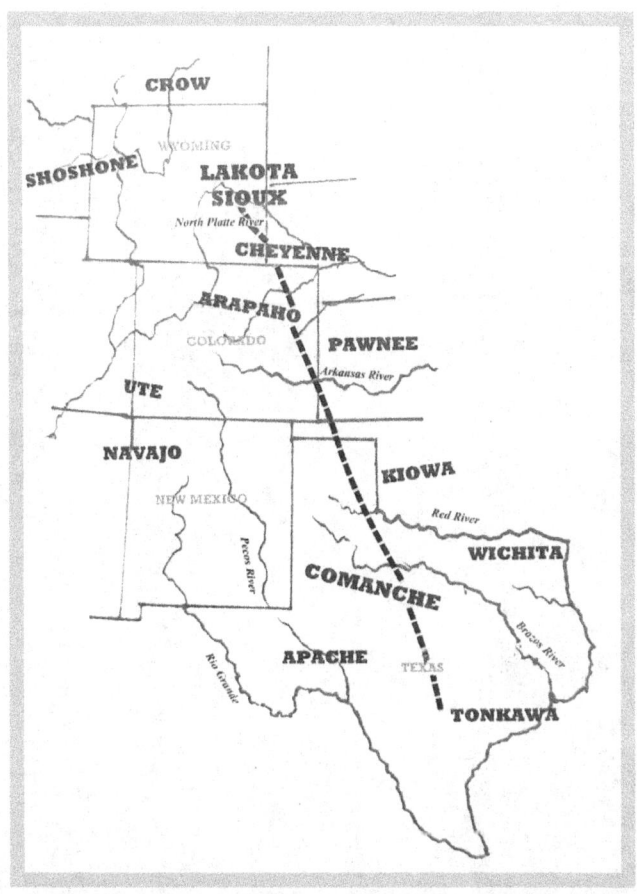

The trail Jack O'Toole and Spirit Talker use to drive cattle from Texas to Wyoming, meeting challenging landscapes and many tribes known to be hostile. The trail is to the west of what became known as the Western Trail. (Map by Mark Greathouse)

YOU ARE INVITED

Dear Reader,

If you've read *Perilous Trails* and *Wyoming Calls*, it's likely my story has fully grabbed you. This part of my tale occurs in 1857. You recall that back in '55, I had been thrown alone and vulnerable by events beyond my control onto the Comancheria, the most dangerous part of the frontier by a factor of 10x. I was now only seventeen years old. The Comancheria with its savage Comanche warriors, was a virtual no-man's-land for White settlers.

Longhorns North: Jack's Great Trail Drive is the third book of The Frontier Chronicles and continues my adventures, further testing my courage, faith, endurance, and pure grit. In this chronicle, we take a herd of five hundred longhorns from Bandera, Texas to Fort Laramie in Wyoming. It sure taught me a ton of life lessons. Do keep in mind that my story incorporates history not found in most school history books. This book relates my tale as driven by fate and guided by God.

I met up plenty with Indians, especially Comanche and Lakota Sioux, so you'll find me using some of their language throughout *Longhorns North*. I have provided a handy glossary of Comanche and Lakota words toward the back of this book.

I'm a devout Christian, but I tried to grasp the Comanche and Lakota religions to better understand them. The Indian religion was based upon what is referred to as animism, in which every common natural item from fish and animals to plants, trees, waterways, and mountains were believed to have souls or spirits. The spirits and traditions connected with them guided the Comanche and Lakota. Their passion for their spirits no doubt gave them their fearlessness as fed by the belief that they were protected in everything they did. Would they kill to defend their beliefs? Let's say that theirs was not a religion of love and forgiveness.

Could Indians like the Comanche or Lakota become Christians? I have intended for my story in *Longhorns North* to unfold at the intersection of faith and culture. Historically, it was not unlike Saint Patrick's conversion of the Irish to Christianity by folding many of their less-offensive heathen rites into the Catholic faith. The British derisively referred to the Irish as "Black Catholics." Would this work with the Indians? Well, it's part of the story I'm sharing with y'all.

As you follow my adventures, ask yourself whether you might be up to meeting the challenges I take on. Dangers? Privations? Hmmm. How might you have fared? Through it all, I first relied on the teachings from my family, then went on to learn from the raw and risky experiences I faced. I learned to trust in instincts forged from my biblical lessons.

To be straight here, I had no idea that my story was

going to fill multiple volumes until I began to write it all down. I invite you to follow my often perilous adventures on America's western frontier.

Kindest regards,
  John "Jack" O'Toole

LONGHORNS NORTH: JACK'S GREAT TRAIL DRIVE

PROLOGUE

TEXANS CONSIDERED hiders to be the dredges of society. Hiders rustled cattle, took their hides, and left the carcasses to rot. They profited handsomely from selling the hides, as they avoided the expense of maintaining range lands, feeding and caring for herds of beeves, driving the beasts to market, employing cowboys, fighting off rustlers, and all manner of efforts that went into raising cattle. Most often, but not exclusively, the hiders were Mexicans. The major risk for hiders was that if caught they'd be hung.

Me, my new Comanche wife Blue Flower, and Isaac's wife Sarah were returning by wagon to Rising Cross Ranch from a visit to Bandera, when we discovered hiders ahead of us on the trail. We hid off the trail among trees and grasses and nearly escaped detection. As fate would have it, one of the mules was bitten by a fly and brayed loudly. That got the attention of the hiders.

I readied my Sharps carbine, and Blue Flower grabbed the old Colt revolver from the wagon seat. I handed my own Colt to Sarah who managed to juggle the gun along with her baby. "Lord, give us strength. Protect us from evil," I murmured, earnestly praying that God's strong medicine, the *sunipu* I'd shown with the Comanche and Lakota, would prevail against the hiders. I was extremely fearful of what they might do to Blue Flower and Sarah.

The hiders doubled back upon hearing the mule, and their attention focused on the stand of live oak that partially hid us. The hiders had a veritable arsenal of revolvers and rifles at the ready, as they cautiously approached our hiding place. They laughingly jested among themselves and threw verbal taunts at me and the ladies. *"Hay, mujeres! Dónde estás!"* they taunted. *"Bellezas! Ven aqui!"* Tension filled the air. There was no question as to what the hiders had in mind for what they figured to be hapless victims, especially the ladies.

ONE
GOD'S PROVIDENCE!

I HAD LEARNED in my brief time on earth that meeting the challenges of frontier threats quickly and effectively before giving an enemy second thoughts was critically important. I inserted a cartridge and pulled back the hammer of my Sharps carbine. "Ladies, don't miss!" I pleaded as I aimed at the lead hider just fifty feet away and heading straight at me. I squeezed the trigger. The .50 caliber slug plowed through the center of the Mexican's chest while throwing him back a good ten feet into the waiting arms of a cactus. The roar in that confined space was deafening. There was no recoil, as the Sharps weight fully absorbed the bullet's exit from its muzzle. I quickly slipped another cartridge into the breech, aimed at a second hider, and fired but missed.

Blue Flower and Sarah opened fire. Hardly aiming at all, they nevertheless figured to give the hiders reason to question the wisdom of their attack.

The remaining four hiders saw their compadre fall. *"Madre de Dios!"* shouted one. Mother of God, indeed!

Second thoughts instantly ran through their heads. This was far more than they had bargained for.

A second hider fell back, blood flowing from his arm thanks to one of the ladies' poorly aimed but effective shots.

Shots began to ring out from the hiders' right flank. This was getting far too hot for their tastes. It was as though they faced a veritable hail of lead. They were outlaws by any measure, but they were realizing that staying alive trumped the lure of the young women fortified behind the live oaks. Better to be a live coward. They broke and ran to their horses and the wagon full of hides.

Charging at full gallop from the tall grasses and firing their guns came Sam Collins and the cowboy who'd stuck with him following the earlier skirmish with a Comanche hunting party that I had diffused.

I leaped onto Big Red and followed the cowboys in pursuit of the remaining hiders.

Didn't take long.

The hiders tossed aside their guns and stood beside their wagon with arms raised. There was no fight left in them. They looked like the sorriest lot of ne'er-do-wells that could be conjured.

I caught up with Collins as he and his cowhand kept their guns trained on the four hiders.

Two of the four were wounded and whining and groaning in their pain.

"Much obliged to you showing up, Sam," I offered while striving to catch my breath.

"Heard the gunfire, an' had a sense y'all might be in trouble." Collins smiled. "From what I saw of you an' that there Sharps, you likely would've whupped'em yerselves."

"Shall we save these folks for Captain Benton?"

"We could save the Texas Rangers some trouble," said Collins with a wink.

One of the hiders apparently understood enough English to realize what was being suggested. *"Madre de Dios! Por favor!"* he pleaded for his life.

"Bunch of *cobardes*, snivelin' cowards all," observed Collins.

In the silence that followed the attack and not hearing any further gunfire from the direction I rode off to, Blue Flower boldly climbed back up onto the wagon seat and drove the rig back onto the trail. They diverted their eyes as they passed the dead hider embraced by the cactus. Upon reaching the trail, they saw us men holding the hiders at bay. "Jack!" she called.

In the excitement and rush of joining Collins in pursuit of the hiders, I had momentarily forgotten my primary responsibility to protect Blue Flower and Sarah. The cries of Sarah's baby punctuated the vulnerability of the scene.

"Let's tie these men behind their horses and bring them and their prized hides up to Rising Cross. I reckon it's not so far as the Circle C," I suggested. "We can hold the hiders in a stall in our barn to await Benton."

"What about them hides?" asked Collins.

The hiders' wagon held a load of roughly fifty hides. It was tempting to divvy up the spoils from having captured the lawbreakers—a reward of sorts. "I expect Benton might want some evidence," I said with a wry smile. "But he won't need all of them. There's talk of building a schoolhouse in Bandera. Maybe we could sell the hides and donate the proceeds to the school."

Collins thought seriously on that. He sighed. "Guess I agree. I like yer style, Jack."

Blue Flower and Sarah drove closer with the wagon.

I caught the pained expressions on two of the hiders who suffered from nasty but not life-threatening gunshot wounds. "Sarah, please take some of that liniment we got from Klappenbach and those cotton strips and see whether you can stop these prisoners' bleeding. I'd like to keep them alive for Captain Benton."

"Can they walk to Rising Cross?" asked Sarah, concerned that blood loss was weakening them.

I sighed. "Okay, we'll tie the wounded into their saddles."

Blue Flower and Sarah climbed down from the wagon and did their best to treat the wounded hiders. I could feel Blue Flower's eyes following me admiringly, as I tied up the two hiders that weren't wounded.

Upon finishing tying up the two, I paused and returned her gaze.

There was pride in Blue Flower's eyes; pride that she had married a true warrior, a protector of women and children. Yet a hint of perplexity crept in at my showing mercy to the hiders and coming up with a worthy disposition of the hides. I sensed that she wondered what my God was all about. The concept of mercy to breakers of the law was not common to Comanche thinking.

I eased over to her and wrapped my arms around her. She seemed to melt with relief, as I felt the tension of the moment escape. This was the vulnerable side of Blue Flower that I especially loved.

"You brave, Jack," she whispered before pushing away. She gave me that look and smile of hers that could have melted steel.

As I tied the two wounded hiders to their saddles and secured the ropes on the two that would walk on tethers behind them, Collins and his cowhand kept their guns aimed on them to ensure that they tried nothing stupid.

With the prisoners secured, I could finally take a deep breath of relief. "Let's get home," I said, turning to Blue Flower.

She gave the mules their head, and they surged forward. The hider prisoners followed with the wagon of hides, Collins, and his cowhand pulling up the rear.

———

AS FATE or God's will would have it, we were drawing right close to Rising Cross when Captain Benton and his Texas Ranger company came into view. I felt relieved that we likely wouldn't have to house and keep our prisoners. I reined in Big Red and pointed to Benton off in the distance.

Collins nodded and smiled. I expect he was similarly pleased with the prospect of having the hider problem behind us.

Benton and our entourage arrived at my cabin at just about the same time.

"What you got there, Jack O'Toole?" he exclaimed.

I figured it was sort of obvious.

Benton off-handedly waved for Collins to come in. "You with this bunch, Sam?"

While Collins rode up from the rear, Isaac and Buck emerged from the barn to greet the sudden gathering. "Buck, see to Big Red while we chat with Captain Benton." I reckoned it might be best for his young ears to be spared any difficult conversation with the Texas Rangers.

"Mr. O'Toole here put a hurtin' on these hiders back a few miles, Captain," explained Collins. "There were five, but Jack's Sharps dispatched one. Bert here and me, we jus' help a bit. We figured to save these scoundrels fer yuh, Captain. I'd as soon as hung'em back yonder."

Benton shook his head. His gaze went from Collins to Jack to the ladies. "I'll be pleased to relieve you of the prisoners. Much as I like Sam's solution, we'll take them in to stand trial." With that, he turned to Jack. "You and the ladies okay, Jack?"

"Appreciate your concern, Captain. Yes, God was looking out for us," I responded. "Er…Captain?"

"Yes."

"We were of a mind to sell the hides and donate the money to Bandera for a school." I could see Benton doing some sort of financial calculation in his head, as he examined the stack of hides in the wagon.

Benton looked over at Collins.

Collins nodded.

"Tell you what, Jack. Donating for a school is downright worthy. We'll take the hider wagon and a branded hide for evidence. You and Sam here can handle the rest." He urged a couple of his Texas Rangers forward to secure the prisoners with manacles. "How 'bout you and Sam keep the dead hider's cayuse. We'll send the other horses back after we deposit the prisoners in Austin. Consider it a reward."

"Care for some coffee, Captain Benton," offered Sarah in a well-intended show of hospitality and gratitude.

Benton smiled. "Thanks kindly, ma'am. I expect y'all need to settle and rest, so we'll be on our way." He turned to me. "What happened to that fine Comanche escort, Jack?"

I couldn't help displaying a mischievous smile. I knew they'd headed home, and it was obvious that Benton hadn't seen them. "I'm sure they were watching us all, Captain."

Benton gave me a puzzled look as though trying to decide whether I was serious. "Wouldn't surprise me none, Jack." He rode over to me and leaned down.

This was odd.

"Just a heads-up, Jack, for your Indian friends," he confided. "Austin folks are looking to bring on more Texas Rangers to put an end to Comanche hostilities. Could get right nasty."

I nodded. "Thanks, Captain." Maybe Benton wasn't a total Indian hater after all.

Benton pulled back and scanned the yard to be satisfied that the prisoners and evidence were secured. He thanked us, gave a nod to Blue Flower and Sarah, and headed his Texas Ranger company eastward toward Austin.

By this time, Kate emerged from the cabin and greeted us with an understandably quizzical expression. Buck walked over as I dismounted. He shrugged at all the goings-on, took Big Red's reins, and led the big stallion off to the barn.

That left the rest of us to take a deep breath and try to grasp all that had happened in the past couple of hours.

"What happened?" asked Kate.

"Long story," I responded. "Tell you in a bit."

———

BUCK SOON STROLLED out from the barn. "Big Red's in the corral, Jack," he advised proudly.

"Thanks Buck. Could you help your sister and Mrs. Fisher pull together some grub while we unload the wagon? Mr. Collins and Bert here will join us."

"Where were those mean looking men from, Jack?" asked Buck. He didn't miss much.

"Tell you at dinner," I said with a smile. "You go help the ladies. They're tired from our travels and need your help."

It occurred to me that I hadn't actually invited Collins to join us. "Er, Sam. You and Bert up for some grub?" I nearly found myself lapsing into asking in the Comanche tongue.

Collins slid from his saddle, hitched his horse, and loosened the cinch. "Wondered if yuh'd ever ask," he said with a chuckle as he pushed his weather-beaten hat back on his forehead. "We can talk 'bout that cattle drive o'er a home-cooked meal." With that, he and Bert began to help unload our wagon.

We got to know Collins better over a scrumptious meal and began to cement both a friendship and business arrangement. Importantly, he was up for contributing up to fifty head to the cattle drive and would spare one of his wranglers to join us.

Good humor prevailed as highlighted when Collins discovered that we had named our prize longhorn bull Atlas. The rancher thought it was appropriate, though it was likely based on what our beloved longhorn was tasked to do with the cows. Kate and Sarah blushed, Blue Flower laughed, and Buck hadn't a clue as to what we were talking about.

Naturally, we shared our encounters on the return from Bandera, though we cut out some of it to spare young Buck's ears. No point in him having nightmares. It was bad enough that he occasionally dreamed of the horrors of the Comanche attack on our home so many months back and his and Kate's captivity. I was ever grateful that the Lord saw fit to helping me free them and that my friendship with Spirit Talker and marriage to Blue Flower helped heal any festering wounds.

––––––

IT HAD BEGUN to sink into my thick skull that here we were reckoning on gathering a herd and driving them to Wyoming, and I was what might be generously described as a tenderfoot so far as my cowboy skills. Oh, I had rounded up a passel of horses and knew how to ride, but I was unschooled so far as the skills of rounding up and driving cattle. I didn't know one saddle from another, didn't own a pair of chaps, didn't know a rawhide reata from a grass rope, was an abject failure at lassoing anything more than ten feet away, and never wore spurs because they didn't fit over my moccasin boots. What I did have was a willingness—nay, a full-bore enthusiasm —to learn the art of handling cattle. Collins hinted that I had what he called the "something." It was apparently a God-given gift that's born in a person rather than acquired. As Collins put it, a cowboy with the "something" could work magic with livestock even though he might be a mediocre roper and less-than-expert horseman. In a way, I expect he was right. I felt as though I had a sense of the inner workings of a the brain of a bull or cow—even a horse. I surely had such a gift as concerned humans, too. Maybe, this was part of the strong *sunipu* that Spirit Talker attributed to me.

Well, I set to work building on the "something" that Collins had identified in me. I would ride out to the pasture near and select a longhorn for my target, then wore the poor beast ragged practicing lassoing from the cast to the catch to loop closing. I even hogtied a long-horn or two, being ever watchful of those dangerous horns that could reach eight feet or more in tip-to-tip span. The older beeves with the wide horn spreads were called mossy horns. Thanks to a Mexican *vaquero* that Collins sent over to educate me, I even learned how to tail an errant longhorn. Tailing is handy but very dangerous exercise used when a longhorn goes a tad crazy and charges off on its own to escape the herd and any cowboys. It's a trick aimed at bringing an ornery dogie to heel by riding up behind the escaping critter, grabbing the tip of its tail, wrapping it around the saddle horn, and bringing your horse to a sudden halt. The reluctant longhorn is brought to a halt with a resounding thump to its belly. While the critter is momentarily stunned, the effect is to calm him down sufficiently enough to easily guide him back to the herd. The alternative to tailing was to throw a rope so as to catch a leg or two and trip up the longhorn.

Thanks to the open range, wild beeves often intermingled with broken or domesticated beeves. I learned about rounding up, cutting calves from cows, and branding. It was as much a livestock management process as a social event. Shouts of cowpokes, sharp crack of quirts on leather chaps, braying of beeves, tossing of lassos, and smells of branding iron fires were part and parcel to the roundup event. Bulls were turned into steers via castration, as steer meat was better for human palates. We were ever vigilant to bring in slick-ears, the nickname given unbranded beeves, and mavericks. The laws were rather straightforward as concerned brands and branding and depended on the honesty of the cowboys. Brands were registered locally with a county clerk, along with marriage licenses, oaths of office, sales of slaves, wills, land titles, and more. Naturally, not all cowboys were honest and would even forge an existing brand by using what was called a running iron.

Saddles were another part of my ranching education. I found myself preferring what was called a Texas saddle, an evolution from saddles popularized in Mexico. Collins and his Mexican *vaquero* assured me that the Texas-style saddle was superior for our needs. My saddle was nothing fancy. I preferred a simple leather-covered steel stirrup, a higher cantle to tie necessaries to, and a slightly wider than normal saddle horn.

I was tempted to acquire a pair of sheepskin chaps, as they were effective protection in thorny brush, but I wound up with heavy leather chaps for their all-around utility. I did use a pair of pointed-toe boots for cattle work, as I needed to wear spurs to get optimum performance from Big Red or any bronc I rode. I generally went for smaller rowels at the ends of my spurs, though there was one cayuse that seemed to only respond to the larger spiked rowels popularized by the vaqueros.

I always had a bandanna or two with me. The bandanna was a cowboy essential, as it served as a utility tool. It could be waved as a signal, tied off as a bag, wet to cool a sweaty brow, a shield from trail dust, a bandage, a washcloth or towel, a sling, a napkin, a head covering, and much more as devised by fertile minds. Topping me off was a broad-brimmed, well-stained hat that managed to keep the sun and rain off my nose, ears, and neck most of the time. It could also serve as a tool to move livestock along.

I reckon this all contributed to my turning what Collins called my "something" into actual cowboy skills. As the days drew ever closer to gather for the trail drive to Fort Laramie and the North Platte country, the skills I was developing served to boost my confidence. I felt as though God was ever-preparing me for delivering on the potential of His creation.

Blessedly and when all my cowboy education was nearing a level of reasonable capability, I found an ornery tough old longhorn bull that had the makings of a herd leader. I felt relieved that Atlas could remain at Rising Cross to help grow our herd. I smiled as I thought on how Atlas likely relished the idea of delivering his bullish charms to the cows. I never saw a cow complain.

———

I WOULD RETURN each evening from my chores across the breadth of the Rising Cross Ranch to Blue Flower's welcoming arms punctuated with a delicious dinner and followed by loving reflections under starry skies before turning in. Blue Flower was every bit the capable and supportive wife. Kate and Buck loved her like a mother, and my Comanche wife seemed to accept the role with a certain tenderness. It reminded me that the Comanche culture was matriarchal in nature. However, an Indian woman in a White man's culture had its challenges, as the frontier was rife with prejudices. Blue Flower could be as strong as she was tender.

Still, there was little so precious as lying under the stars with Blue Flower on nights with a quiet only broken by coyote howls and owl hoots. Shucks, sometimes it was so quiet that you could just about hear the stars twinkling. All was good.

TWO
SURPRISES!

SEPTEMBER GAVE WAY TO OCTOBER, and November chills soon began to sweep across the rolling hills of Rising Cross Ranch.

There was no shortage of tasks that needed doing. An operating ranch was a huge undertaking. Livestock had to be cared for, barn stalls mucked, fences mended, buildings repaired, and family and hands fed. Likely the most distasteful for me was mucking stalls. We took turns shoveling out horse and mule droppings. The upside was that the horses and mules showed their appreciation with nickers and nuzzlings. Oh, and they occasionally kicked; a habit we quickly learned to look out for. As temperatures dropped, we took extra care to be sure animals were fed and at times had to break up ice covering the watering holes. By now, we had also managed to burn our distinctive Rising Cross brand into the haunches of our cattle and horses. They were none too happy about it, but it was a necessity out here on the Texas frontier and would be even more important for next year's trail drive.

When I wasn't spending time with Blue Flower, I spent what little solitude I had with my old friend Big Red. He was quite a hunk of horseflesh. Whether currying him or simply offering treats, our best times were spent simply riding around Rising Cross Ranch. As if the journey to the North Platte had not been enough to cement the relationship between horse and rider, these personal interludes sealed our bond.

I was out in the barn one morning when Blue Flower slipped up behind me. She placed her hand over top of the one I was currying Big Red with. "Jack home today?" she cooed hopefully.

Turning gently to her, I kissed her forehead. Big Red whinnied softly, as I stopped my soothing motion across his neck. "Yes...I'm home today," I responded. It struck me that I'd been spending necessary but too much time visiting neighboring ranches to promote my trail drive. Many entailed a night or two away from Blue Flower's loving arms. My business forays would pale in comparison to the months I'd be away on the drive itself, but we hadn't discussed that eventuality yet. "You up for a ride?" I knew she loved to join me riding across the vast expanse of prairie and rolling hills—perhaps 50,000 acres —that now comprised Rising Cross Ranch. In my travels among ranches around the southern Comancheria, I happened upon a beautiful appaloosa mare. One look, and I had to have her. It was so easy to envision Blue Flower astride her.

She looked over her shoulder at Sky Dancer prancing hopefully in her stall. "Ride good. Have what you call picnic?" she urged.

The idea of relaxing with my beautiful wife under a cypress near my old fishing spot had an irresistible allure. "I'll saddle the horses. You fill a basket for us," I said with a broad smile.

Blue Flower pulled away and headed for the cabin to put together a basket of good eats.

I found myself distracted from Big Red as I watched her glide away gracefully and disappear into our home. I'd observed that there seemed to be a natural graceful way that Indian women walked; something about their stride, their very presence or oneness with their surroundings. Big Red nickered and nudged me back to the here and now.

I led Big Red and Sky Dancer to the hitching post in front of the cabin. Blue Flower was taking a tad longer than I'd expected. She must be putting together quite a feast. Far be it from me to think that she might be using that mirror in our bedroom to do what women do for their men. I stroked Big Red. He was anxious to feel the prairie air in his lungs and the wind course through his mane and tail.

"Hang loose, big fella," I said soothingly.

He fidgeted anyway.

My loving sister Kate peeked from the doorway, stifled a giggle, and stepped back. It was unlike her.

I was intrigued. What on earth was going on?

Blue Flower emerged soon enough with picnic basket in hand. She had her hair fixed in two long braids and wore a blue dress barely suitable for riding but too fetchingly beautiful for me to protest.

I was taken aback; just about breathless. Did I deserve such a woman? God hadn't spared Himself with creating this exquisitely lovely vision that was Blue Flower. Did I mention that she had a touch of gold to her skin, making it a shade or so lighter than most Indians? Ah, so beautiful!

She didn't fail to catch my facial expression as she approached Sky Dancer. Handing the basket to me, she easily climbed into the saddle. "Are you coming?" She laughed with dancing eyes.

———

WE RODE out a couple of miles and were soon at what had been my favorite fishing spot. I dismounted and helped Blue Flower down from Sky Dancer.

I spread a blanket under a spreading cypress beside the Guadalupe River and watched lovingly as Blue Flower sat gracefully and opened the picnic basket. She wore an especially demure smile that caught me a bit off guard. It was as though she was holding some mystery. I figured that she must have heard from Spirit Talker.

I took a healthy bite from a jam-laden slice of bread. "Have you heard from your brother?" I said between chews.

She looked at me quizzically, as though I was from some other planet. "You do not know?"

I swallowed hard. "Er...know what?"

Blue Flower shook her head.

"Is there a secret?"

She smiled and took my hand as I was about to take another bite of bread. Her eyes probed mine. "Jack...Jack, we have child."

The bread fell. My jaw dropped.

"Jack happy?" she asked disconcertedly.

My, but I was deliriously happy. I stood and swept her up into my arms. "Happy? Oh yes, I am very happy." I stood there embracing Blue Flower for what seemed like forever. "How do you know?" I finally blurted.

She shook her head. "Women know, Jack." She

paused as though trying to get me to understand. "No bleed," she finally offered with a sigh that said women know these things.

"Do Sarah and Kate know?"

She laughed. "Sarah know...not Kate."

"When will the baby come?" I asked, suddenly realizing that I had a trail drive ahead.

"Seven moons," she responded tentatively.

I sure as shootin' didn't want to miss the blessed event. We'd be pushing to deliver beeves to Wyoming and aimed to be back by the end of July. My emotions instantly became mush. I hadn't quite expected God to bless me with a family quite so soon. Could I postpone the trail drive? Not likely at this stage.

Blue Flower had a habit of reading my mind. "Warriors hunt, wives have babies," she said, seeking to reassure me. Her words were so true. It is our divine destiny, part of our purpose as God's creation.

I gazed into her love-filled eyes and took her in my arms. Words simply could never fully express our joy. We kissed as the sparkling life-giving waters of the Guadalupe River gently flowed past. God had blessed us.

LITTLE COULD I know that a similar scene was occurring many miles to the north.

Running Waters was awakened by a shard of sunlight shooting through the cabin window. She nudged George awake.

"Wha...what is it?" He shook off sleep cobwebs.

"Feel sick," she advised him.

"Something we ate?" he asked.

She sat up and shook out her long dark hair, then fell

back on the bed. Despite her slight nausea, she managed a smile. She took his hand and placed it on her still-flat belly. "Think we have child," she cooed with a mix of English and Pawnee.

George sat bolt upright, eyes wide. A broad smile spread across his face. He had an urge to run outside, beat his chest, and shout to the world, a booming roar that would have echoed clear across the mountains and shaken their very foundations. "Praise the Lord!" he announced, as he turned to his loving Pawnee wife. They embraced with the joy of the moment.

This was to be a story of conquering the frontier and building a family after all. From the overseer's whip in the fields of Carolina to driving Texas cattle to his very own ranch in the majestic Wyoming North Platte country, George found himself blessed. He pulled back from Running Waters. "Have you told Prairie Flower?"

She shook her head.

"We'll have to add a room to the cabin. We don't want her to feel left out."

Running Waters nodded agreement. This was her husband, always thinking of other folks' feelings. Then, she smiled. "Think Spirit Talker return soon," she suggested.

It hadn't occurred to George that there might be feelings between Prairie Flower and Spirit Talker. He scratched his chin as he pondered that eventuality. "It is all good," he said with finality and lit the room with his smile.

———

KATE GREETED our return from picnicking. Her smile

turned to a questioning stare as she sensed a change. "What happened?"

How do women know these things? What is it in their make-up that enables them to sense changes that men would be oblivious to. I dismounted from Big Red and tried to be nonchalant in helping Blue Flower down from Sky Dancer. I smiled as I handed the still-filled picnic basket to Kate.

She hefted it and offered an inquisitive smile. "Have I missed something?"

"You are going to be an aunt," I announced.

Kate's jaw dropped. She paused, then rushed over and embraced Blue Flower. "This is wonderful news. We are blessed!"

Sarah and Isaac moseyed up from their cabin. She could see from the expression on my face and Kate's joyful response that the proverbial cat was out of the bag. She whispered the good news in Isaac's ear, as they approached us.

"Congratulations, Jack," offered Isaac as he shook my hand. His knowing smile told me that I'd soon be experiencing the sort of life change that he and Sarah had when baby Jack was born.

"Just hope and pray I'm back from the drive before the baby is born," I said, expressing my concern.

About then, Buck appeared. He took the Big Red's and Sky Dancer's reins. "What's all the ruckus about?" he asked obliviously.

"You're going to be an uncle, Buck," said Kate.

"Uncle? What's an uncle?"

We all laughed.

"We'll explain later," I said. Please let Big Red loose after you curry him, and be sure to give him and Sky Dancer some treats."

Buck shrugged and led the horses off to the barn.

THREE
THE BIG GATHER

SPIRIT TALKER KNEELED near the trees. He'd taken to arising early to pray to this all-knowing, powerful God his friend Jack had brought him to believe in. As he opened his eyes and prepared to rise, his gaze was filled with a pair of beaded white moccasins. His eyes journeyed upward as he arose to face the banished medicine man Hakan. Rising to full height, Spirit Talker stood a full head taller than the shaman. But how on earth had the medicine man gotten so close without his having heard him? Had his own prayers been so intense?

"*Tosa taa narumi isa wasu,*" hissed Hakan. "*Mukwooru tosa tabu,*" he snarled.

Calling God poison was one thing. Insulting Spirit Talker personally by calling him a White coward was pushing the limits of what Buffalo Hump's son could be expected to endure. It was a racial insult. Spirit Talker leveled a cold, hard stare down upon the shaman.

Hakan ignored the implied warning. The heat from his breath in the pre-dawn hours of this cold March morning spoke of some evil fire that stirred deep within his breast. Fear? Envy? What was driving the shaman? Hakan stood unyieldingly toe-to-toe with Spirit Talker at the edge of the stand of live oak a mere stone's throw from the Pedernales River. His eyes were two black slits framed by black warpaint. Pure evil oozed from his every pore. "*Tosa taa narumi isa wasu,*" he repeated that the White man's God was poison. "Buffalo Hump *kooitu.*"

Bristling at the shaman daring to say that his father's soul was dead from the White man's God was too much for Spirit Talker. "*Ap* tell you go." He held back his rising anger and reminded the outcast medicine man that Buffalo Hump had ordered Hakan from the village. Despite that expulsion, the shaman had hung around the periphery of the encampment and regularly upbraided warriors with his protestations against the White man's religion. Spirit Talker clenched his fists.

"*Tosa taa narumi isa wasu,*" Hakan taunted the young warrior again, as he literally spat the words in Spirit Talker's face.

The spittle nearly froze on Spirit Talker's cheek. He found himself conflicted between his Comanche instincts and his God's call for forgiveness and mercy. This wasn't the first time Hakan had confronted him, but the shaman grew ever-more threatening with each encounter. In a few of days, Spirit Talker would head to Rising Cross Ranch to join with Jack's cattle drive north to Wyoming. He dared not leave Hakan to further influence the Penateka Comanche with his evil ideas. "*Wutsutsuki* leave *numunuu,*" commanded Spirit Talker still holding back his growing rage. Nevertheless, he found himself unable to restrain himself from casting Hakan in the image of a rattlesnake, as he ordered him to leave the people. He'd called the shaman a rattlesnake before and thought of the medicine man as one many times. To Spirit Talker's thinking, the image of the poisonous reptile with its darting tongue and venomous fangs fit the shaman quite well. He recalled Jack sharing the tale of the evil serpent in the Garden of Eden, as it tempted Eve. Hakan was no less an evil tempter.

Hakan's moved even closer to Spirit Talker. His buffalo horn headdress shook with crazed anger. *"Tosa taa narumi isa wasu,"* he seethed once again. His hand grasped the knife at his waist, and he slowly began to draw it out.

It happened in a flash. Spirit Talker's knife spoke in that instant what words could not deliver.

Hakan's eyes widened with surprise and pain. This was not supposed to happen to a warrior of *taa narumi*, the great spirit of the Comanche gods. A glazed look crossed his face as his hand opened and the knife tumbled to the ground. His knees began to buckle.

Spirit Talker stepped aside just in time to avoid the shaman falling into his arms. The anger and fear that drove him to kill Hakan quickly began to subside as it dawned on him that he now had a body to dispose of. He took a deep breath and glanced around furtively. There were no witnesses. He dragged the lifeless body deeper among the trees. "God forgive," he murmured as he took Hakan's scalp. He had already assured the shaman's journey to hell but felt compelled to keep him from the Comanche spirit world as well. Spirit Talker stood over the lifeless body. He could not bring himself to give it the honor of any memorial ritual. He figured it better that the buzzards and coyotes feast as he covering the remains with leaves. He took Hakan's buffalo horn head-dress and flung it far out into the waters of Pedernales River. He stared at the scalp in his hand. It was an unworthy trophy. It joined the buffalo horn headdress.

The deadly confrontation with the shaman served to

hasten Spirit Talker's decision to depart for Rising Cross Ranch. He decided to be gone before and if Hakan's body was discovered. Hopefully, scavengers would make quick work of the corpse. He walked to the river's edge, cleaned his knife, and washed Hakan's blood from his hands. He paused in deep thought. Would the shaman's poisonous blood ever be fully cleansed from his hands? "Must say goodbye to my *ap*," he said to himself, as if a reminder were needed. Buffalo Hump likely expected his son to leave soon. Now, the departure would be sooner.

––––––

THE RISING sun's warming rays cast long shadows on the bustling scene around the cabin. Isaac, Sarah, and Kate had joined forces to feed everyone a delicious breakfast appropriate to the long journey that lay ahead. Young Buck was still expressing his frustration that he was neither old enough or big enough to join the trail drive. Sam Collins and his foreman Bert had ridden in before dawn and enjoyed the breakfast repast.

I had managed to hire on a young teen boy that Klappenbach sent me from Bandera. Apparently, the young man had journeyed from a farm back east where he was a younger child of a family was so large that he saw no promising future. He sought opportunity, and we were pleased to provide it. I assured him that he could have a spread of his own one day, if he worked hard and learned the ways of ranching. He called himself Willard Smith, but we would call him Will. He was tall and had a bit of a gangly appearance as though his bones were waiting for his muscles to grow. He seemed honest enough for Klappenbach, so that was good enough for me. Importantly, Isaac would have some help while we were gone.

The air was filled with the mooing, snorting, bellowing, and grunting of a tad more than a hundred head of longhorns. Pulling the herd together had been a challenge unto itself. Most of the beeves we rounded up had lived free and were pretty much wild animals. They were game; not unlike deer or antelope. They kept mostly to the seemingly impenetrable dense brush during the day. Despite the thick brush, the longhorns could crash through it at top speed even with as much as a six-foot horn spread. Anyway, they'd stay in cover during the day and sneak out at dusk to devour the prairie grasses. It took a lot of talent and a tough spirit roundup. Now, we had a herd of the finicky wild beasts branded, fixed, and ready for my first trail drive. We'd be driving them to Bandera for what I called a big gather. In addition to our beeves, we had three pack mules and a half-dozen extra horses. I prayed that Mr. Klappenbach would fully deliver on his promises in Bandera.

I stood outside the cabin, unable to find the words to say goodbye, as I held Blue Flower at arm's length and gazed deeply into her loving eyes. Her slightly bulging belly already gave evidence that meeting the nexus of my return from the trail drive and the birth of our first child might be a considerable challenge. "*Kamakuna*," I finally managed to utter with a crack in my voice that betrayed how much I would miss her.

"*Kamakuna*," she responded. Yes, we loved each other.

We walked arm-in-arm to Big Red who snorted and nickered with anticipation. Longhorns snorted and mooed behind us. It wasn't exactly a romantic parting, but it was memorable in its stark reality.

Isaac would be staying back to manage Rising Cross and his own spread. They reckoned their good relations with the Penateka Comanche and the Kiowa plus occasional visits by Captain Benton's Texas Rangers would keep them about as safe as might be expected.

I shared a goodbye kiss with Blue Flower. As I mounted Big Red, I heard a faint shout from the west. I spun Big Red about to see Spirit Talker about a quarter mile off and riding in at a trot.

Like me, he was decked in buckskins and moccasin boots but set off with the mountain lion necklace with its carved cross. Two eagle feathers were affixed to the back of his head, as two braids hung halfway down his back. As he pulled up in a cloud of dust, he dismounted to greet his sister Blue Flower with an exuberant hug. He quickly pulled back, realizing that she was with child. He turned to me and let out a big smile.

"About time you got here, brother," I chided.

Not to be outdone, Spirit Talker responded, "What we wait for?" He laughed and looked about as though everyone else was causing the delay in departing. He quickly hugged Kate and Buck; nodded to Isaac, Sarah, and the new hire; and remounted his pony. The pinto pranced a bit, as though finally realizing his old friend Big Red was standing near. Spirit Talker looked down at his sister. "Blue Flower *wa'ipu*," he observed. Indeed, she had become a woman in Comanche eyes.

I was overjoyed to have Spirit Talker with us. I sighed and made a final scan of the ranch buildings. Our prize longhorn Atlas bellowed a goodbye from the corral as though wishing he was joining the drive north. Little did he realize what was to become of his fellow four-hooved beasts. I waved my hand to silence everyone. "Lord, we ask your blessing on this venture. Please keep everyone at Rising Cross safe and bring us home safely. We ask that you continue to bless us with your bounty. Amen." I kept my head bowed and eyes closed for another moment, then opened them and caught Blue Flower's loving eyes. I sighed deeply, even longingly, then took a deep breath. "Head'em out!" I shouted as I turned Big Red toward the trail to Bandera. Doggone, but it hurt to leave Blue Flower; hurt to leave the ranch.

Last I'd heard from Klappenbach in Bandera, he'd mustered five men from some troops mustering out of Camp Verde, a cook, and enough basic grub to sustain us for at least a couple of months. We'd be eating some of the beeves we were delivering, and there were still buffalo to feast upon. I had managed to get commitments from ten ranches around the southern Comancheria and down toward the Medina River. I figured we'd be driving roughly four hundred head to the North Platte country, assuming all of the ranchers came through with their promises. We held prayerfully to the premise that the folks at Fort Laramie would enthusiastically welcome fresh beef on their dinner plates. We figured to let the longhorns fatten up and recuperate up at George's spread. Of course, the term "fattening a longhorn" might be thought of as what's called an oxymoron, a contradiction, as they tended to be naturally lean critters. Still, a mature "lean" bull could weigh in at twelve to fifteen hundred pounds. Of course, most were no longer bulls. They had become steers.

Out here on the wild frontier of the Comancheria, I had by necessity matured faster than most kids my age back east. I was seventeen years old going on twenty-something. I had given plenty of thought to what lay ahead of us on this cattle venture. We'd be facing plenty of hazards from lack of trails to nasty folks intent on mayhem. Rivers would likely be swollen with snowmelt, making crossing them with our beeves, horses, and cowboys a struggle. Likely as not, we'd be facing spring thunderstorms that would stampede our herd of wild-eyed, temperamental longhorns. It could be feast or famine, as there would surely be waterless stretches to test our grit. As though the livestock and elements weren't enough, we would be crossing territory featuring Indians and bandits determined to take our measure by force. I had visions of Lakota or Cheyenne war parties taking their toll on us and rustlers looking to steal a few beeves to satisfy their greedy lusts. I suspect it was my appreciation for the reality of all that lay ahead that led ranchers in the region to take me and my cattle venture seriously. I could only pray that our longhorns, valued at roughly two dollars a head, would fetch us a profit up north. I had heard that packing houses were paying upward of twenty-five dollars but didn't expect nearly so much from a remote Army outpost like Fort Laramie. In fact, I'd adjusted my plan by figuring to sell beeves at outposts and forts along our route. Sounded plenty sensible to me, so long as we maintained accurate records of sales.

As we began to move our contribution of beeves southward, I quickly became aware of the clouds of trail dust even our modest herd of beeves could kick up. Sam Collins's cowboy, Bert, took drag for the first few miles and was soon caked nearly white with dust. He was a sight to behold. Of course, we'd each be taking a turn, so we held back any laughter.

We reckoned it would take at least two days to cover the ground to Bandera. It seemed cattle tended to have a mind of their own as to how fast they cared to ramble along. The lead bull that I had chosen appeared to have been a good choice. I was still pleased that Atlas would not be winding up as someone's dinner; at least, not yet. Gathering strays also tended to slow our pace. Keep in mind, these beeves still had a wild side, and every now and then one or two would try to stray off and have to be redirected by virtue of some hard riding by one of us. There was a technique called tailing that only the very best cowboys were capable of, as it could be tough on man and beast. I'll spare the detail and say that it involved grabbing the wayward longhorn's tail on the dead run and bringing it to a sudden earth-shattering halt. Assuming horse, cowboy, and longhorn were unhurt, the beast would generally forget what it was running from and saunter lazily back to the herd. Tailing was a last resort.

About every five miles or so, we all switched horses to give our primary cayuses a well-deserved break. It was no exaggeration to say we stayed very busy.

Collins rode up front with Spirit Talker and me. We didn't talk all that much, especially once we realized that opening your mouth risked choking on trail dust. The weather warmed up right quickly, and we found ourselves wetting bandanas and draping them around our necks to stay cool. All moved along right well. It would take a few days to truly become acquainted. I called it a feeling out time, when we'd begin to find out who was good at doing what. We camped about five miles north of the Medina River. The longhorns stayed calm through the night, and we felt blessed that there were no thunderstorms or prairie fires to deal with. So far, so good. I was feeling confident that God was watching over us.

The next day was overcast, but the sky didn't seem especially threatening. The cloud cover had a refreshing cooling effect that was heightened by our first crossing of the frigid Medina River. By early afternoon of the second day, Bandera came into view. Glory be, but we were greeted by hundreds of cattle. I guessed that we were looking at more than four hundred head not counting our own. Our ranchers around the region appeared to have delivered on their promises and then some. Praise the Lord, this was going to be a big gather for sure.

We found a space among the gentle hills to let our beeves recuperate and graze after the push to Bandera. Given that it was hardly more than a hundred head, it served as a sort of practice drive for us. Collins and Spirit Talker joined me in the short ride into Bandera where rosy-cheeked August Klappenbach awaited us. Within the hour, we gathered together all the men who would be joining us on the trail drive in the back room of Klappenbach's store. The weather was warming, and we were grateful to Klappenbach for opening up the windows to let a breeze through the room. Actually, it was likely Stella's way of fending off the stench from a bunch of sweaty, trail-dust-laden cowboys as mixed with the pungent odor of "bouquet of cattle." Couldn't hardly blame her.

FOUR
STICKY DETAILS

AS WE GATHERED in the heavy air of Klappenbach's back room, there was plenty of chatter. Plenty until Klappenbach brought a hammer down on an oak table in the middle of the room. The hammer served as a most effective gavel. The proprietor turned to me. "They're all yours, Jack."

Silence. I hadn't prepared any kind of speech. I suddenly found myself tongue-tied. I scanned the gathered men while gathering my thoughts. Call them cowboys, cowpokes, vaqueros, buckaroos, or any of another half-dozen or so appellations, these life-toughened men would be drovers for the next three months. They would be answering to me. From the expressions gracing some of their grizzled faces, I was a young whippersnapper. Hopefully, they would reserve judgment. I felt there would be plenty of opportunity to prove myself to them. After all, Klappenbach had no trouble with my youth.

"Thet Injun comin' with us?" came a husky voice

from the back of the room. It came from a tall lanky gruff-looking cowpoke standing behind two others.

Well, that got my attention. I found my voice. "That brave Comanche warrior is my friend Spirit Talker. He will serve as our scout, hopefully to keep us from being ambushed by Indians," I stated firmly. "And he speaks perfect English," I added.

The cowboy shuffled his feet. "Only good Injun is..."

One of the cowboys in front of him stomped on his foot, putting an end to his prejudiced comment.

I cleared my throat. It was time to take charge. "My name is Jack O'Toole, and I run this outfit. Anyone having a problem with that is welcome to leave now with no hard feelings. Sam Collins here is in charge, when I'm not around." I let that settle on the gathering. "We'll be spending the next three months together, so let's begin with introductions. I like to connect faces with names, so just tell me who you are for now."

The Injun-hating cowboy with the yellow trooper stripe up his pants spoke first. "Name's Hank Johnson," he groused.

Each cowboy introduced themselves in turn. They were a motley crew so far as appearance, all wearing a mix of well broken in broad-brimmed hats and black US Cavalry hats with gold braid bands. Some still wore their chaps from the morning tending of the herds. Chaps, leather, fringed or fur were a must on a trail drive where all manner of brush seemed to reach out to tear up a drover's legs. Their pants were tucked into well-worn boots sporting various styles of spurs. The men who'd mustered out kept their military-issue trousers with yellow stripes down the pant legs. Many wore shirts that had seen better days, though a couple of the men had availed themselves of Klappenbach's inventory. Mostly Colt 1852 Navy revolvers protruded from waistbands or in holsters and nearly all had large knives hanging from their belts. I didn't know whether to feel safe or scared.

As introductions wound down, a bandy-legged Mexican-looking man with broad mustache stepped forward. "*Mi nombre es Juan. Soy tu cocinero.*" Juan Perez stepped forward proudly and looked around the room, as a couple of the cowboys guffawed. "*Madre de Dios,*" he said. "Be careful or Juan put *mucho pimienta* in your stew," he said mostly in English and punctuated with a big laugh.

I had heard there were peppers that could turn your insides ablaze. At least, our cook had a sense of humor and believed in God. We'd get along.

With introductions completed, I continued my introductory remarks. "We're headed through dangerous country and must work as a team, if we expect to make it to Fort Laramie. This is a risky venture, and some of you might not make it. If you have any personal concerns you need to wrap up, do so." I felt a shudder go around the room, as the possibility of not returning dawned on the men. "You are responsible for your own weapons, horses, and personal effects. Mr. Klappenbach here should have a full tally of the contribution of cattle. Y'all get paid, when we deliver and sell the beeves." I scanned the room. Faces were all dead serious. "We leave day after tomorrow. Any questions?" Nothing save for scattered coughs and nervous shuffling of feet. "Y'all can head back to tend your beeves," I said in conclusion.

The cowboys and cook filed from the room, with Collins and Spirit Talker hanging back with me.

I turned to Klappenbach. "Thought that went well," I said.

"You did well, Jack. I'd keep an eye on Hank. He has

some hard feelings about Indians, but he pretty much listens to reason."

I thoughtfully rubbed my chin. "I'll keep an eye on him. Did you get a tally of beeves?" I asked.

"Need to count yours, Jack," he responded.

"Between Sam's Circle C and my Rising Cross, we brought a hundred and fifteen head but do take a count just to be official," I said. I turned to Collins. "Spirit Talker and I have something to tend to. I'll join you with our herd. You might double-check that we have all we'll be needing for the trail drive." I motioned Spirit Talker to follow me.

———

I FIGURED we had what I call sticky details to tend to, if the drive had a prayer of success. One of them was Hank Johnson.

"What you do, Jack? Where we go?" asked Spirit Talker with a slight bit of trepidation, as I led the way off to where our drovers had gathered at a close-by corral. Inside I was saying a heartfelt prayer that all would go well. I had acquired a serviceable belt and holster for my Colt revolver but left them behind so as to not encourage gunplay.

I nodded to Juan as we strode by.

Juan smiled, grabbed his shotgun, and followed at a distance. Seemed he was a security guard in addition to his cooking skills. I appreciated that he apparently had a sense for difficult situations.

The drovers were chattering away intensely with an occasional expletive thrown in.

Johnson was loudest of the group. "I jus' might quit afore we start," he announced. He looked up to see Spirit

Talker and me approaching and gave me what some call the "hard eye." It was a challenge.

I moved close in with as much confidence as I could muster. "Howdy, men. Figured it might do to clear some air before we head out to spend nearly three months together."

"What you got on yer mind, boss man?" challenged Johnson in a slightly derisive tone. He seemed of a mind to test what sort of man Jack O'Toole was.

I reckoned that if I could turn Johnson's thinking around, the others would follow. I took a deep breath. Here I was, a mere seventeen years old about to deliver an admonition of sorts to these older grizzled life warriors. I locked eyes with each in turn, ending with Johnson. "A couple of years back, my family's homestead was attacked by Comanche; the very same tribe that my friend Spirit Talker here is from. My mother, father, and a sister and brother were killed and another sister and brother taken captive. My home was burned to the ground. Anger, revenge, guilt, and fear took over the very core of my being. I was raised in a Christian home, but it all took a back seat to the pure hatred that welled up in my very soul. I was determined to single-handedly save my captured sister and brother and take out my anger on the Comanche." I paused. I had already grabbed the full attention of the men, having counted on delivering my message with humble sincerity. Any hint of bravado or insincerity surely would not have worked. "I expect you'll all agree that I had every reason to hate all Indians and especially the Comanche to this very day. Forgiveness and mercy were not in my thoughts. In the days that followed as I sought to free my brother and sister; however, experiences would grow my faith in God and enable me to triumph over my vengeful hatred of the Comanche."

Johnson shuffled his feet and nodded agreement. "How'd you hook up with this Injun varmint?" he asked, waving a hand toward Spirit Talker.

Spirit Talker stood close to me, never even flinching. The scars from the mountain lion attack did grow just a tad redder.

"I saved Spirit Talker's life. It was by pure instinct— saving another human being from an attack by a mountain lion. That necklace around my friend's neck," I said, motioning toward the decoration around Spirit Talker's neck. "It features the claws from that mountain lion on either side of the cross that represents the faith that he has accepted. My saving his life was God's way of breaking through my vengeful spirit. Spirit Talker and I developed a trust and became friends. He helped me free my sister and brother from his people. We have ever strengthened our trust in God's spirit and power and in that of the Son and Spirit. We have witnessed God's raw power, his strong medicine protecting us time after time in our journeys. Today, I am married to his sister."

That last sentence fell heavily on the men, yet there were mostly nods of acceptance. Mixed marriages were often the way of the west, most of them because women-folk tended to be scarce.

"Yuh become an Injun lover," observed Johnson with a bit less contempt in his voice.

I shook my head. "No, Hank. I'm a God lover. And I suggest that you and anyone else on our team think hard on that. Leave any prejudices and hatreds behind. We'll be spending long days working hard and must have full trust in each other. Our very lives will depend on it."

The other drovers nodded collectively.

Johnson hesitated, gave an awkward foot shuffle, and nodded. "I'm with yuh, boss...er, Mr. O'Toole."

"We're pulling out day after tomorrow, men. Be sure to get your affairs in order," I said. It had occurred to me again that some might not make it back.

In my peripheral vision, I saw Juan return the shotgun to the wagon. He caught my look and winked. I had a feeling I'd be relying on him.

Spirit Talker placed a hand on my shoulder. "Strong *sunipu*, brother," he assured me. "Now, me scout," he added with a laugh.

"Topsannah," I chided.

He blushed ever-so-slightly. What could he say? We walked back to Klappenbach's store.

"How Blue Flower?" asked Spirit Talker. We'd departed Rising Cross so quickly upon Spirit Talker's arrival that he'd barely had time to greet his sister.

"She's with child," I said with a broad grin.

He stopped in his tracks. "I know. Is good. She *wa'ipu*."

I turned to face him. I immediately felt a sense of guilt at not having shared the news sooner, especially back at Rising Cross Ranch. "I forgot to mention it in the rush to leave," I said with head hung just a bit.

Spirit Talker laughed easily. "I know when hug. Buffalo Hump be pleased," he said.

FIVE
HEAD'EM OUT!

AUGUST KLAPPENBACH CHOSE the moment we were about to drive our herd of precisely 524 head of beeves northward and delivered a bonus that would significantly improve the chances of our trail drive being successful. He stood proudly on the wooden walk that served as a dust and mud barrier in front of his store, smiled broadly, and motioned to his left.

I sat curiously astride Big Red as Juan emerged driving a team of oxen pulling a wagon from around the side of Klappenbach's store.

A chorus of yahoos rose up from the gathered drovers and the grin on Juan's face couldn't have been broader.

"You've outdone yourself, August," I responded.

"Love to take credit, Jack, but it was Stella's idea. Oxen can be slow, but they're reliable. Figure that rig ought to keep up with the herd."

In addition to cooking supplies and a couple of water barrels, the wagon had space for bedrolls and most other gear the drovers figured to bring along. A canvas shroud over top mostly protect contents from rain and trail dust.

"*Es muy bueno*, boss," intoned Juan with a big wink to emphasize his pleasure. He'd known about the wagon, but kept it a secret at Klappenbach's urging.

"Those boys heading herds to California would envy us, August," I said with greater confidence.

Stella emerged from the store toting a big basket. "Hopefully, these will last a day or two," she said with a laugh as she handed it up to Juan.

Juan peeked inside, and his eyes grew wide. "Cornbread!" he announced as he stored the precious basket beneath the wagon seat.

"Thanks right kindly, Stella," I offered up. I nodded to Klappenbach who smiled back. With that, I looked about. "Let's get to it, men. Time to head'em out!" I shouted and put gentle spurs to Big Red just enough to lead our drovers at a gallop toward our gathered herd.

———

RIDING IN FRONT OF A SWAYING, mooing, snorting, bellowing herd of longhorns is an incredible experience. I felt as though I was contributing per God's direction in Genesis, when he tells mankind to subdue the earth and extract its potential. This was surely in fulfillment of that directive.

Spirit Talker rode point roughly a half mile in front of us. Given the slow pace of the herd, he had the luxury of not having to rush. Now and then as we moved northward, he would allow us catch up and give a report as to any concerns ahead.

Amazingly, we actually made about a dozen miles our first day out.

Johnson sidled up to me, as we were scraping off our

dinner plates. "Did I see a bow and arrows hanging off yer saddle, boss?"

I turned and smiled. "Nice alternative to the Sharps, Hank."

"Yuh akchully shoot the thing?"

Despite his curiosity, I sensed that my apparent love of Indians still stuck in Johnson's craw.

He shook his head. "Gun's quick," he stated firmly.

"And loud," I responded. "Sometimes, silence can save your life," I responded.

"Ever kill a man with it?" he asked.

"Yep," I said with quiet assurance. It was enough said.

Johnson shuffled his feet; a nervous habit he seemed to have. "Can ya teach me?"

"To shoot, yes." Something told me that Hank Johnson was coming around. "Shooting deer with a gun is easy," I advised. "Hunting with bow and arrow? That's true hunting." I smiled.

Johnson seemed impressed. "Thanks, boss," he said.

"Via con Dios, Hank," I threw in.

"That too," he said and headed off to ride night guard. I was soon to learn that Johnson had a smooth easy-going singing voice, which he exercised for the enjoyment of the cowboys but mostly to help keep the beeves calm during the night.

As I turned away, I came face-to-face with Spirit Talker who had ridden in rather stealthily. I quickly learned why he'd been so cautious. "Kiowa watch us, Jack," he said with due seriousness. It was only the first day of the drive, and it seemed we might have hostiles to contend with. "Count twelve," Spirit Talker continued. That meant there could be more.

"Should we ignore them?" I asked.

"Kiowa curious," he said with slight smile. "I think," he added.

"We should let Sam know. We don't need any surprises."

"If attack, will be *kaahaniitu*...a trick for us to chase them into trap. Men must know not to follow Kiowa that run."

We had eight drovers, and my fervent prayer was that none would get over-zealous and pursue any attacking Kiowa. The emotional and physical rush that comes with being attacked can all too easily cause men to lose rational control. "We need every man we have; can't afford being ambushed," I said as if to reassure myself. "It's going to take strong *sunipu* to get safely past the Kiowa. God willing, we'll get through this." Indeed, I could only hope and pray that we could avoid an attack.

———

I COULD HEAR the dulcet tones of Johnson's serenading the beeves as I eased on over to where Collins was laying out his bedroll to catch a couple of hours of shuteye before his night guard duty. "Sam?" I said perhaps too quietly, as he spun around, startled.

"Dang, Jack! Don't do that. Make some kind of noise when you're coming up behind me," he chided.

"Spirit Talker tells me there's a party of Kiowa stalking us. Guess they're trying to figure out what we're up to with so many beeves."

"Trouble already?" he responded with an incredulous expression.

"We need to warn the men that if they attack, they will quickly retreat to lure us into following them into an ambush. Under no circumstances are the men to pursue retreating Indians."

Collins nodded. "I'll be sure they all know, Jack."

"Just in case, have a drover ride shotgun alongside Juan and our wagon."

"Good idea. Cookie's far too important to risk losing him…or the wagon."

———

FOR THE NEXT TWO DAYS, we rode with the creepy feeling that not-so-friendly eyes were following us. The Kiowa apparently were having trouble deciding what to do. I liked to think that they were warriors we had encountered before, they recognized Spirit Talker and me, and were disinclined to test our strong *sunipu* again. In any case, I prayed earnestly for God's protection.

We'd made an incredible forty miles through some of the most hilly countryside of Texas. As we settled in for the night, I found Johnson once again standing beside me. "Howdy, Hank. You looking to talk?" I asked.

"Reckoned to catch yuh afore I do night guard."

"Been missing your singing the past couple of nights."

Johnson actually smiled. "Did yuh really lose yer family, boss?" Apparently, the question had been weighing on him, since my speech back in Bandera.

"Yes. Still hurts to think on it."

Johnson did one of his nervous shuffles. "Lost my wife and son to Apache," he confessed.

Little wonder that Collins had come to hate Indians.

"I joined the Army to get away. Stuck me with a bunch of danged camels," he said, lending credibility to

Klappenbach's observation that the soldiers hated the Army's camel experiment at Camp Verde.

"Sorry for your loss, Hank," I said with earnest condolence.

"Did yuh really forgive them Comanche?"

"Forgave but did not forget. God punishes evil in what often seems like strange ways. He set a mountain lion on Spirit Talker to kill his friend and to claw him unmercifully but sent me to save his life. As to freeing my brother and sister, God taught the Comanche that they could not barter for human life."

"And yuh don't wanna kill them Injuns?"

"Not Spirit Talker's people. They've come to understand God, and some even accepting Christ. I've forgiven them their past evil deeds." I saw that my words were having a deep impact on Johnson. "There's evil Indians and Whites likely worth killing. Yes, I've killed bad men. Did I forgive them?" I gave Johnson a slight grin of assurance. "They didn't give me a chance. In sum, Hank, forgiving doesn't eliminate punishment for evil. And you can't lump all people together over the bad deeds of a few."

"Yuh truly believe that?" Johnson asked.

"Yep. Worked so far," I assured him. "In the case of the Indians, I have come to consider that they see us as invaders of their country. I can understand them wanting to protect it, but forgiving enemies isn't part of their religion. They only know violence to protect themselves. Spirit Talker and I are trying to change that, though I never really thought on it that way."

"Thanks, boss," offered Collins. "Gotta think on this."

I knew that I had barely scratched the surface of the issue of forgiving versus punishment. It was so simple yet so complicated. "Don't let that stop you from sere-nading the beeves, Hank," I cajoled with a broad smile.

Johnson shuffled off to cut his horse from the remuda. He was already humming a tune.

———

I HAD JUST FINISHED a turn at drag and was trying mostly in vain to beat the trail dust off with my hat, when Collins came riding up.

"Spirit Talker just told me that the Kiowa are gone," he informed me with relief in his voice.

I took a swig from my canteen and spit out a muddy mess. It wasn't enough to clear the grit from my mouth. "Great news, Sam." I scanned ahead through the dust. "Sun's getting low, there a place ahead to rest our outfit?"

"Spirit Talker found a place another mile ahead with water and plenty of grazing. Might be tough to get the beeves to leave," he said with a laugh that spoke of minds being eased at having dodged the Kiowa threat.

Having experienced this journey to Wyoming, I knew there would be plenty more challenges ahead. Still, I reckoned this night might offer a chance to relax.

SIX
STORMY WEATHER

WITH THE HILLS BEHIND US, the prairie ahead served to open our line of sight to what lay ahead. We were graced with a full moon and an endless blanket of stars.

I was pretty much dead asleep when Spirit Talker nudged me. I awakened a tad groggy but got my eyes into focus.

"Look, Jack," he said, pointing off to the northwest. "*Ekakwitsụbaitụ*," he said in a near whisper.

"Lightning?" I responded and looked out in the direction he was pointing. Sure enough. Lightning was way off on the horizon.

He nodded. "Come this way. Plenty *umaru*." Plenty of rain headed our way.

In learning about cattle, especially longhorns, I had been told that the slightest out-of-the-ordinary event could set them to stampeding. "We need to warn our cowhands. I'll get Sam. You tell Juan to hook up the wagon and head west toward the storm." I figured the beeves would likely run away from the storm, but there was no way to be sure. The night was growing ever blacker.

Of a sudden, everyone was roused and preparing for the worst. As I understood, the best way to handle a stampede was to let the critters run a bit, head them off, and then turn them to circle in on themselves. They could be expected to mill about in a circular pattern and finally settle down…until the next lightning bolt.

Just about the time Juan had begun moving the wagon out and a couple of cowboys were heading our valuable remuda of horses out of harm's way, the wind picked up and there was a flash and a boom that nearly jolted me from Big Red's saddle.

Johnson's night guard serenade faded away quickly, lost in the braying, huffing, and snorting of better than five hundred beeves blindly setting off on their panicky run. Wild-eyed and desperate with fear, the startled beasts rushed madly away from the fearsome bolt of lightning punctuated by another earth-shattering rumble. Another bolt and another quickly jagged their way across the dark gray sky followed by crashes that would put cannon to shame.

Our drovers did their best in the driving rain to alter the direction of the herd, waving hats or blankets, firing guns, and shouting at the tops of their lungs. Bushes, brambles, and scrub oak hadn't a prayer against the thundering herd. A thousand hooves pounded blindly ahead. Blessedly, the beeves fell in behind our lead steer, making it just a hair easier for Collins and Johnson to begin trying to turn the leaders.

"Heads up!" yelled Collins's cowhand Bert as he galloped between me and a charging stray. He nearly knocked me over but likely saved me from a disastrous confrontation with the crazed steer. A couple of feet of a longhorn's horn spread could do a lot of damage. I didn't have time to thank Bert, as I spurred Big Red out of harm's way. The driving rain in the darkness made visibility close to zero, but we had to move with the stampeding beeves. The occasional bolt of lightning was a blessing in the sense that they would blight up the pandemonium spread before us.

The herd had run roughly two miles and showed no sign of slowing. I paused on a piece of higher ground to try to make out the shadowy forms running amok before me.

Spirit Talker pulled up alongside. "Need strong *sunipu*," he observed with a hint of exaggeration. I guess this was Comanche sarcasm.

I pointed ahead. "Looks like Collins and Johnson have turned them," I shouted in between what turned out to be the final shards of lightning and claps of thunder. "There's our *sunipu!*"

"No sleep tonight," added Spirit Talker. He was becoming a master of understatement.

"See if you can find Juan and the wagon," I urged. "Hopefully, he dodged the stampede."

Spirit Talker grew serious for a moment, as he surveyed the milling herd. "Bad like buffalo, but horns bigger."

It was a valid comparison, except the buffalo were generally hundreds of pounds heavier and stood taller. too. As I understood it, the Indians hunted them by running herds off cliffs, or what were called buffalo jumps. They would butcher the broken carcasses and feed their tribes for months. They used just about every bit of the buffalo, so there was little or no waste.

I put my spurs to Big Red and headed toward Collins

and Johnson at a gallop, while Spirit Talker searched for Juan.

Sure enough, the beeves were beginning to circle and appeared to be under some semblance of control. We could only hope the restraint would last. It seemed like forever before the final drenching remainder of the storm passed. The clouds parted, but the dim light of the moon and stars was insufficient to allow us to assess the extent of damage that had been wrought. Far as we could tell, none of our men or their cayuses had been hurt. Juan and our wagon avoided the stampeding herd altogether. We'd be taking inventory at daybreak, round up strays, dry out the best we could, and resume the drive.

I finally paused enough to take a deep breath. Big Red and I were caked with mud and soaked to the skin. That I'd managed to keep my hat through it all was a testament to its tight fit and durability.

———

THE DROVERS BROUGHT the herd together sooner than expected the morning after the stampede. Only two beeves had been injured seriously to have to be put down. We lost three calves that were crushed in the galloping melee. Juan packed as much of the beef as possible into the wagon. We would be especially well fed for a few days. Importantly, we resumed our northward journey. There was surprisingly little damage and the warm rays of the sun dried us out right quickly. We were lucky to have avoided greater trampling. Turned out that stampedes were a far greater hazard than I'd dared imagine. God's *sunipu* was evident was surely evident in our survival.

Shorty McBride came riding up. He was grimacing

with pain, as the rowel on one of his spurs had caught in a bush during the stampede and wrenched his leg something awful. Apparently, nothing was broken, but he figured to ride the day out in Juan's wagon.

The spur incident with Shorty led me to consider my own spurs. Most of us, Shorty included, sported the large rowels popular with the Mexican *vaqueros*. They were effective toward getting a cayuse to hightail it in a hurry or in quick bursts of speed gathering beeves for branding, but not so much in the heavy brush of the prairie. My answer was rather simple. I removed the rowel. The naked shank and chap guard were plenty sufficient for a drover's needs. I modified Shorty's spurs, and everyone else followed suit. As I've said, this trail drive would be a learning experience.

We had to deal with occasional stretches of mud for a couple of hours. Juan managed to avoid bogging down the wagon in the mire. By afternoon the drovers at drag were once again eating trail dust.

I had to admit that I was right proud of the performance of our men. The stampede had the effect of bringing us all together as a team.

The drive was now headed through arguably the flattest segment of our journey. Heavy brush and grass laid before us so far as the naked eye could see. There really wasn't a trail to be had. Five hundred beeves had the effect of carving one. The vastness of the landscape had the effect of making the sky seem especially huge. In my mind, it was God's glory in full display.

I was amazed that no Indians had engaged us yet. Other than the Kiowa threat that disappeared of its own accord, Comanche, Arapaho, Navajo, and Apache were not to be seen. Word of the humble exploits of Spirit

Talker and I could not possibly have dissuaded all of the tribes from trying their coup sticks on us.

––––––

WE WERE a couple of days south of the Red River when we happened upon a Pawnee hunting party headed by our old friend Man Who Steals Horses. The warrior was very pleased when we cut out a longhorn cow as a gift. It didn't hurt that we were honoring our promise from the day a few months back, when Man Who Steals Horses had applied a life-saving poultice to Spirit Talker's rattlesnake bite wound. Our drovers watched with apprehension, but nobody protested. I made sure the bovine bore the Rising Cross brand.

The Pawnee were happy. Word of these sorts of honoring of promises did tend get out among the *numunuu* of the many tribes in the region.

––––––

THE RED RIVER could be seen off in the distance. We were about three weeks into our drive, and all was going to plan. The beeves kept on the move, there was plenty of foliage for livestock to graze, and no more storms were encountered. The drovers seemed to be getting along; at least, to the extent that no one appeared to be getting on anyone's nerves. Juan managed to stretch the meat from the aftermath of the stampede and mixed in other delicacies that seemed to keep everyone happy. Juan's ability to come up with menu variations with his sort-of-secret blends of spices and vegetables likely served to spoil us all. On the rare occasion that we'd stop for an extended rest, Juan would come up with a sweet dessert to further cement his essential role with the men. He wouldn't let a soul inside his wagon, so there was no telling what unexpected foodstuffs were lurking in the drawers and boxes within his bit of trail drive heaven. I do recall one of the drovers shooting a rattlesnake and tossing it toward Juan as a joke. There remained the ever-lingering suspicion that the snake found its way into our beef stew.

Reaching the Red River would place us nearly halfway to our destination. Our trail drive would bend to the northwest a bit. In a few days, we'd reach the Canadian River and soon after cross the Texas border into Indian Territory.

SEVEN

ATTACK AT RED RIVER

ARAPAHO AHEAD! Who'd have figured? And just shy of four weeks into our drive. Had I been wondering where the Indians were? Well, those musings were about to be answered!

Spirit Talker came charging toward me at a full gallop. Dust kicked up in my face, as he came to a skidding halt beside me. "Arapaho!" he warned.

On cue, Collins came galloping over to us. "What's up, Jack?" he asked, questioning the obvious.

At least three dozen Arapaho lined the rise ahead. Far as we could see from roughly a quarter mile off, they were a fully-decked-out war party. They meant business. Blessedly, I could see no rifles among them, so we had the advantage of greater weaponry.

My first thought was to ask for a parley. Maybe, a couple of beeves would persuade them to go in peace. I turned to Spirit Talker. "Parley?" I vainly asked.

"We fight," responded Spirit Talker.

"Sam, circle the herd. Put a couple of men with horses. Under no circumstances follow the Indians, if they retreat. They might lead us into a trap." I knew the toughest part might be keeping the cattle calm, as guns blazed near them.

As Sam rode off, I drew my Sharps carbine from its sheath and placed it across my lap. I double-checked the loads in my Colt revolver. In my peripheral vision, I saw Spirit Talker applying a broad black stripe of warpaint across the upper portion of his face.

My Comanche brother caught my surprise. "God good," he assured me, as he finished applying the pigment. It gave him a decidedly savage appearance. I prayed it scared the Arapaho as much as me.

With three drovers guarding the livestock, it left the rest of us to face the Indians. We were outnumbered about six to one so far as I could figure. About this time, I felt blessedly fortunate that Hank Johnson, Shorty McBride, and a couple of the others had served in the Army. It brought with it a certain discipline and confidence.

The Arapaho began to wave lances, whoop and yell, and prance about as they built up their courage for a charge. The air was pregnant with anticipation. The sun was nearly at its peak, when one of the warriors rode round in a tight circle, raised his lance, and led a charge toward us.

We held fire until the Arapaho were perhaps fifty yards off and coming on fast. The smoke and concussive explosions from the muzzles of five rifles coupled with well-placed arrows from Spirit Talker's bow brought the charge to a halt. Surprised expressions crossed Arapaho faces, as they fell back. The prairie was littered with the bodies of at least seven savages and several ponies.

Spirit Talker rode over beside me. "Shaman lie," he said with an air of finality. "Shaman say they do not die."

The Arapaho were gathering at the top of the hill for some sort of powwow. There was plenty more of that whooping and hollering, hands and lances waved high, and ponies prancing about. Whatever their conversation, they kept looking at us and gesticulating with all manner of false bravado.

"What do you think?" I asked, turning to Spirit Talker.

He smiled knowingly. "We wait," he added.

Soon enough, a trio of Arapaho warriors rode toward us with lances lowered and a hand raised in a sign of peace.

"Sam, y'all watch our backs," I cautioned. Spirit Talker and I rode out toward the hostiles, while Collins and the rest of our men held rifles at the ready.

"You talk, me translate," advised Spirit Talker.

I knew from past chats with my Comanche brother that there was no love lost between the Comanche and Arapaho. It made good sense that the Arapaho should parley with me and not a longtime sworn enemy.

Glancing over my shoulder, I saw Johnson aim his rifle at the approaching Arapaho. "Hank! Hold your fire! This is a parley!" I cautioned him.

Johnson lowered the gun, but suspicion was writ large across his face. He held no trust for these savages.

The Arapaho leader halted within talking distance. "Whites big medicine," he said in Arapaho. He then pointed to himself, "Buffalo Killer." Beneath the warpaint, there was something about his eyes that caused me to agree with Johnson that the Arapaho were not to be trusted. I strove to hold my suspicion in check.

Spirit Talker turned to me. "He admits you have strong *sunipu*. His name is Buffalo Killer."

With that, I reckoned that I had the stronger hand in

this parley. "Tell Buffalo Killer that many more Arapaho will meet their great spirit."

Spirit Talker turned back to the Arapaho chief and delivered my message.

Buffalo Killer nodded in acknowledgment. "We take bodies," said Buffalo Killer. "Leave Whites in peace." Again, Spirit Talker relayed the message.

I thought it strange that Buffalo Killer had not asked for any price for passage. Apparently, he was far more impressed with our firepower than I had expected. I felt a warning tingle up my spine. This could be a trick, a *kaahaniitu*. I nodded. "Go in peace." Instinctively, my hand grasped the butt of my Colt revolver.

Buffalo Killer said something to the two braves beside him. The three turned as if to leave, then spun about.

"*Kaahaniitu*, Jack!" shouted Spirit Talker. It was a trap.

My senses had been true.

Arapaho savages came charging over the hill. Buffalo Killer charged directly at me, but Big Red jumped aside, and the savage's lance missed. A bullet from Collins's rifle didn't miss, as the Arapaho and his pony fell in a heap. We were suddenly surrounded by the hostiles! My Colt blazed fire and lead into the melee, and Spirit Talker's war club crushed more than one enemy skull. Collins and the men held their line and picked off Arapaho at will. There was a loud cry from one of the warriors, and the remaining savages went into a full retreat. The prairie was now littered with perhaps a dozen or more hostiles in addition to their losses from the initial charge. Their shaman would surely have questions to answer.

When the dust had finally cleared, we took stock of our situation. Blessedly and perhaps incredibly, no one had even been wounded. Collins rode over to where

Spirit Talker and I were sucking air in an attempt to recover from the intensity of the battle. "Never seen nothin' like it," observed Collins.

I simply pointed heavenward.

"They go," chimed in Spirit Talker. He didn't have to say more, as our strong medicine had been quite obvious.

I nodded to Collins. "Their medicine man likely told them that the White man's bullets wouldn't hurt them. He lied," I offered with a hint of a satisfied grin.

"You're the real deal, Jack. All Klappenbach said you'd be."

That was a big admission from the cowboy. He was likely speaking for all of our men. Apparently, I had passed some sort of informal test; a baptism under fire so to speak.

———

WE WASTED no time moving on from the Red River. Spirit Talker assured me that the Arapaho would retrieve their fallen brothers once we had moved on. We did mercy kill a couple of wounded horses. Incredibly, our herd mostly stood fast during the battle. It didn't take long to round up a couple of wandering beeves and resume the drive.

Our trail drive had developed a routine by now, and that was fortuitous given the rougher landscape ahead. Lord willing, we'd make Fort Laramie as planned. We were yet a long way from celebrating. We kept a wary eye out for more Indians. Johnson was especially worried that the Arapaho would come back, as though even a defanged rattlesnake might still bite. Most of the men simply rode with heightened awareness.

We'd survived a Kiowa threat, a thunderstorm, and an Arapaho attack. So far, so good. We still had a tad better than a month of drive ahead, assuming all went well. From Spirit Talker's and my journey last year, we knew there would be days ahead when the trail would barely permit a half-dozen miles of progress. We were blessed with ever-warmer, but that was a mixed bag given the increased possibility of spring storms.

I rode out with Collins. We were a hundred yards or so in front of the mass of better than five hundred snorting, occasionally bellowing longhorns. Now and then, a sharp ear could hear horns knock together. As we headed the drive through a shallow valley of sorts, I saw Spirit Talker off in the distance waiting for us. We had put a few days between us and the Arapaho encounter, and I was in anxious anticipation of what news he was about to deliver. Since he wasn't galloping back to us, I figured there was no immediate danger.

We finally reached his position. Collins fell back to bring the herd to a halt, as it was clear that my Comanche brother had some serious advice to impart.

"River *kobe*," Spirit Talker advised, comparing it to a wild horse. Rains and snow melt apparently had the Canadian River near to overflowing. He pointed eastward. "Better that way. Maybe one day," he urged.

This detour would set us back, but a safe river crossing was paramount. Keeping livestock and drovers from drowning was far more important than some vague schedule. Juan would be happier, too, as his wagon had proven itself a critically important part of our trail drive. I nodded to Spirit Talker. "Anything more to worry about?" I asked.

He grinned. "Think on Topsannah."

I fully understood the pangs of love he was feeling.

Prairie Flower would be awaiting us at George's ranch. Spirit Talker was likely more frustrated by delay than me, though for an entirely different reason.

Turning the herd was a challenge given the proximity of the river and the faint smell of water in the air. Spirit Talker had been right about a better river crossing downstream. I like to think it served to further cement respect for him from the likes of Hank Johnson.

———

WHILE WE WERE DRIVING our herd ever northward and a goodly distance from Fort Laramie, Otaktay and Mato sat tall astride their ponies as they observed the lumbering wagons heading ever-westward on what was called the Oregon Trail. The bright colors of warpaint across their cheeks stood out vibrantly in the midday sun. Their thoughts were filled with a mix of fear, anger, and frustration; mostly unbridled anger. The White man's treaties had proven worthless. The Great Father in Washington had no conception of the Lakota culture, that the land belonged to the Great Spirit and was not bought and sold in parcels. While they were pleased to accept any bounty from the White man, even that was not often delivered as promised. Perhaps worse, dependence on the White man's largesse was turning warriors into lazy burdens on their families. They quickly forgot how to hunt; how to fend for themselves.

"*Kize!*" declared Otaktay through clenched teeth while turning to Mato. There would be a fight. There must be a fight, a *kize*. The wagons must not pass unchallenged. "*Wasichus katá!*" The invaders must die. It was a small wagon train; a fairly easy target that would put few warriors at risk.

Mato nodded agreement. They needed to move quickly, as the point riders had already sensed danger and begun to circle the wagons to form a defensive perimeter.

Otaktay grinned. The wagons could not move fast enough.

The two subchiefs turned their ponies and joined the warriors assembled below. They had boosted their fighting spirit the night before, dancing with wild abandon around a blazing fire. The warriors were decked out in bone breastplates, leggings, and breechcloths. Lances, clubs, and bows and arrows were held at the ready behind leather shields. A couple of the Lakota even had carbines, though ammunition was scarce. Otaktay and Mato aimed to teach the folks in the wagon train a lesson they'd not soon forget; make them pay for taking their land, killing their buffalo, and bringing their deadly diseases.

"*Wasichus katá!*" Otaktay shouted as he led the warriors forward at a gallop. They presented a fearsome sight. Nearly a hundred Lakota charged at the wagons.

For their part, the wagons had not yet completed their defensive circle. They did the best they could upon seeing the crazed savages charging at them. The defenders opened up with sporadic gunfire from the wagons, as men unlimbered weapons and women and children dove beneath the wagons for protection. The air suddenly seemed full of arrows whizzing every which way.

A lone figure clothed in a black robe stood solemnly a few feet in front of the nearest wagon. His long black hair and full beard framed an intense gaze aimed skyward. The man held a cross high toward the heavens and droned some sort of religious chant. The bright sun caught the polished cross and its silver chain such that his hand seemed to alight with white fire.

Otaktay paused and stared curiously before charging his war pony full tilt at the black-robed apparition. "*Sapa unk*," he growled at the black devil. He drove his heels into his pony's sides, snatching the cross from the man as he galloped by.

The man fell to his knees and held his clasped hands high as though praying.

Otaktay spun his pony, slammed the silver relic to the ground, and galloped back toward the man. He swung his club, but, luckily for his victim, he delivered a blow that barely grazed the man's skull.

The Lakota warriors by now had easily breached the semi-circle of wagons. A defender fell victim to a Lakota lance. A scalp was lifted. Bullets and arrows flew in virtually every direction. Dust, sweat, gunsmoke, blood-curdling screams, and rallying shouts filled the air. Mules brayed and horses stomped in panic.

As Otaktay was about to make another run at the black robe, his attention was diverted. "*Tashunke!*" he hollered as he saw the opportunity to steal horses.

Arrows from a dozen Lakota quickly dispatched the two men guarding the horses, and they drove the cayuses off in a great cloud of dust.

Otaktay pulled up and surveyed the battle scene. He was pleased. "*Ayústan!*" he directed, calling off the attack.

The Lakota charged off in a cloud of dust and gathered out of range of sporadic gunfire from the defenders that yet survived. The Lakota had stolen many horses, counted plenty of coup, and taken scalps. "*Wash tay*," intoned Otaktay to Mato beside him. Indeed, it was good.

The wagon train had shuddered and quaked under

the savage attack, but at least there were survivors that would live another day. There were six wagons still serviceable from the original nine; enough to make it to Fort Laramie. One wagon was in flames and two in splinters, most of their horses were gone, several oxen were dead, and at least eight men and two women had been killed. Children either cried inconsolably or stood in silent shock. Women did their best to comfort those grieving the death of loved ones. Others cared for the wounded.

The black-robed man arose and staggered back to the wagons.

"Dang, preacher but yuh nearly got kilt," observed one of the defenders.

The preacher shook his head. "God protected me," he stated in unequivocal terms. "But we have sinned. God delivered his wrath on our people. He has punished the sinners among us." He laid accusatory eyes on anyone bold enough to challenge him.

"Preacher Rollo, get Miz Wilson to bandage that wound on yer head," directed the wagon train boss. John Kenny had seen his share of Indians back when he was with the Army. He was relieved that they'd fended off the attack, though it was at the price of settlers, wagons, and horses. Now, he would have to convince these folks to carry on, to endure, to reach Oregon. He strode toward Preacher Rollo.

It was then that the preacher realized that blood—his own blood—was staining his black frock. He raised a crucifix in feigned supplication. "God is good...God punishes the sinner." His voice trailed off, and he fainted.

The preacher had proven the bane of Kenny's existence on this journey. The trail boss had his misgivings about Leon Rollo, when the train first departed Independence, Missouri. They were now nearly halfway to their destination, though they yet faced the challenge of the Rocky Mountains. Preacher Rollo had scared off game several times with his heartfelt but loud incantations. Kenny found himself wishing that the Indian's club had found its target. To his thinking, Satan's horns held up Rollo's halo. In any case, there would be no turning back.

On the ridge above, Mato turned triumphantly to Otaktay. "*Wash tay*," he agreed. Indeed, it had been good.

The chief agreed, but concern swept across his face. Tasunke Witko would not be pleased. Crazy Horse had counseled restraint. For the moment, however, the passions of Otaktay and the Lakota warriors had been satisfied. Returning to the village with horses would salve the pain of not having followed Crazy Horse's counsel.

Otaktay watched as the wagon train reassembled. There would be many more coming. He felt a sadness coupled with frustration and anger course through him.

EIGHT
GOODBYE PANHANDLE

WITH THE ARAPAHO and Red River crossing behind us, we made great progress. After crossing the Canadian River, we came upon the remains of the Adobe Walls trading post and followed Bent's Creek northward. Soon we would be crossing the Arkansas River and then the Santa Fe Trail. There would be plenty of water and forage for a few days.

Spirit Talker and I lingered for a few minutes at Adobe Walls. Apparently, its founder William Bent had grown frustrated with Indians killing his livestock and blew the place up back in 1849. It now served as a landmark to travelers. "Guess he didn't get along with your *numunuu*," I chided my Comanche brother.

Spirit Talker shrugged. "*Kaahaniitu aitu*," he said with a derisive laugh. Indeed, deception was not good. Apparently, the Comanche didn't feel that Bent treated them fairly. "No God," he added.

I don't know whether William Bent was a man of faith or not, but it already felt as though the goings on at

Adobe Walls had faded into history so far as we were concerned.

We took a final look at Adobe Walls, turned our cayuses north, and headed off to catch up with the herd. The Texas Panhandle would soon be left behind in our trail dust. It would be a milestone in our journey but not likely one we'd take the time to celebrate.

———

IN A COUPLE OF DAYS, we drove our beeves across what was called the Cimmaron section of the Santa Fe Trail. We rested for a few hours along the gentle waters of Sand Creek before pushing on. The landscape was becoming ever more rugged and hilly. In a few days, the Sangre de Cristo Mountains would be looming off to our west.

Spirit Talker continued to scout the trail ahead. We had been blessed to not run into more Indians, and we were spared prairie fires and further thunderstorms. The weather grew ever-warmer, though it didn't diminish the trail dust eaten by drovers riding drag on the herd. Finding strays and turning them back to the herd was a constant, though most beeves followed along right well.

Now and then, a steer would get its dander up, tossing horns and pawing the dust before ambling off with no particular destination in mind. It was then up to one of our swing or flank drovers to veer off from the drive and persuade the beast to return to the business at hand. It didn't matter that the steer would be someone's dinner in a few weeks. Dinner had to be delivered. The longhorns weren't especially mindful of the nature of the landscape, and pursuing cowboys would have to nego-tiate all manner of obstacles to corner the steer, sometimes lasso it, but use whatever wiles at their disposal to return the longhorn to the herd.

Another challenge was that cows would occasionally drop a calf. At the risk of sounding heartless, fact was that the little ones simply couldn't keep up with their mamas. We had no facilities for transporting them, so they were left behind or picked up by Juan for a future meal.

As I was cogitating on our progress, Spirit Talker rode up. "Plenty water ahead. Watch for Cheyenne and Ute. Plenty them, too."

I nodded. He knew that I was well aware of the eyes that were likely watching us at this very moment. We had successfully fended off the Arapaho, but there were plenty more tribes to be on the lookout for.

Johnson came riding up to join us. He'd been riding swing alongside the herd but still managed to sport a light coating of dust. "Say boss," he greeted me, as he wiped his brow and swiped sweat from the inner hatband of his hat. "Found this in the grass." He held out an arrow toward me.

Spirit Talker's eyes widened. "Cheyenne," he quickly intoned.

Johnson handed me the arrow, and I passed it to Spirit Talker to inspect it more closely.

"Clean," said Spirit Talker. "Cheyenne close."

Now, it was Johnson's eyes that widened. More Indians! "Place be crawlin' with savages, boss!" he stated the obvious with finality. "You be right 'bout this trail."

"Hank, go alert Sam. We'll need to be keeping a watchful eye." Knowing there were no active military forts between us and our destination, I gulped at the realization that we were our own final line of defense.

As Johnson rode off, Spirit Talker turned and confided

to me. "Maybe they Cheyenne we fight many moons ago. They fear strong *sunipu*."

My Comanche brother was likely right. As if on cue, movement on the horizon to our west caught my eye. A band of about a dozen Indians sat watching us astride their ponies. I surmised that they were the Cheyenne whose arrow Johnson had found. "Hunters," I said definitively, as they were close enough for me to discern that there was no warpaint on their faces.

Spirit Talker looked off for a moment and turned to me. "No hunt us," he added.

"Shall we leave a peace offering?" I asked with a nod to our herd.

Spirit Talker laughed. "Cheyenne like buffalo. No like longhorn." He put heels to pony and headed out to resume his scouting duties.

I shrugged. "Let's keep moving," I said to myself.

Keeping especially keen eyes out for Indians would be the order of the day from this time until we reached Fort Laramie.

I CALLED in most our drovers for an after-dinner meeting. Only Bert watching the horse remuda and a cowboy performing first night guard were excused. Juan had outdone himself with chili and biscuits, so the men were drinking plenty of water and in good spirits.

I nodded to Juan, and he banged on a frying pan to get the men's attention. But for a mumble or two, conversation halted. I stepped forward. "Men, we're just better than halfway to Fort Laramie and the North Platte country. It'll be teeming with Indians." We all knew that was an understatement. "Our drive has been blessed so far. We haven't lost anyone to Indians, stampedes, or river crossings. Rustlers are a danger, but most don't venture where we're heading. I reckon God is looking out for us." I motioned for Spirit Talker to join me. "The Indian tribes ahead of us can be right nasty. A few have rifles, but most still use lances, clubs, and bows and arrows. It's lances and arrows that we need to worry about. I've asked Spirit Talker to explain."

The men jostled around a tad, as my Comanche brother stood front and center. Johnson rolled his eyes a little, but remained respectful.

"*Isa wasu,*" began Spirit Talker.

Blank expressions crossed the cowboy's faces.

Spirit Talker smiled, then grew deadly serious. "Poison. Indians use poison on tips of arrows and lances. If arrow not kill, poison kill." He had the drovers' undivided attention. "Navajo, Blackfeet, Cheyenne, Oglala Lakota...no matter. Use snake venom or rotten meat to paint arrows and lances with poison."

"Do they always use poison?" asked Collins.

Spirit Talker ruefully shook his head. "Don't know until you sick and die."

Johnson went into full foot shuffle mode. "Heathen savages!" he opined with a low growl.

"There more," offered Spirit Talker.

By now, he had the rapt attention of the gathering. No matter personal feelings about Indians, the information Spirit Talker was imparting sent involuntary shivers up the spines of these rough-edged cowpokes.

"Torture," he carefully enunciated. "Many kill selves before capture by my people in Texas. Is same here. Torture is slow death."

A murmur of alarm spread through the men. The men who'd served in the Army had experienced the aftermath of Indian torture so knew of what Spirit Talker spoke. It was horrific by any measure. They hadn't signed up for these levels of danger but intuitively knew they were a possibility. Getting killed and scalped lingered on drover minds as a constant as well. There was no shortage of possible danger to be encountered.

"Question?" asked Spirit Talker.

Johnson stepped forward. "Yuh done any of that?" he boldly asked.

Spirit Talker glanced over at me, and I nodded. "Christ save me. Strong *sunipu*, strong medicine. Spirit Talker has taken scalps. No poison, no torture."

Johnson extended his hand. "Peace," he proffered.

Spirit Talker smiled broadly and took Johnson's hand. "Peace," he replied. "But duck arrows," he added with a laugh that eased any tension among the men.

Collins shook his head. "You waited long 'nough to talk about arrows an' torture, Jack," he observed.

I couldn't contain an aw-shucks sort of grin. "Reckoned we reached a point of no return, Sam." I couldn't admit that we'd waited so as not to scare off our drivers.

The men dispersed to take up their chores and, thanks to Juan's chili, answer nature's call.

———

AFORE LONG, the Arkansas River and Bent's Fort came into view. The old fort had been abandoned in 1849, but Bent had built a new stone fort on a higher-elevation bluff not too far off and at a place called Big Timbers in 1853. Collins said he'd heard that the old fort was abandoned as a result of a cholera epidemic among the Cheyenne and other area tribes. The new fort was actually a trading post and served as a stopping point along the Mountain Route portion of the Sante Fe Trail where the location was ideal for regional trade. We decided to seize the opportunity to rest men, horses, and longhorns. Other than providing dinners and breakfasts for us, most of the herd was intact. At last count, we had five hundred and one head. I maintained a detailed written accounting of how many beeves under each brand. It was critically important that due credit be kept for the final ultimate sale.

We still had about four weeks of trail drive ahead of us, and we would be facing arguably the most dangerous part of our journey. I found myself praying just a tad more often.

I was becoming ever more appreciative of the various talents my drovers contributed. There were a couple, like Collin's man Bert and like Hank Johnson that exhibited what I call a special something. They had a God-given talent for handling longhorns akin to climbing into the beasts' heads and knowing what they were going to do before the steers even knew. A top cowboy can ride into and through a herd, cut out a feisty maverick, get his hooves cooled, and let the steer think it had come up with the idea by its lonesome. Same for calming a herd at night or spacing a thirsty herd out along a river or watering hole so all had their fill. Yep, they are special cowboys. Collins himself was a master with the lariat. I counted God's blessings that we had men such as these.

We had concerns, too. We realized that we needed more than three horses per man per day. The result was that the cayuses tired and took ever-longer to recover. We'd have to double the remuda of horses next trail drive. Another shortcoming was having only one team of oxen pulling Juan's wagon. They were big and strong but were also subject to fatigue. If an errant – or not-so-errant – arrow or bullet were to wound or take down an ox, we'd be in a bad way.

There were a few travelers lingering at Bent's Fort. I can't say as I especially liked the look of five of them in particular. They were supposedly headed to California, but were traveling pretty-light for so long a journey. Additionally, a west-bound wagon train pulled out at about the time we were arriving, and the five exhibited no inclination to travel with the settlers.

"*Tosa aitu,*" observed Spirit Talker as he rode up beside me. He pretty much read my mind. These White men were no good, if we were to judge by appearance and the way they carried themselves.

"Better keep an eye on them," I rejoined.

Collins rode up about the time I finished my own observation. "There be somethin' familiar 'bout a couple of 'em. I could swear I've seen 'em before an' not under pleasant circumstances. I suspect there be a few nooses on their family tree."

Bert joined our little gathering. "Sam, weren't a couple of them fellas in that saloon brawl in Laredo?"

Collins nodded.

"Laredo? Brawl?" I asked.

"Local sheriff broke it up. Got shot and nearly killed doin' it," responded Bert.

"Trader at Bent's says they claim to be heading to California to look for gold," I said thoughtfully. "They're carrying a lot of guns for simple miners."

"Nothin' simple 'bout 'em," responded Bert.

Collins nodded.

I turned to Spirit Talker. "Expect we'd better get on with scouting the trail ahead. It's beginning to make no sense to linger here." Up here in Kansas, there would be no Texas Rangers around to rescue us and the Army was absent.

———

WE WERE GATHERED around a campfire shortly after dinner, when we were approached by three of the travelers.

"Hail the camp," shouted the apparent leader. He was a big swarthy man with dark hair and mustache, squinty eyes, a scar across his cheek, and a pair of revolvers in his waistband.

"See if you can figure where their other two men are," I told Johnson who was standing closest to me. I kept my eyes riveted on the visitors. "Come on in," I invited.

The leader's hands hovered a bit too close to his guns, and the same went for his companions. "Comin' in," he said.

My own hand covered the butt of my Colt. "Y'all are welcome to some coffee. But keep your hands clear of those guns, my friends." I wasn't getting a friendly feeling from our visitors.

The leader moved his hands away from his guns as he came within the reach of the firelight. "Where y'all headed with all them beeves?" he asked.

"Like to know whom I'm talking with," I responded.

"Don't matter none," he responded with a dark gravelly tone.

I heard the click of a hammer being pulled back followed by a thump, a grunt, and a thud.

"What the...?!" shouted the ringleader as his right hand moved toward one of his guns. Two shots rang out from behind me, and he froze. His hand hovered nervously over the gun. The men on either side of him had taken leg shots and lay wounded in the dust.

Another hammer click behind me, and another arrow did its work.

Spirit Talker stepped from the shadows with another arrow nocked in his bowstring.

Gunsmoke wafted from the barrels of Collins's and Johnson's guns.

The ringleader's hands raised above his shoulders. "I...I surrender. Please...please don't shoot," he begged in a no-longer-dark voice. His eyes darted furtively around the scene. Of the five ne'er-do-wells, he was the last one standing. Two were dead or dying and two were wounded.

I glanced from Collins to Johnson to Spirit Talker. Seemed what came next was my call. I can't say as I had forgiveness and mercy at the forefront of my thinking. "Sam, please relieve this gentleman of his weapons."

While Collins disarmed the man and his two wounded companions, I had time to think. "Any trees around?" I semi-seriously.

The ringleader's eyes grew wide and his jaw just about dropped to his belly. "Yuh...yuh wouldn't!" he implored.

"Law of the frontier, isn't it, Sam?" I winked at Collins.

"Got a perfect rope, Jack," he responded.

I looked over at Spirit Talker. "You need more scalps?"

By this time, the ringleader had actually soiled his pants. The thought of being scalped nearly made him faint dead away. I could see that he was unsteady on his feet.

"I asked your name," I said with a hard look into the ringleader's eyes.

"Er...Jack...Jack Bowles," he responded shakily.

"Bert...Hank...please haul the dead and wounded up to Bent's Fort. I don't know what they'll do with them, but we can't have them soiling the grass our livestock must eat." With that, I walked up just about nose-to-nose with Bowles. I was about a head taller and likely half his age.

"Wha...what are yuh gonna do with me?" he pleaded as Collins tied his hands behind his back. He was on the verge of tears as he watched his companions being draped over their cayuses to be led off to Bent's Fort.

"See yonder tree, Mr. Bowles."

Bowles watched my motion to a tree about a hundred or so yards off.

"Sam, do you think that tree would work?"

The look of sheer panic that swept across Bowles's face nearly made me feel sad that we wouldn't actually be hanging him.

"I recall that Christ forgave the sinner, but didn't necessarily keep him from punishment."

We pushed and half dragged Bowles over to the tree. We tied a rope under his armpits and flung the loose end over a branch. We pulled him up so his feet were barely touching the ground. A combination of fear and relief oozed from every pore of Bowle's body.

"The folks from Bent's Fort will likely find you in a day or so, Bowles. If we see you again, we might not be in such a forgiving state of mind," I said with a serious tone that left no doubt as to what might happen to him were our paths to cross again.

"What about varmints?" he pled, as he thought on the likes of snakes, coyotes, or worse.

I shrugged. "Good luck."

———

WE PULLED out in the morning. Nary a grumble was to be heard about missing our intended rest at Bent's Fort. There was far too much to do and time was a-wasting. The Arkansas River had been a bit of a challenge, swollen as it was with rains and snowmelt. Juan's wagon nearly got caught in a strong current and would have been swept downstream but for the quick action of a couple of our men with well-placed tosses of their lariats.

In the evenings with the herd settled down, I occasionally took some time to teach Johnson the art of the bow and arrow. I had a dual purpose in engaging him on this, as I sought to turn him from his prejudice against Indians. It was in one of those evenings that our conversation took an unexpected turn.

"I built this bow myself and made my own arrows, Hank. Spirit Talker patiently taught me how. A man's relationship with his bow is very personal. It doesn't have to be perfect, but we accept that and compensate for the imperfections. It's like we humans. We aren't perfect, but we try."

Johnson nocked an arrow, pulled back the bowstring, aimed, and let fly. He missed. The cowboy lowered the bow. "Guess I need my own bow. Sights on yers don't work," he said with a chuckle. He paused and took a deep breath. "Would yuh get yer Injun' friend to show me?"

I gulped. "Er...sure."

"What's the North Platte like, boss?" he said, shifting the subject.

"Fort Laramie is not exactly perfect," I said with a broad grin. "Teepees and huts surround the place.

Command is weak. Indians and even Whites are sick or starving."

"Yuh think they be buyin' our beeves?"

"With more folks heading west on the Oregon Trail, we expect the garrison to be strengthened. They need our beeves. There are ranches around, too. We'll be seeing a friend of mine with a big spread north of the fort," I was beginning to think that just maybe I was sharing a bit too much information.

"Cattle ranch?" asked Johnson.

"Nice spread. Lush grass. Plenty of water," I responded. "Folks can have second chances; start new lives. Pretty much like Texas...or most of this country we've driven our beeves through."

Johnson scratched his chin and did his habitual foot shuffle. "Tried to raise cattle once already," he said solemnly.

I had inadvertently reopened the wounds from losing his own family. I had to admit that I wasn't fully over my own loss, so he and I had something very much in common. "I believe that with loss, God gave me opportunity, Hank."

He shuffled his feet.

I looked off at the sun sinking at the horizon. "By my reckoning, Hank, man is often the most cruel, thoughtless, selfish critter in God's kingdom. This vast space around us that folks call the frontier tends to make evil less obvious to the naked eye. Sometimes, you must turn over rocks to find the venomous snakes among us. Rocks turn to dust, snakes die, and the grasses grow lush. One day, the range will be over-crowded, and our imperfections more clearly seen. It's like I mentioned about the bow and arrow. When you make your own, you compensate for its imperfections. We are not perfect, but with

God's help we can try to be as perfect as possible." I took a deep breath. "So far, God hasn't let me down."

"Even after losin' yer family?" Johnson enjoined.

"Yes," I said emphatically.

———

"RUNNING WATERS!" shouted George.

She came running to the cabin door. "Yes?" she responded.

George pointed off to the northernmost boundary of his ranch; to where the Oregon Trail ran beside the North Platte River.

Six tattered wagons lurched along. Men and women, shoulders slumped in defeated hangdog postures, trudged beside them.

"I'm going to ride out there and see what I can do," said George.

Running Waters nodded. With a child growing within her, she wasn't quite up to horseback riding these days. "Have plenty food," she assured him.

George saddled up promptly and headed out to meet the wagons. He slowed to a trot, as he drew near.

The lone point rider brought the caravan to a halt. He appeared to be just about as weary and downtrodden as the folks in the wagons trailing behind him. One black-robed man with a bandage around his head did stride in front of the lead wagon. He held a Bible and seemed to be saying something that George couldn't make out.

"Hail the wagons!" called George. As he rode closer, it became obvious from shredded canvas wagon covers and the bandages on some of the men and women that the wagon train had been attacked by Indians; likely the nearby Oglala Lakota. A few arrows remained embedded in a couple of the wagons. He rode up beside the point man. "My name is George Freeman. Live yonder," he said, motioning toward his cabin with smoke pirouetting from its chimney. "Y'all need some help?"

"From a nig—" The man caught himself. He was too tired, too defeated to even express his prejudice against Blacks. He glanced back at the forlorn-looking wagon train behind him. "Yes," he finally confessed.

"Tell your folks that you're turning south. I'll get my wife to cook up some grub and get fresh bandages. Looks as though your horses and oxen could use some rest, too."

"My name is John Kenny. I head this train. What about them Injuns?" asked the train boss.

George scanned the horizon. "Don't appear to be bothering us today, John," he responded with a wry comforting sort of smile.

Kenny turned his horse about and rode off to tell his charges that help and comfort was at hand.

The Black rancher watched the man ride off. The fact that the wagon train had moved on from its encounter with the Lakota seemed to speak well of their fortitude. It was a very necessary characteristic toward survival on the frontier. George would counsel them on whether it would be best to move on or double back to Fort Laramie and await another caravan of settlers headed west. There was a degree of safety in numbers, and six wagons might be just a bit lean for traveling on. They'd surely be less likely to endure another large-scale Indian attack.

NINE
FIRE!

WE FELT RIGHTLY RELIEVED at having escaped the incident near Bent's Fort. We were already better than a full day north of the Arkansas River, and the trading post was well behind us.

The lead steer must have caught a whiff of it first. Doggone, but those beasts had sensitive noses. I saw Spirit Talker heading toward me about as fast as his pinto pony could carry him. He drew up in a cloud of dust and horse lather.

"*Kuuna! Kuuna!* Fire, Jack!"

I gazed off at the northern horizon and could barely make out a dusky-gray haze blanketing the far-distant prairie ahead. Strong winds were already bending trees and grasses not far from us. Any fire could quickly grow to cataclysmic proportions when fed by strong winds. We were in the southern portion of the region between the Arkansas and South Platte Rivers; in a no-man's-land so far as any water refuge. The landscape had begun to feature what knowing folks called hogback ridges with intervening valleys. Much of the terrain north of the

Arkansas had been smoothed out over the centuries by an almost constant cover of windblown sand and silt. There were sand dunes and gentle ridges of sand so far as the eyes could see as covered sparsely by sand-sage prairie vegetation. Could we turn the herd back and make a run for the Arkansas River? Could we outrace a windblown prairie fire? All this was running through my head while Spirit Talker pranced about on his pony. "We gotta run for it!" I finally blurted and pointed south.

Spirit Talker brought his pinto under control. "No run!" he stated in no uncertain terms. "Turn west," he added, pointing emphatically in that direction.

I gave him a quizzical look. "West?" I challenged.

"*Kuuna* on wind. Pass north. Strong *sunipu*."

What could I say? Strong medicine? The Indians had been dealing with prairie fires for centuries, even did controlled burns themselves or used fire to drive buffalo. I could see that our beeves were already getting nervous at the faint aroma of the smoke beginning to hang in the air. Cattle bawled with a hint of distress and tails flitted about nervously even as the longhorns kept moving forward. Being around these beasts long enough, I had begun to learn of their instinctive tendencies, even their personalities. This situation would test those sensibilities. "Sam! Bert!" I shouted. "Turn the drive west! Do it fast! There's fire ahead!"

They didn't question my orders. Not a moment's hesitation. Me? I prayed to God that Spirit Talker was right and the fire would indeed pass us by. I couldn't imagine the chaos from a stampede in the midst of a blinding hot prairie fire. No telling how many beeves or drovers we might lose, much less how much suffering might be endured from burns.

The herd obliged, as our lead steer needed little

persuasion to turn. There we were, moving five hundred doggies west at a run with a crystal-clear vista to our south and smoke-filled skies to our north. As the beeves moved off cooperatively at a decidedly faster pace than we'd typically push them to, I realized that Juan and our supply wagon were still lumbering along to the rear. Oxen were being oxen; plodding along at their normal slow measured gait. They were strong but not built for speed.

I rode back to encourage Juan to get the most from the oxen. If the fire were to turn southward, the result could be tragic. I pulled up alongside the wagon. "*Rápido*, Juan. Use the whip."

Juan shrugged. "Whip no help. Oxen slow," he said with a hint of resignation and frustration born of sheer helplessness in the face of the looming conflagration.

I looked to the north. Smoke on the horizon hung thick. Thus far, the fire was headed due east just as Spirit Talker had figured. I thanked God that we weren't in the midst of the blaze. I began to see all sorts of varmints fleeing in our direction. Deer, coyote, pronghorns, bobcats, lizards, rattlesnakes, prairie dogs, all shared a common panicked flight from the danger.

Juan caught my observing of the escaping wildlife. "Dinner," he said with a wry grin. He gave the whip a crack over the heads of the oxen after all.

A deer appeared no more than ten feet from me. The doe paused in her panic. I pulled the Colt from my holster and dispatched her with two shots. The herd was far enough off, that I figured gunfire wouldn't be starting a stampede. I glanced at an approving Juan. A couple of coyotes paused to watch me with hungry yellow eyes. There was no time to waste. I snarled at the critters and quickly dismounted, did a quick field dress, and threw the deer carcass into the back of the slow-moving wagon. There'd be venison on this night's menu, and the coyotes would have to have to be satisfied with deer entrails. As I went to remount Big Red, I narrowly avoided stepping on a rattlesnake. Dangers seemed to lurk pretty much everywhere, though the fire did seem to be passing well off to our north. I tipped my hat to a smiling Juan and headed off to catch up with the herd while praying that the wind didn't make a sudden shift southward.

It didn't take long to rejoin the cattle. Collins and the men were managing to keep the running mass of longhorns just shy of stampeding. We ran them at a goodly pace for a few miles before turning them into a milling circle well clear of the prairie fire that was moving east as borne on strong winds.

Spirit Talker finally signaled that we were clear and began heading northward.

Collins rode up beside me. "We gonna rest the herd, boss?"

It was still early in the day, and we were losing precious time. I looked around at the sparse vegetation and considered the lack of plentiful water. I shook my head. "No," I said firmly. "We need to find water and grazing. Head'em out."

Collins gave me a look as though thinking he might challenge my decision but turned and galloped off shouting, "Head'em out, boys!"

————

AS WE TRAVERSED the burned-out landscape left in the wake of the prairie fire, I found myself especially grateful for my Comanche brother. It had to be God's will that we managed to eke our way out of so many deadly scrapes.

We cleared the area consumed by the fire and turned the herd to the northeast to bring us back on the trail. Spirit Talker was doing his best to keep us well away from the Sangre de Cristo Mountains, where the trail would be more challenging for our longhorns. He and I communicated regularly, as the need for decent forage and water was growing to concerning proportions. Juan's water barrels were nearly empty.

We remained ever-mindful of Indians. I couldn't shake that lingering sense of being constantly watched. It's not an easy feeling to shake, as it grabs my very core. I pray frequently and rely on my faith but am unable to escape that tingling unease, that angst tearing at my insides.

We were able to occasionally relax in the evenings. Johnson would entertain us with a ballad or two, but Shorty's offerings were special. He had this device he blew through called a pipe organ—I later learned it was called a harmonica—that he'd play while dancing a jig around the fire. He even got Johnson to tap his toes instead of shuffling. Shucks, I even felt the urge to dance. Of course, as we hit dry stretches of the trail as we were now, our lips and throats suffered along with Shorty's pipe organ playing.

Did I say dry? We learned not to lick our lips during stretches when water was scarce, as saliva dried and tended to encourage cracking and blistering made worse by trail dust seeping into the tiny wounds. Lack of water was the bane of a drover's existence. It caused us to be ever on the alert, as longhorns seemed able to smell water at considerable distances. Once a herd decided it was thirsty and smelled water, there really was no stopping them from satisfying that thirst. It was all we drovers could do to head the beasts where we wanted them to go. Typically, the lead beeves would arrive first and savor clear waters. By the time the drovers had a chance to slake their thirsts, the water generally got quite murky. Collins sidled up to me on one occasion and observed that he could just about chew his water. After that, we tried to drink upstream or at least get ahead of the lead steers. This trail drive was ever a learning experience. This is all fair enough to think on, but right now everyone was thirsty.

The longhorns are a hearty breed, but they need water. One day we were blessed with a light rain, but it did nothing to slake thirsts of man or beast. We even failed to gather a significant amount of rainwater in Juan's barrels. We had extended our daily drive into the darkness of night to take advantage of cooler temperatures. The thinking was that not sweating would reduce our thirst. Nope. I daresay that a couple of our men were so thirsty that they thought seriously on cutting their arms and drinking their own blood or killing a longhorn for its blood. Others gave consideration to drinking their own urine.

On about the seventh day of what I judged as one of the toughest tests of our trail drive, Spirit Talker came riding in. He didn't have to, as longhorn noses were lofted on high catching the tell-tale scent of water. "Water, Jack!" he called out upon approaching. We had apparently reached the South Fork of the Republican River. Despite the dearth of rain, it would surely be flush with snowmelt.

It was all the drovers could do to keep the herd from stampeding. If left to their own devices, the beasts would make a panicky run to the river. Collins and the men were hard-pressed to force the beeves into a gradual process of slaking thirsts a few at a time.

As I watched from a bluff, the longhorns waded into the waters. The drovers took turns heading upstream to avoid swallowing muddy mouthfuls of the life-giving water. All of us took the opportunity to immerse ourselves in the refreshingly chilly current, washing off the sweat and trail dust built over the past few days.

There was also enough forage around to make it worth our while to let the herd rest and eat. We were approaching the final segment of our drive.

TEN
MORE INDIAN DANGERS!

THE CHEYENNE chief's words spewed forth with venom. Fires of hate shot from his eyes. "Tonight, we eat!" he assured the dozen warriors around him. Beneath the savages, ponies pranced with excited anticipation. The buffalo herds had moved off, and Jack's herd represented easy pickings to feed his hungry people.

Spotted Tail scanned the herd and assessed the cowboys driving it northward across his lands. The reassuring words of the White man still stung, words that guaranteed that the Cheyenne would have dominion over these lands forever. Despite the promises the Whites kept coming. There seemed no end in sight. The cowboys driving this herd were well-armed, but the day was hot windy, and their attentions were focused on keeping the longhorns on the trail. More accurately, the longhorns were cutting a trail through virgin lands. The chief's war party was small, but these were among his very best warriors, and his enemy was outnumbered two to one.

The Cheyenne chief wondered about the identity of lone Indian leading the drive. He was neither Cherokee not Pawnee, tribes normally friendly with the Whites. The Indian was surely not Arapaho or Lakota. Perhaps, he would dispose of the scout himself, and he told his war party so. "Scout for Whites...mine," he said, making his intentions crystal clear. The scout was well-armed and would be no easy victim.

Meanwhile, Spirit Talker had already spotted the war party and had turned to ride back and warn the drive.

Spotted Tail was not to be denied his warrior blood lust. His emotions had taken command of his rational senses. He directed his warriors to attack the trail drive, while he sprinted off at a gallop to intercept Spirit Talker. In his hatred, he foolishly stripped the attackers of his leadership.

I HAPPENED to glance up from coaxing a steer back into the herd. A dozen hostiles decked in warpaint were descending on the herd, while off to my right, a lone warrior was chasing down Spirit Talker. Making a quick assessment, I pulled the Sharps carbine from its scabbard, loaded a cartridge, and eased off a shot in the general direction of the charging savages. The booming report got the attention of Collins and the rest of the drovers. The shot naturally roused the beeves, as they were instantly startled into a near stampede. My shot hit thin air, but the sound alerted the attackers to their potential victims' readiness to defend themselves.

Spirit Talker also saw the attack unfolding before him. Any warning was too late, and it was clear that he had an immediate need to defend himself from the Cheyenne chief. While at full gallop, he nocked an arrow in his bowstring. What followed seemed like forever, though it was merely fractions of seconds.

Just as Spotted Tail drew close enough to count coup, Spirit Talker's arrow found its way deep into the charging savage's chest.

The Cheyenne chief's eyes grew wide with surprise, as he found himself involuntarily spinning from the back of his pony. He landed with a thud that momentarily knocked the wind from him. As he struggled to catch his breath, his eyes focused on the arrow shaft protruding from his chest.

Spirit Talker wheeled about and leaped from his pony. In but a heartbeat, he stood, knife in hand over Spotted Tail's body.

The Cheyenne chief's face contorted with pain, as he drew his own knife. A quick glance beyond Spirit Talker revealed that the attack by his warriors had failed. His foolish pride had cost them any chance at victory. "Who are you?" he struggled to ask while grimacing in agonizing pain. The arrow having penetrated a lung, his breathing came in short gasps.

Spirit Talker would have none of the Cheyenne attacking with a knife. He deftly moved his foot, pinning the chief's knife-gripping hand. He pressed down extra hard with his foot.

The savage tried to grasp the Comanche's knee, but his strength was waning. He released the knife. "Who?" he asked again.

"Me Spirit Talker, son of Buffalo Hump, mighty chief of the Penateka Comanche," he informed his dying prisoner.

"You take hair?" Spotted Tail asked.

It was all Spirit Talker could do to contain his birth instincts. A Cheyenne chief's scalp would be a worthy adornment. It was Spotted Tail's lucky day. Spirit Talker shook his head. The Cheyenne warrior beneath him was breathing his last. Taking a scalp would have been easy. Instead, he looked off at the Cheyenne war party gathered a couple of hundred yards away on the bluff overlooking the passing cattle herd. There were now ten warriors. Spirit Taker slid his knife back into its sheath and cautiously backed away from Spotted Tail's body. He mounted his pony and waved derisively at the warriors before riding off to catch up to Jack and the trail drive. The Cheyenne would not soon forget this encounter. Did it serve as threat or warning?

I SLOWED as Spirit Talker rode in beside me. I laid a grin on my Comanche brother. "That went well," I chided.

"No trouble from Cheyenne," assured Spirit Talker with a broad smile of his own. Somehow, he was finding it ever-easier not to scalp his battle victims. "God good. Strong *sunipu*," he added.

"The Oglala Lakota still lay ahead," I reminded him.

"See George soon," he replied with feigned ignorance of the possible dangers lying ahead.

"Topsannah," I said with a laugh.

Spirit Talker blushed, or at least the old scars from the mountain lion attack turned a deep pink.

ELEVEN
CROSSING THE SOUTH PLATTE

WE WERE at times grudgingly learning the dos and don'ts of driving a herd of beeves over uncharted territory. I heard someone once way that there's no learning from the second kick of a mule. If you haven't learned from the first kick, you deserve the second.

I could tell from the way the longhorns were behaving that the South Platte wasn't far off. As rivers went, the South Platte meandered along like most. There'd been no rain, though the river would be fed by snowmelt. We were depending upon Spirit Talker to find a good crossing. With any luck at all, we'd reach Fort Laramie in about ten days.

If a person believed in fate; trust me, it now intervened. We had stopped for the evening and were finishing dinner, when Juan took me aside.

"Boss, look at this," he said, pointing to the rear axle of the wagon.

"What?" I asked.

He placed his finger on a long crack. "Is getting worse," he advised.

"Can we lighten the load?"

Juan shook his head. "We need a new axle."

I looked around. There were a couple of cottonwood trees nearby, but it would take hours to fashion an axle, and there was no guarantee that the thing would be strong enough. The cottonwoods grew near the water, and I wasn't sure how well an axle fashioned from green wood might perform.

Juan looked at me questioningly.

"Let's go cut down one of those," I said, pointing to a cottonwood. "I'll get Hank and Shorty to help out."

Blessedly, Juan had the foresight to have brought a saw and wood plane among other tools, though it would take hours to make the axle to precisely match the broken one. Then we'd have to prop up the wagon to accomplish the replacement. All the while, we'd be praying that this fix would work.

Spirit Talker rode up, as we were preparing to cut down a cottonwood. "What happen?" he asked.

"We'll be stuck here for a few hours. The axle is broken."

He shook his head.

I could tell that he was both anxious to get to George's ranch and the lovely Topsannah and concerned that we might be a stationary target for any roaming bands of Oglala Lakota or Blackfeet.

———

THE AXLE REPAIR took longer than expected. The piece of cottonwood tree we'd cut was fairly easy to shape, and I must say that it ultimately mirrored the size and shape of the broken axle. A time-consuming difficult came with us having lifted the back end of the emptied wagon and propped it on a tree stump. Twice in fitting the new axle, the wagon teetered on the brink of falling over on its side. It took five of us to set it right each time. We salvaged the iron fittings from the old axle, so that did make the replacement process just a tad easier.

Once the axle was in place, lubricated, and wheels reattached, we performed the laborious task of repacking the wagon. It took a while, because Juan was very precise about where the wagon contents were stored. Part of that was owing to a need to balance the load and partly because Juan was obsessed with organization.

We ultimately lost a day with the wagon. I hoped and prayed that it would hold together for the remainder of the trail drive. The cottonwood was green lumber, and I feared that it would shrink or even split as it seasoned.

Importantly, Juan was smiling, and the oxen kept up their slow, plodding, but ever-sure pace.

WE FINALLY DREW up to the South Platte River. Given that it was late in the day and the crossing would require extra energy, we decided to spend the night on the south side of the river.

I was sacked-out laying fully-clothed atop my blanket with my head propped on my saddle and Colt revolver within easy reach. I was asleep under one of those incredibly magnificent skies so typical of the frontier west. Stars stretched as far as the eyes could see and but for the lowing of cattle and occasional owl hoot or coyote howl, I could almost hear the stars twinkle.

I was dead asleep, when a wet nose nudged my cheek. I slowly opened one eye and found myself staring into a pair of blue eyes set in a furry gray face. I had not seen *isa* for many months. Here he was having found me once again. It was uncanny how this particular wolf could find his way to me.

Isa nuzzled me as though urging me to get up.

I obliged but paused. I had obligations now. I slipped over to Spirit Talker.

"Brother," I said softly.

He looked up at me through sleep-heavy eyes.

I motioned toward *isa*.

Spirit Talker's eyes grew wide.

"I must follow," I whispered.

He nodded. "See you in morning," he added with a nonchalant tone as though the appearance of the wolf was no surprise. Spirit Talker had come to accommodate my relationship with wolves, especially this wolf. To him, it represented strong *sunipu*, a force bestowed on me from a higher power, from God.

I turned, grabbed my Colt and bow and arrows, and followed *isa,* who was waiting impatiently. It was more like I followed his shadow in the moonlight. He'd pause now and then and look back to be certain I was keeping up.

We must have traveled a couple of miles, when I saw the distant flickering of a campfire.

Isa now slowed. He finally stopped and sunk to his haunches while I caught up.

It didn't take long to figure why he'd stopped. As we drew near, I could hear snoring and then saw three blanket-covered forms lying around the campfire circle. Their horses and a couple of pack mules were tethered nearby. So far as I could make out, there was no sentry. A sniff of the air gave a big clue as to the cause of their careless-ness. There had been some heavy drinking. In the combination of moonlight and firelight, I made out a stack of furs bundled for transport on the mules.

Isa stealthily traversed the campsite and pawed at the furs.

I rightly figured there was no way these men were waking up any time soon. A herd of longhorns could have crashed through, and they'd never have awakened. Nevertheless, I traipsed cautiously across the campsite to the furs.

Isa looked at me desperately, nuzzled a stack of furs, and let out a soft whine.

Upon cutting the ropes and freeing the furs, I quickly realized the source of isa's concern. One of the furs bore the scars of an old arrow wound and now the recent hole made from a bullet. This had been isa's mate, the one I had rescued many months back. It's important to understand that wolves mate for life, and they are very loyal to and protective of the pack. The Comanche admire the wolf for these characteristics. I lifted the wolf pelt from the stack and spread it before me. What happened next served to fully blow my mind.

Isa pushed the fur toward me. He nosed it to my feet with clear intent. I knelt and stroked the fur. With that, he began licking my hand and nuzzling me.

I wasn't sure what isa was trying to say. I lifted the fur and his licking and nudging became more earnest. It was as though he was giving me this pelt, this last vestige of his mate, as a gift. I wrapped it over my shoulders.

If a wolf's eyes could express gratitude, then isa's blue eyes were very much alive with thanks. I reached out to pet him. Instead of shying back or even running away, he allowed my hand to caress his neck and back. There was a comfort shared between us, a closeness. If this was God's doing, then strong sunipu surely hung in the air.

The wolf, *isa,* was the leader of a pack. I sensed a certain tension, as though he wanted to be with me but had responsibilities.

"It's okay," I said, as though he could understand my words.

About this time, one of the drunken trappers stirred. He apparently had to answer nature's call. The man stood shakily and staggered a couple of steps in our direction.

Isa growled. His hackles went up, and, with fangs bared, he presented a fearsome sight.

The man reacted as though he'd seen a ghost. He answered nature's call right then and there without dropping his pants. He then passed out.

There was part of me that wanted to punish these men, but they'd done nothing illegal so far as man's law. I reminded myself to not give human characteristics to animals, even those to whose spirit I seemed to be drawn. The wolf pelt would surely have fetched a pretty penny at whatever trading post they dealt with. Despite this, I felt led to give a warning. My arrows were marked to resemble Comanche shafts. I nocked an arrow and shot it into a tree beside the horses and just above where the furs had been stacked. I hoped it would throw just a bit of a scare into them.

Isa nudged me a final time and darted away, likely to rejoin his pack.

"Zeb," I whispered after him. I felt led to give *isa* a name, and Zeb, short for Zebedee in the New Testament, translated to "gift from God." I had a feeling I'd be seeing him again, as I wrapped the wolf fur around my shoulders and headed back toward our camp.

I arrived just before sunrise and encountered Spirit Talker.

"Strong *sunipu*," he said upon seeing the large fur draped over my shoulders and then shifted his gaze behind me. "Jack have friend," he observed.

I looked behind me.

Zeb's blue eyes were riveted on mine.

Spirit Talker smiled and shrugged. He began saddling his pony to scout the trail ahead but paused long enough for me to share what happened with the trappers.

I gave him the short version of the incident and Zeb's role.

"Have to find Comanche name for Jack," he said with sincere solemnity.

I figured it was about time. I hoped and prayed that a Comanche name might be so powerful as to strike fear into any enemies.

"Me think on this," said Spirit Talker as though reading my mind. With that, he mounted his pony and was off. Characteristics like loyalty, family, fierceness, protectiveness, and cunning were part and parcel to the way Comanche revered the wolf.

I nudged Big Red's sides and headed for Collins and the herd. I took a couple of brief looks behind me, and Zeb was following. I wondered how the drovers would react to a wolf in camp.

The sun was peeking from the horizon and the campsite was swarming with drovers grabbing biscuits, jerky, and coffee before heading out to get the herd moving. No one paid any attention to the wolf pelt still draped over my shoulders until they saw the beast trailing behind me.

Collins was first to react. "Whoa, Jack. You've got company!"

I let Zeb catch up with me. He looked around warily at the drovers, yet seemed fearless. "He's attached himself to me, Sam," I said loudly enough for all within earshot to hear. "I've named him Zeb."

"Just keep him away from me," said Hank Johnson with a strong hint of fear in his tone.

Juan smiled. "Wolf kill own meal," he said, recognizing that wolves were not carrion eaters.

"I think he can fend for himself," I assured the cookie. Of a sudden, I realized that I hadn't slept. No matter. There was work to do. I folded the fur and tied it behind my saddle for now.

I ultimately made a vest of the wolf pelt. It wasn't appropriate fashion for the warm daylight hours but sure could take the chill out of the night. When I did don the vest, it made me quite a sight in combination with my bear claw necklace set off with mountain lion fangs and featuring a cross dead center. Of course, the image was significantly enhanced by Zeb. A companion wolf was not exactly common, and Zeb was large as his kind went. Little wonder that he'd been the Alpha male of his pack. Oh, I did wonder what became of Zeb's pack. He wasn't talking, and I knew he wouldn't have simply left the pack even for me or his mate. Something serious had happened. In any case, I firmly believed that God had placed Zeb in my life.

––––––––

MEANWHILE, dark eyes were watching us. "*Katá wasichus,*" muttered a voice behind the dark eyes. *Katá wasichus,* to kill White men, was the venom that captured the warrior's soul. This warrior was of the Lakota tribe that the Whites called Blackfeet. They were of the Sihasapas subgroup of the Lakota Sioux and were known for a brand of horrific savagery matched only by the

Comanche. Folks attacked by the Blackfeet saved a bullet for themselves rather than endure torture if captured.

"*Kize,*" intoned one of the warrior's companions. He was anxious to fight; to get the attack underway.

"*Wash tay,*" responded the warrior. It was good, and they would attack soon. He was being cautious, as he had no idea whom he was dealing with. No herds had passed this way before, so he was unfamiliar with this new activity by the Whites. His war party was small; barely outnumbering the well-armed drovers. The Blackfeet needed to find a place with topographical advantage from which to attack the *wasichus*. He pointed off in the distance to a ravine through which the herd would have to pass. From the high ground on either side, the warrior figured their numerical disadvantage would be offset. "*Katá wasichus,*" he repeated with a snarl. With that, he turned his pony and led his war party off at a gallop. Killing *wasichus* and stealing cattle might get him recognized as a chief in the Blackfeet nation.

Spirit Talker saw just a hint of dust off to the west. It wasn't nearly enough to have been kicked up by buffalo or even a herd of mustangs. This dust was being kicked up by humans, most likely Indians. Which tribe was yet to be seen. He looked ahead and noted the same ravine to which the dust cloud seemed to be moving. The young Comanche turned his pony and raced back to intercept the trail drive.

Spirit Talker pulled up beside Jack and Collins. "Ambush ahead," he warned.

"Are they Lakota or Cheyenne?" asked Collins.

"Too far away. Head for ravine. Attack from high."

I pondered Spirit Talker's warning. Considering how strung out the herd was and the unlikelihood of finding another route given our commitment to that very ravine that lay ahead, I had to figure how we might best defend ourselves. "Plenty dust?" I asked.

Spirit Talker shook his head. "Little," he stated. That meant any war party likely lacked any numerical advantage. However, they'd have the high ground, and that was decidedly a strategic advantage.

Collins was watching me expectantly. What were we to do?

"Sam, we're going to split up. We only need a couple of drovers to keep the beeves headed through the ravine. You take Hank and Shorty and head for the higher ground to the right above where the Indians will be waiting to ambush us. Spirit Talker, Bert, and I will do the same to the left. It's the last thing those savages will ever expect." I put on a brave front, but my knees were quaking. I hope and prayed to be alive to return to Rising Cross in time to greet my new son or daughter into this brutally tough world.

Collins looked befuddled for a moment, then realized that splitting was our only chance. We would ambush the ambushers.

"Is good plan, Walks with Wolves," added Spirit Talker. He had revealed the name he had unceremoniously chosen for me.

"Walks with Wolves?" Collins asked.

"Long story, Sam. Tell you after we put a licking on these savages," I assured him.

In a matter of minutes, our strategy was underway.

About halfway down the sides of the ravine a dozen Blackfeet warriors awaited the appearance of the *wasichus* with the cattle and horses the Blackfeet would prize after slaughtering the drovers. They were totally unaware that their prey had become the hunters.

My men approached stealthily on either side and high

above the hidden Blackfeet. I had ground reined Big Red, and Spirit Talker and Bert had done the same with their mounts. Zeb followed me closely and protectively. I decided to use bow and arrow, figuring to surprise the ambushers with silent death. Collins and his men would necessarily be shooting, though I had seen Johnson take his new bow and arrow with him. He'd actually used the bow and arrow to bring down a large buck a few days back.

The Blackfeet were fully focused on the herd as the lead longhorns began to pass below them. Imagine the surprise, when one of my arrows found its way square into the back of a Blackfoot warrior. He screamed with pain as he flinched with the impact and then looked down to see the arrowhead protruding from his chest. His gasping shout signaled the start of our attack.

An arrow from Spirit Talker's bow found the next victim, as confusion was sowed among the Blackfoot warriors. Their attentions shifted from the ravine below to some unknown attackers from above. Worse, their force was divided.

Our herd was moving quickly through the narrow ravine. Any element of surprise by the Blackfeet was totally lost. The herd below prevented them from joining forces and retreat was cutoff by the attackers from above. They tried in vain to find cover. Every time a warrior tried to move to protect himself from arrows and gunfire raining in from above, he'd risk near-certain death or wounding. Adding to the confusion was the dust kicked up by the longhorns as they passed. The clouds of grit shielded the Blackfeet on one side of the ravine from seeing their warrior brothers on the other side.

To make matters worse for the hostiles, it turned out that my first arrow had killed the war party leader. Chaos swept through the leaderless war party. Those still alive began to use the dust to shield their retreat to the south from whence they had come.

I signaled Spirit Talker and Bert to return to the horses. My hope was to head off any escaping Blackfeet. I wanted any survivors to know whom they had tangled with.

It took but a few minutes to head off four remaining Blackfeet. As I moved to cutoff their escape, Collins and the others pulled in behind them. They were surrounded, yet looked as though they were ready to fight to the death. I harbored no doubt that they would.

At this moment, Spirit Talker rode up. By now, he had painted a scary looking broad black band across the upper portion of his face. It was the typical warpaint of a Comanche warrior. He stood tall on his pony and clasped his hands in front of his chest in the Indian sign for peace.

The Blackfeet paused with astonished expressions on their painted faces. Their eyes showed a strange mix of fear and defiance.

Spirit Talker had them stopped. Now what? "*Isa!*" he snarled and bared his teeth. He motioned over toward Zeb standing beside me with fangs bared. Combined with the scars that yet remained from the mountain lion's attack and the black warpaint, my Comanche brother looked about as fearsome as any man might be.

I dismounted and stood beside Zeb. It was obviously a moment of strong *sunipu*.

Spirit Talker pointed to me and signed my name as Walks with Wolves. He was telling the Blackfeet that their situation was hopeless; that they were beaten by the strong medicine of the wolf. He then pointed upward. *"Taa Narumi,"* he said and signaled the protection of an all-powerful God.

The Blackfeet seemed even more dumbfounded that we hadn't yet killed them all.

I stood beside Zeb and donned my wolf vest. *"Isa,"* I hissed in as tough and forceful a tone as I could muster. As Spirit Talker had done, I clasped my hands in front of my chest as a sign of peace. With that, I signaled our circle surrounding the Blackfoot warriors to open.

The defeated warriors initially couldn't believe that they were being set free.

I motioned for them to leave. Two of them tentatively made the peace sign to us, as they backed away toward their ponies.

"They come back for dead warriors after we go. Blackfeet tell others of *sunipu* of Walks With Wolves," assured Spirit Talker. "Now we journey in peace through Blackfoot lands."

"About time you gave me a warrior name," I chided Spirit Talker.

He laid a wise, all-knowing smile on me. He didn't have to say another word.

I began to remove the wolf-skin vest, finding myself folding it with a touch of reverence. The image of the Zeb taking me to the pelt of his mate was ever embedded in my brain. By now, I was convinced that my wolf protector was indeed God's doing.

"How'd you come by that wolf-skin vest, Jack?" asked Collins, as he glanced apprehensively at Zeb.

"I promise to tell you later, Sam. You likely won't believe it," I said with a slight shake of my head. It was still difficult for me to fully grasp *isa*. "Let's catch up with the herd."

Shorty called out as we turned north. "One of them

heathens got me, boss," he said through gritted teeth. "Hurts like blazes."

I looked to see an arrow stuck clean through the fleshy part of his forearm. It was partly broken off, as only the arrowhead stuck out through his shirtsleeve.

Spirit Talker rode over. "Me see," he pretty much demanded.

Shorty recalled the young Comanche's warning about poisoned arrows. Sweat beads began forming on his forehead at the mere thought. He turned his head away and held the arm up for Spirit Talker to inspect.

"Pull out. Will pain," warned my Comanche brother.

We slipped from our horses, and Shorty sat cross-legged. I slipped behind him and gave him a piece of wood to chomp down on to help endure the pain of what was to come. I held the drover down best I could and nodded to Spirit Talker.

With that, he yanked the shaft from Shorty's arm.

As Shorty tensed from the pain, it was all I could do to keep the man from going for Spirit Talker's throat. He fought me for a moment but realized the arrow was out and I managed to calm him.

Spirit Talker was nonplussed, as he examined the bloody shaft closely, especially the arrowhead.

Shorty sat his saddle, in pain and mouth agape in anticipation of the result of Spirit Talker's examination.

"Poison," Spirit Talker uttered solemnly.

Shorty's face went white.

"Must clean," advised Spirit Talker. "Need fire, need iron," he added.

"My brother, you and I will stay behind with Shorty." I looked up at Collin. "Sam, keep the beeves moving. We'll latch on with Juan and the wagon and make it to camp tonight." I saw it as my job to take care of my men, as well as keep the herd moving. Spirit Talker would know best how to treat Shorty's wound. Treating it speedily and properly was critically important. There were no doctors out here on the frontier, and my Comanche brother was Shorty's best hope for survival.

———

JUAN SAW US COMING, pulled the wagon up under a nearby tree.

"Juan, we need a fire. Shorty's been wounded," I announced.

The cookie hopped out and began to build a fire. The fire had to be a plenty hot one to get the branding iron red hot. Shorty's wound required exceptional care to clean out any poison residue and then be cauterized to ensure against infection and stop bleeding. We aimed to save the drover's arm and prayed to that effect. To say this was a painful procedure would be a gross under-statement.

Shorty was sweating buckets partly owing to the heat of the day and partly the prospect of treatment of his wound.

Juan dug into his secret compartment in the side of the wagon and fished out a silver flask. "Good whiskey," he assured us, as he handed it to Shorty.

I think tears came to Juan's eyes, as he watched Juan drain the flask of its precious contents.

Spirit Talker went about mixing a poultice, but a nasty part of the treatment yet remained.

I gave Shorty another piece of wood and had him clamp his teeth down on it. Juan and I held Shorty down, while the teen Comanche slid his knife into the wound. Shorty flinched, gasped, and passed out. Spirit Talker went to work gouging about in the wound to clean it as best possible. He finally looked to me and nodded toward the branding iron. "Must burn out bad spirits," he assured me.

The odor and sound from burning human flesh is distinctive, and I took no pleasure in cauterizing Shorty's wound. Both Juan and Spirit Talker looked away. Shorty passed out. Hopefully and God willing, it would heal well, and he'd be back to dancing and playing the harmonica sooner than later.

Spirit Talker applied a poultice to the wound to promote its healing.

"What do you think?" I asked.

"Think it good. No *isa wasu*, no poison." Spirit Talker answered. He still had a habit of translating his Comanche language for me, even though I was speaking it quite well by now.

We lifted Shorty into the wagon and slipped a blanket over him. He was chilly despite the early afternoon heat. I would later learn that the chill was a symptom of shock. I tied Shorty's horse to the back of the wagon, and we headed out to rejoin the trail drive.

The wagon moved so slowly as to test our patience. Oxen were slow but reliable. Spirit Talker and I rode out front, keeping keen eyes on the trail ahead. Zeb followed along, providing an extra set of eyes. We weren't totally convinced of the now peaceful intentions of the Black-feet. I hoped the word would go out to stay clear of Walks With Wolves.

———

IT WAS JUST ABOUT SUNSET, when we pulled into camp. You would have never thought that our men had fended off a Blackfoot attack earlier, as they milled about waiting for Juan to cook dinner. They did manage to start a fire to move the feeding process along.

Shorty woke up, and his groans emanating from the wagon immediately let everyone know that he was in pain. We endured the sounds for a few minutes before I'd had enough. I rifled through Shorty's bag and grabbed his harmonica. With no ceremony whatsoever, I stalked to the rear of the wagon and put the instrument in the wounded drover's hand. "Play this and stop complaining," I ordered. "You're going to start a stampede with all your fussing."

Relief swept over the faces of the drovers standing around the campfire. Relief quickly turned to guffaws and downright laughter, as the stress of the day was released.

Just as the sun was about to disappear below the western horizon and dinner was finally about to be served, a rattlesnake showed up. Nonplussed, I drew out my knife, threw it, and pinned the rascally serpent's head to the ground. I don't know that I could have repeated that feat in a million years, but it sure impressed my drovers. Even Spirit Talker's mouth went agape. Perhaps even more scary was Zeb cautiously easing over and beginning to chow down on the still-writhing serpent. The drovers shared my own amazement.

Again, there was the laughter of relief all around. I reckoned that this day would be the talk of the entire region by the time the trail drive was ended. It would surely be embellished, and my new Indian name would get legs and, coupled with now having a wolf companion, garner even greater *sunipu*. It would be tough to keep my wits about me; to stay humble. Not to worry, the frontier has the effect of keeping its people humble.

TWELVE
HOMESTRETCH

BETWEEN THE SOUTH PLATTE RIVER and Fort Laramie lay a landscape featuring plenty of challenges. I found myself confronted with the reality that we would soon be delivering five hundred longhorns. The drovers would have to be paid, and that depended on selling the beasts. Had they regarrisoned Fort Laramie? Did the Army still want cattle? Would they fetch a decent price? There were so many questions to be answered. August Klappenbach had offered plenty of advice, but he wasn't here by my side to help negotiate. I harkened back to God's direction in Genesis to subdue the earth and extract its potential. How much potential would I be extracting? Upon extracting that potential, would the Lord see me safely back to my family. I regularly reminded myself to stay respectful of the dangers inherent in my frontier surroundings.

Sam Collins rode up beside me, as I contemplated these weighty considerations.

"Looks like the weight of the entire world is hanging round your shoulders, Jack."

I turned to him and nodded. Big Red gave a snort, as though his own load had become heavier.

"Ease up, Jack. This is only our first trail drive," he reminded me. "We sell a few beeves, and I'll be happy."

"Hope so," I responded.

"For a God-fearing man that's emerged unscathed from so many scrapes and has a wild wolf for a pet, I'm surprised that you have doubts. You have that thing called *sunipu* that Spirit Talker always invokes."

"Strong medicine," I replied. "I expect you're right, Sam."

"And what about this wolf business you keep putting off telling me about?" he asked with an eyeball at Zeb.

"Hmmm. *Isa*," I said with a guilty-as-charged smile.

"Guess that's the Comanche word for it. What about it?" Collins asked. He nudged his horse along to keep pace with the long strides of Big Red and kept a wary eye on the lead steer rambling along behind us.

"I'll try to make a long story short," I said with a thoughtful scratch to my chin. I felt as though there were some spiritual things between me and *isa* that were just as well unsaid. "You must not share this with anyone, Sam. Can I have your word on that?"

"Cross my beating heart, Jack. Won't tell a soul."

We both looked around, as though there'd be anyone eavesdropping out here on the frontier with only five hundred longhorns to hear my story.

I urged Big Red closer, so as not to have to shout. "One night back when Spirit Talker and I were getting acquainted, this big wolf awakened me. I didn't know what to make of it. He made signs to follow him, so I pulled on my boots, grabbed my gun, and cautiously snuck along behind him. He led me to a female with an arrow sticking from her side."

"You're kiddin'," observed Collins.

I shook my head. "I pulled the arrow out. Didn't have any poultice or anything for the wound, but it was apparently enough. She got up and ambled off behind her mate. He even looked back a time or two as though thanking me."

"Seriously?" asked Collins with an incredulous expression.

"Come daylight, Spirit Talker followed the wolf's tracks from me to where the female had laid wounded," I said by way of lending credibility to my tale. "Months later, the same *isa* appeared and scared off a bunch of Indians we were fighting. The tribes admire the wolf and fear it. *Isa* is held in very high esteem. A few nights ago, *isa* appeared and led me to a campsite where trappers slept. Seems they had shot and killed his mate. He took me to her pelt while the trappers slept, and he gave it to me. That's how I came upon the wolf-skin vest." With that, I unfastened the vest from the cantle of my saddle and showed Collins the arrow wound scar and the more recent bullet wound.

Collins's mouth hung fully agape.

"That's about it, Sam. Now, Spirit Talker has given me my Comanche name Walks With Wolves, and *isa* has attached himself to me."

"You think this is a God thing, Jack?"

"I don't doubt it for a second," I assured him. "He's a gift from God."

———

WE WERE DRAWING EVER CLOSER to Fort Laramie. Likely four days out. While I normally tended to be optimistic, my memories upon departing the fort last year caused me concern. It had been and might still be a rather depressing place. The Indians and poor Whites that dwelled around the periphery of the fort seemed to be the dredges of their respective cultures. The Great White Father in Washington had yet to learn—and likely never would—that the best way to get along with the Indians was to leave them to their own ways. I was resigned to the fact that our government leaders were hellbent on changing the Indians into what they felt was best for them. My pa used to tell me that if you give a man a fish, you feed him for a day; but, if you teach a man to fish, you feed him for a lifetime. The government was big on giving the Indians "fish," what they referred to as annuities such as blankets and food. Consequently, warriors became dependent and lost both the skills and the will to provide for their people, their *numunuu*. It was unlikely that little old Jack O'Toole would ever change the White man's views about Indians, and this hard reality haunted me. Could Spirit Talker and I change anything. Could Good triumph over evil, right over wrong? We would do our part. We would need to provide for ourselves and those who trusted In us. Would our faith see us through? Likely, it would, but God would need us to be willing servants. Meanwhile, we had longhorns to deliver. Had the Army refreshed the garrison? Would they buy our beeves?

I fell back behind the herd with a saddled horse from our remuda in tow and awaited Juan and the wagon. I hadn't ridden drag in days and was quickly reminded just how nasty that role was, as dust found its way into every crevasse and opening of my clothes, tack, and body. Even Zeb hung far behind. I was chewing on trail grit, when Juan finally came into view. The oxen plodded along, and took note that the new axle seemed to be working just fine.

"*Buenas días, Juan,*" I called out after taking a swig of canteen water and spitting out the grit. "How's Shorty?"

Juan smiled and rolled his eyes. "Get him on a horse, boss. His music; it is killing my ears,"

"I heard that!" shouted Shorty from the wagon bed.

Juan pulled the wagon to a halt, and I made my way to the rear.

Shorty grinned sheepishly at me, and it was clear that his arm was well along in healing. There was no redness or swelling, so indications were that Spirit Talker's treatment of the poison arrow wound seemed to have worked. "Howdy, boss. Guess you need me back in the saddle," he understated.

I gave a wry sort of smile. "I was kind of thinking along those lines, Shorty. You up to it?"

"I'm a tad shaky walkin' but can ride. Just git me a saddled bronc, boss."

"Well, lookee here! I just happen to have one ready for you," I replied with a grin.

Shorty was quickly back in the saddle, the harmonica stuffed in his saddlebag.

Juan urged the oxen forward and gave me a relieved look as I rode back toward the herd.

———

I WAS GETTING the sense that we were all finally working together as a team. Cowboys were anticipating and solving problems before they became serious. We could quickly rally to successfully defend ourselves. I began to hope that I could draw on these men for future drives. Shucks, I was already thinking of pulling together a substantially larger drive in a year or so. It would depend on how much reception there was up this neck of the woods for Texas beef.

I wondered now and then as to whether Otaktay was watching us from afar. I expect he would be curious as to what the crazy Whites were up to with all the cattle. Weren't the buffalo enough? Actually, Otaktay and his Lakota might have begun to worry about the onset of the cattle industry across his ancestral lands. Soon enough, herds of beeves would replace the buffalo. The vast free range was simply too attractive for folks like myself. It drew cattle like a great magnet.

THIRTEEN
MORE SURPRISES!

AT A TYPICAL STOCKYARD, we would be selling our longhorns by weight. But southeastern Wyoming had yet to see the arrival of railroads, much less stockyards. I didn't expect the Army to be concerned with weighing our longhorns, though I felt led to pause a couple of days south of Fort Laramie to allow livestock to rest. It wasn't enough time to fatten up the beeves, but they might present a tad better to buyers.

The region abounded with the sort of wildlife that had made it attractive to fur trappers just a decade or so earlier. Beaver, buffalo, and more were hunted for their pelts. We set up Juan's wagon in the shade of a small grove of green ash, boxelder, and cottonwood trees. Spirit Talker and I reckoned to find plentiful alternatives to our typical mealtime fare.

The longhorns seemed to sense that the end of the trail was not far off, as they enjoyed lazily grazing the gentle rolling hills surrounding us.

If Otaktay was watching us, he surely had to be very curious as to what we were up to. I doubt that he had ever seen a longhorn, so I'm sure some of the horn spreads would amaze him. The buffalo was a hefty hunk of beast, but its difference from the longhorn was quite striking from nose to tail. He would likely be considering the wolf that had become my close companion, and word of my warrior name surely would have reached him.

I headed out on Big Red with Spirit Talker riding alongside and Zeb following. We optimistically brought a packhorse upon which to haul the bounty of our hunt. I daresay that Collins and the other cowboys were a tad jealous of us venturing out. However, they had jobs to do.

Spirit Talker and I caught sight of the fresh tracks of a small herd of deer. We figured that Juan would welcome venison. We dismounted to better track our prey. It was an exceptionally warm day, so we went shirtless, even ditching our leggings for only breechcloths. We moved silently on moccasin-shod feet with bows and arrows at the ready. We decided not to use guns, as Indians were surely in the area and there was no point in unduly stirring them up with loud noises echoing through their hunting grounds. There was a fair chance that we hadn't even been spotted by any hostiles. We hiked at least a mile with horses in tow.

I led the way up a rise and peered through the trees at the crest. I found myself face to face with a rarity of the frontier. Not fifty feet away was a white buffalo!

Spirit Talker came up alongside. "Strong *sunipu*, Jack," he whispered.

I had an urge to shoot the buffalo, but there was something hauntingly spiritual about the moment that caused me to hesitate.

"No kill," advised Spirit Talker. "White buffalo strong *sunipu* to Lakota. Make angry, if you kill."

I had to agree that needlessly upsetting the powerful Lakota in the region was foolhardy. It wouldn't do to attack the religious and spiritual trappings of the Indian culture as represented by that white buffalo. The thing was sacred. Tempting as it was, it was hard to argue with my Comanche brother. I waved my hands to scare the beast off. It wasn't going to be that easy. Instead of shying away, the buffalo turned toward us and lit up into a full charge. We dove for the cover of a tree, and it charged on past barely missing us and nearly running into our packhorse. Blessedly, the buffalo kept on running. I got a good look at the horns as he ran past and had no desire to deal with them. He was big, and any close-in fight would likely not have ended well for me or Spirit Talker. I hoped that, if any Lakota were watching, they appreciated our respect for their sacred animal.

We made certain the sacred white buffalo had left the area before resuming our hunt. We quickly rediscovered the deer tracks. I was looking down at the deer tracks, when Spirit Talker grabbed my arm and pulled me to a stop.

He pointed to the ground to our left. Moccasins! And they weren't ours. We counted as best we could and figured it to be a hunting party of no more than five. Instinctively, we nocked arrows in our bows and surveilled the area as we moved forward. The lure of venison overrode any fear of encountering hostiles. We stepped carefully down a slight wooded incline to a gentle creek.

As if the possibility of running into Lakota or Cheyenne weren't enough, we found ourselves facing a pair of grizzly cubs. The cubs were cute and cuddly but dangerous. It didn't take a mental giant to figure that momma bear had to be nearby.

I glanced at the Sharps carbine sitting in its scabbard attached to my saddle on Big Red. A .50 caliber slug could have a decent effect on any angry adult bear. Certainly, it would be preferable to a couple of puny arrows or even the .44 caliber slug in my Colt revolver.

Spirit Talker saw my glance at the carbine and shook his head.

So far, the female hadn't appeared. Could the cubs be orphans?

We decided to backtrack up the hill. We were about to reach the top, when we heard low voices interspersed with bird sounds. I looked at Zeb. His hackles were up. The sounds were obviously signals. A few guttural growls mixed in with the signals were followed by a full-fledged roar. Was it the momma grizzly? Likely. We dropped to our bellies and peeked over the top of the rise. The hunting party turned out to be Lakota, and their hunt was focused on the large female grizzly they had surrounded. She was a big one. We could see at least four arrows protruding from her. Beneath her feet was a very dead Lakota hunter. A second warrior lay curled up with painful tooth and claw wounds and was bleeding out nearby. The sow must have been angered, sent her cubs off, and turned on the Lakota. What to do? Was the bear mortally wounded?

I looked over my shoulder. The cubs had stopped cavorting and were impatiently waiting for their momma. I figured it wouldn't go well if they decided to try to find her. I could see that Spirit Talker's mind, like mine, was racing through alternatives. I could kill the bear with the Sharps or pump more arrows into her and take our chances with the Lakota or we could skedaddle from here as far as we could get. I retrieved the carbine. I was taking no chances.

In mere seconds, the scenario changed drastically. A crashing of underbrush from the woods off to our left grabbed our undivided attention. We saw the Lakota freeze. They heard it, too. Zeb hunkered down. This was far too much for his tastes.

Spirit Talker and I looked at each other with the same horrified expressions. Some eight hundred pounds of male grizzly stood snarling at us all. He stood at least ten feet tall.

"Need strong *sunipu!*" blurted Spirit Talker.

Strong medicine for sure. We dared not run. I very slowly eased the Sharps around in the direction of the bear. "Dear God, please help that grizzly make the right decision. Amen," I whispered to myself.

Spirit Talker had his eyes closed and was praying, as well.

Would the grizzly come after us or the Lakota hunters harassing his mate? Maybe, he'd simply come through us to get to them.

We became spectators to a battle unfolding before us. A Lakota began to run, the grizzly moved with lightning speed and had the luckless hunter in his grasp in mere seconds. With the Lakota's head in his jaws, he snapped the hunter around like a rag doll. We could hear bones snap. Assured that he'd killed his foe, the grizzly turned back to the remaining Lakota. Total fear swept their faces. There was no pretense of bravery. The hunters pumped arrow after arrow at the big bear. Meanwhile, the female grizzly rejoined the fray. Outnumbered, the Lakota were desperate.

I hated the idea of killing the bears. They were only defending their family. I had no choice. I turned to Spirit Talker, and he nodded.

I aimed the Sharps at the great bear and fired.

Stunned, the huge grizzly froze. He'd digested a .50 caliber slug to the center of his great chest. I slipped another cartridge into the carbine, aimed, and fired again. The grizzly growled, slapped at the fresh wound in his neck, moaned, and keeled over in a heap. The female, arrows dangling from her great furry body, sniffed briefly at him before charging over the hill past us and gathering her cubs. She seemed to sense the opportunity to escape. Protecting her cubs was most important. As she rumbled off into the woods with cubs in tow, Spirit Talker and I stood to survey the damage. Three Lakota remained standing, one within mere inches of the dead grizzly's massive paws.

The hunters looked up at us. Any pretense of hostility was absent. I had just saved their lives, and they full-well knew it. *"Unktehi mato,"* uttered one pointing at me.

Indeed, I had killed the bear. I propped the Sharps against my leg and clasped my hands in a sign of peace. Zeb joined me, and his move to sit calmly beside me sent a clear message.

The hunter who had spoken returned the gesture and nodded toward Zeb.

We approached cautiously.

"Iya Tate Wanbli," said the Lakota hunter pointing to himself and signing his name as Eagle on the Wind.

"Walks With Wolves," I said in return, signing as best I could.

"Mukwooru," offered Spirit Talker.

The Lakota gave each of us a visual once over. We were clad in our buckskins and wearing moccasins. Along with my carbine and revolver, we both sported bows and arrows. Coupled with a wolf, I expect we posed a bit of a conundrum to these lords of the northern plains. *"Oglala Lakota,"* said Eagle on the Wind.

"Penateka Comanche," said Spirit Talker, pointing to himself. He pointed to me. "*Isa* kill *wasápe*," he intoned while motioning from me to the grizzly. "*Sunipu*," he concluded with finality.

I was a tad relieved that they weren't Blackfoot Sioux, the dreaded Sihasapas Lakota. What next? I had begun to figure that Collins might be wondering when we might get back to the herd. But we were dealing with a delicate situation.

The Lakota talked briefly among themselves. I reckoned they were realizing that I was connected to wolves and had medicine strong enough to have killed the bear. Of a sudden, the three turned. All clasped their hands as a peace sign. "*Wasichus wasanke tanka*," uttered Eagle on the Wind. "*Mato*," he said and pointed to the grizzly.

"He recognize you as strong medicine, Jack. Spirit of *isa* strong. They are giving you the bear."

The grizzly was huge. Even with our packhorse, there was no way that we could haul the entire beast back to camp.

We didn't know what the Lakota word was for share, but Spirit Talker signed as best he could.

Lakota smiles were plenty of evidence that the idea was a winner.

With momma bear and cubs long gone, we set to work on the bear. The Lakota made a great ceremony of presenting me with the claws and the grizzly's hide. Having gifted a bearskin to Spirit Talker's father months back when I had brought the horses for Blue Flower, I was more fully able to appreciate the gesture. The Lakota packed most of the meat. We took just enough bear meat to add variety to Juan's stew. Spirit Talker also scooped up some of the fat from the bear, as it made for an excellent lubricant when properly rendered.

Most folks happening on the five of us working in harmony to tackle the reaping of a harvest from the big grizzly would have been amazed. Any hostilities or animosities had been cast aside. Even Zeb enjoyed a taste of fresh-killed bear meat.

In the end, we packed out all we could take. The Lakota reverently placed their blanket-wrapped brothers over their ponies and rode off with their bounty and a story to tell at their campfire about Walks With Wolves. We had parted ways in peace; all grateful that events had turned out as they did. If they were of Crazy Horse's encampment, I doubt they would convince Otaktay of our peaceful intentions. In any case, we hoped we had made some progress toward peace.

Spirit Talker and I watched the Lakota depart. "Wonder what happened to those deer we were tracking?" I said with a chuckle. My humor brought us back to reality. We would be satisfied with bear meat for now, and the Lakota wouldn't be the only ones telling a great story around a campfire.

"God good," offered Spirit Talker.

Big Red seemed happy to be headed back to camp. I'm sure my big friend had not been especially pleased at the proximity of the grizzly family. Zeb pranced behind acting more like a pet dog than fearsome predator.

———

WE FIGURED to rest one more day, before the final drive to Fort Laramie. I must say that we had encountered little to no settlement through the wild frontier of western Kansas. There were occasional abandoned cabins and spots where travelers had camped, but no active homesteading within sight of our trail drive. The fur trade had died out years back, and settlers were moving westward at more of a trickle than a wave. Unbeknownst to us, it would be another year before gold was discovered in the hills near Pike's Peak. Gold and cattle would be having a major impact on the western frontier economy, and I was just ahead of the curve with my cattle drive.

The drovers thoroughly enjoyed our tale of encountering the grizzly bears and the Lakota hunting party. We didn't feel led to embellish the story. It was nearly unbelievable without adding to it.

Juan was overjoyed to add bear meat to the stew, and the drovers appreciated a little variety of culinary fare. Juan also was pleased to render the bear fat. He knew that bear fat was pretty much the best of lubricants and that bear oil had many non-cooking functions like preserving leather, lubricating guns, and fueling oil lamps. As I understood it, bear oil also didn't go bad so quickly as pork lard and could be used for most any cooking applications. Yes, Juan was well-pleased.

We set to work tanning the bear hide. It began with removing any meat, fat, scar tissue. This is followed by rubbing plenty of salt into the hide. Once dry, the hide is ready for the tanning that turns it into a supple blanket or coat. Given that we'd be moving on, we rolled the dried bear hide and figured to wait until we reached George's ranch before tanning it. Meanwhile, we drilled holes in the bear claws, and I soon had a necklace to lay over my mountain lion necklace. I was getting to be a fearsome sight with those necklaces dangling around my neck. Oh, and an ever-thicker neck it was. I had grown, since first meeting Spirit Talker. I had no measuring stick, but Collins assured me that I was at least four inches over six feet. My frame was filling out with muscle, too. The rough life of the trail drive combined with Juan's cooking had helped put a few pounds of muscle on my bony frame. My Comanche friend was big as his people went, but I was now plenty bigger than he. I had to believe that Big Red felt the difference; not that he ever complained.

It had been a while, since Hank Johnson and I had any in-depth talk. Driving cattle tended to isolate folks except at meal times. I was taken a bit off guard, when he sidled up to me after I'd rolled the bearskin. "Must've been a whale of a scrap, boss," he offered by way of starting a conversation.

I looked up from hoisting the bear hide to my shoulder so as to dump it in the wagon. "Pretty much, Hank," I responded. "How you getting on? Been practicing with the bow and arrows?"

"Didn't come to talk 'bout that, boss." He shuffled his feet, as he measured his words. "Couple of us been talkin'," he said thoughtfully.

"What's on your mind?"

"Like to hitch on at Rising Cross, if'n you'll have us," he offered. "Figure yuh got more drives in mind."

I was momentarily taken aback.

Johnson looked at me questioningly.

"Let's see where we are, when we've delivered this herd, Hank. But, yes, I'd sure consider such an arrangement in a positive way."

Johnson nodded. "Fair 'nuf," he responded. He shuffled his feet again. "Did that *sunipu* yuh keep talkin' 'bout have anythin' to do with killin' thet bear?"

I nodded. "God's work, Hank. Bear could have attacked me and Spirit Talker or the Lakota. He chose them."

"Yuh truly think yer faith saved yuh?" he asked.

This talk had taken a fascinating turn far as I was concerned. "I try to follow God's will, Hank. If you have faith without obeying that God's word, such faith might as well be dead. My pa told me that action without faith is sinful. Spirit Talker and I pray for strength of faith every time we face danger."

Johnson nodded. "Heavy, boss." He shuffled those feet of his again. He looked over at Zeb, the wolf's blue eyes seeming to know where the conversation was headed. "Yuh ever afraid; I mean scared outta yer wits?" Hank asked.

"Faith has worked for me, Hank. Faith helps lighten the burden," I added. "We might have made friends of those Lakota hunters. Who knows? They might even sway that Otaktay fellow to ease up." I grinned broadly at that thought, though I doubted Otaktay's feeling could be changed any time soon.

Johnson laughed and stopped shuffling his feet. "Yer a good man, Mr. O'Toole. First, yuh get me to rethinkin' my feelin' 'bout Injuns, then help me make bow an' arrows, an' now yer laying this God thing on me so tight I can feel it in my bones." He began to amble off but paused. "Thanks kindly, boss," he said. "Gotta git ready fer findin' strays." He took another step and added, "Like that pup of yers, too."

I blinked. It had been quite a powerful conversation. I was touched that Johnson had felt the strength to approach me about faith, as that was clearly his underlying purpose. The rest of his talk was pretty much frills on the cow.

———

WITH THE SUN creeping over the eastern horizon and revealing the majestic vista ahead, we began the home-stretch to Fort Laramie. The beeves were pretty much trained by now. Drovers, too.

Spirit Talker continued to scout well ahead of the herd. There were still hostiles about, so he was ever alert to any signs of trouble. Part of me figured that he relished being in the lead because he'd get to be with Prairie Flower sooner. He was sure enough incentivized to get us all there safely.

It would be great to see George again. He'd plunked himself up on the North Platte in the midst of some of the roughest frontier to be found. Challenges posed by the frontier these days were more than about the land-scape; there were the ever more hostile Indians coupled with the onslaught of settlers who lacked respect for both Indians and the countryside. George, like us, was being tested...constantly. I recall the Bible telling us that tests often follow triumphs. And it simply will never do to run from a test, as you will surely face another. It was what life was about. Through all our tests, we drew upon our faith to endure. We fully relished the upsides; the friendships, loves, successful hunts, birthing calves and foals, tilling the soil, and more, as we extracted a bounty from God's creation.

Zeb joined us, as though he had adopted us as his pack. He sure lent credence to the Walks With Wolves name that Spirit Talker had blessed me with. I was yet uncertain as to what God had in store for me with Zeb, but reckoned to find out. Maybe, I was oblivious to something that God was already working within me.

FOURTEEN
ARRIVAL AT GEORGE'S RANCH

SPIRIT TALKER WAITED PATIENTLY for us to catch up, as he sat astride his pony on the south bank of the North Platte. We figured to water and graze the herd a few days before moving on to Fort Laramie which was but a few more miles to the northwest. Beyond that would be George's ranch.

I rode up beside Collins. "Sam, how about you minding the herd, while Spirit Talker and I ride ahead to George's ranch. He likely can bring us the latest of goings on at Fort Laramie. Ought to be wise before we descend on the fort."

Collins nodded. "Don't figure no problems with Indians this close to the fort, Jack. Hurry back."

"Expect I'll be gone a couple of days," I advised. This was big country, and destinations tended to be far apart much like our journeys in Texas. Travel was measured more in days and weeks than miles or hours.

I nodded and rode off to join Spirit Talker.

"Rest herd?" he asked upon my riding up alongside him.

"Collins is in charge. Should be no problem," I stated flatly. "Figure to visit George before we visit Fort Laramie."

Spirit Talker lit up. I could almost make out his heart pounding through his buckskin shirt. Prairie Flower was ahead, and he would be seeing her just a tad sooner than expected.

I must admit that I was beginning to be concerned that if we tarried up here too long, I wouldn't make it back to Rising Cross and Blue Flower's birthing of our first child. "Let's go," I said while gently pressing spurs to Big Red's flanks.

We aimed to skirt wide of the fort, as we stuck to the banks of the river. There was no point in arousing any attention just yet from the military or the folks residing around the fort.

We kept a sharp eye out for threats. I especially appreciated Zeb as he provided an extra set of senses.

"PREACHER ROLLO, WHAT BRINGS YOU WEST?" asked George, as they sat on the porch sipping post-breakfast coffee. John Kenny had already shared his opinion of the preacher, but George was looking to hear what Rollo had to say. George stroked Bear's back. The dog usually stayed away, but something drew him to his master's side this day. He cast wary eyes on Rollo.

"I'm here to convert the heathens to Christ," Rollo responded. The tone came across like a script.

George reckoned right off that he wasn't dealing with a man of truth. "Mr. Kenny tells me those so-called heathens nearly killed you."

Rollo squirmed just a bit. "Didn't figure the Lord's work to be easy."

George tried his best to smile. "You figure screaming scripture at them in the midst of a battle is going to bring them to Christ, preacher?"

"What are you driving at, Mr. Freeman. You a man of God?"

George thought on the preacher's response aimed at turning the conversation upside down. It wasn't totally unexpected coming from this man whom George figured to be a gospel pretender. Something didn't ring true with this Rollo character, and George hadn't yet been able to figure it. The man dressed the part, could quote a Bible verse or two, and was unarmed so far as he could tell. "Why do believe that you must ask?" answered George. He knew how to turn Rollo's reasoning back on him.

The preacher seemed momentarily tongue-tied. It was as though he was in a card game, and the ante had just been upped. "Well...er...just wondering." He tried vainly to regain control of the conversation.

"How well do you know the Sioux or Cheyenne, preacher? Have you studied their culture? Do you have any idea what, if anything, might draw them to faith in God?"

Rollo sat quietly.

Bear growled just a bit, so George stroked him reassuringly. George fought to control his distress at dealing with the sort of Christian this preacher claimed to be. He felt as though Rollo was hiding something. He decided to shift the conversation. "Do you know the folks you're traveling with? Are they folks of faith? Do you share their hopes and dreams?" He wanted to ask whether the settlers were giving Rollo free passage in exchange for his providing preaching services. George was more concerned with his observation that the preacher was a handsome man with a smooth manner who seemed to hold inordinate sway with the ladies of the wagon train. He shook off the concern...for now.

Again, there was an uncomfortable quiet. Rollo stood up. He wasn't used to answering so many questions; to being challenged. He reckoned that his higher calling protected him from such inquiries. "What are you implying, Mr. Freeman? They're a bunch of hypocrites thinking only of themselves," he said, his voice trailing off upon slowly realizing that he was convicting himself of what he was accusing his fellow travelers of. He was a self-serving hypocrite hiding behind God's word for his own ends; whatever those ends might be.

George took a long sip of coffee. "Any day now, some friends of mine will be arriving. I hope you're around to meet them, preacher."

Rollo looked quizzically at the Black man and finished his coffee. "Er...I'm going to the river to pray," he announced, reverting to the holier-than-thou role he'd fashioned for himself. He strode off as fast as his legs could carry him.

George shook his head. Bear stood, sniffed warily after the preacher, and laid back down.

John Kenny emerged from the cabin just as the preacher departed for the river. "Think some of them hostiles might..." his voice trailed off, and he shook his head resignedly. He was stuck with Rollo.

George cast a jaundiced eye on the wagon boss. "He's misguided, Mr. Kenny. I haven't quite figured him out just yet other than being full of himself. Not sure what he's really up to." He smiled broadly. "Bear here is a pretty good judge of humans, and he doesn't trust the preacher a lick."

"Let me know, if you figure it out," responded Kenny. "He begged to join us back in Independence. My gut instinct was to say no, but a couple of the ladies thought having a man of God along would be good. Rollo has played that hand ever since, but like he was dealing from the bottom of the deck."

"As I told the preacher, I'm expecting some friends any day now. If they arrive before you leave, they may figure out Mr. Rollo," George said, as he smiled and scratched an itch.

"You done well here, Mr. Freeman," said Kenny. He seemed to be developing newfound respect for George. "I saw your scars this morning, when you were washing before breakfast. Slave?"

This was getting a tad personal for George. "Long past, Mr. Kenny. Have a wife, family, friends, and am living in the very best part of God's creation."

"Injun, ain't she?"

"Pawnee. Love of my life."

Kenny backed off. There was going to be no riling the big Black man. Better to have George as an ally, in any case. He shrugged and began to walk toward the corral. "Let me know, if you figure the preacher."

———

"SHOULD BE AROUND THE NEXT BEND," I assured Spirit Talker.

We'd continued to follow the North Platte. Fort Laramie was actually set on the Laramie River not far from where it was joined by the North Platte. We had crossed to the north side to avoid engaging with anyone at or near the fort. There'd be plenty of time to reconnoiter the Army post after we met with George.

Our trek had changed just a bit from last year. There was more sign of wagon trains having passed through. Graves, discarded furniture, and wagon wrecks littered the trail. Yet, the wagon trains kept coming. We paused for an hour while Zeb killed and then feasted on a fawn that had separated from its momma. It served to remind us of the natural order of life. In a way, it was akin to America's settlement, as the Indians gave way to the onslaught of us Whites with our land ownership, farming and ranching methods, sophisticated towns and villages, deadlier weaponry, and the like.

As George's spread came into view, the midday sun seemed to focus on a black-robed White man kneeling and chanting forth some unintelligible incantations.

Zeb offered a wary growl, as he took a wider track away from the man.

Spirit Talker tapped his head as though indicating that the man was crazy. "He call Lakota to take scalp," he said with a wry sort of smile. The Lakota actually tended to shy from folks they figured were not of a sane mind.

"Maybe, George knows him," I suggested. We were close to a hundred yards from the man, yet could hear his ravings. He was caught up in some seemingly maniacal chants and was totally unaware of us so far as I could tell. "Let's get on to the cabin," I urged.

Spirit Talker needed no persuading.

I urged Big Red forward just as Bear came romping up. He made no sound, but it was clear that he remembered us. He came to an abrupt halt upon seeing Zeb. Bear looked at us and then at the wolf. He obviously was working hard to suppress his natural protective instincts.

Zeb also paused to evaluate this four-legged interloper that was every bit as large as he. He cocked his head.

I dismounted, and Zeb trotted over to me with wary eyes on Bear. "Bear is okay, Zeb," I said soothingly. I motioned Bear over. Yes, it was a crazy action, but it was already doggone strange that a wolf had latched onto me in the first place. It took a few minutes, but the apex hunter in Zeb eventually made him bold enough to take a sniff at the big dog.

For his part, Bear crept up low with ears pinned back. I never expected it of the big tough pup, but Bear was telling Zeb that he was no threat. He was signaling his recognition of the wolf as dominant. I could only pray that the two would get used to each other over time and become friends.

With introductions over, Bear was soon leading the way to the cabin while Zeb pranced along beside us. As I looked down at my new companion, I wondered whether his recent feasting on the fawn had tempered his meeting with Bear. I sure wouldn't have wanted to see the two of them fight each other. I'd have hated for George to lose his dog.

About this time, we noticed a circle of a half-dozen wagons. As I recalled, the rigs were called prairie schooners, because their white canvas covers made them look from a distance like sailing ships. Compared to the old Conestoga wagons, the prairie schooners were far better for traveling long distance over rugged terrain. We wondered why they were camped near George's cabin. It didn't take much brain power to figure a connection between the wagons and the black-robed man. Spirit Talker and I shrugged curiously and rode on.

George had just arisen from his spot on the porch, when he spotted us off in the distance. His broad smile was about enough to add plenty of extra brightness to the day. We could see him calling Running Waters and Prairie Flower to come see us visitors.

Soon enough, we pulled up to the cabin and quickly slid from our saddles. Hugs and tears of joy filled the scene. I couldn't help but notice that Spirit Talker and Prairie Flower hugged just a tad longer. They finally parted with blushes painted on their faces.

"Welcome, my dear friends," said George. "Been too long. God bless that you made it." He gave Spirit Talker and then me great hugs.

"Great to see y'all, dear friend," I said with joy in my heart. Hugging me had brought on a low growl from Zeb.

George glanced at Zeb. "That...that's no dog, that's a wolf," he stammered.

"Not just any wolf. This is Zeb. He's a gift from God," I responded.

George looked at me quizzically.

"Long story, George. Zeb here has adopted me," I said with a smile. "My ma used to tell me the story of Androcles and the lion, where he pulled a thorn from the lion's paw and the lion later protected him. Well, this here is pretty much the same. I saved Zeb's mate many months back."

George shook his head. "Enough! Let's get your horses cared for, and we'll do some eating and talking. Gather you brought that herd you promised. Plenty to talk about."

The couple of folks from the wagon train standing nearby looked rather dumbfounded but said nothing.

George caught my questioning expression. "They're camped yonder waiting for the next wagon train. Ran into a Lakota war party and limped this far. A few were wounded but figure to continue on to Oregon."

I laid a judgmental gaze on the remnants of the wagon train off in the distance. The women appeared to be bustling about making repairs and preparing to continue their journey upon arrival of a larger contingent. White women? They were likely facing a far tougher situation than they faced back home. The land wasn't nearly like back east with its little wooded hills. The west featured ice-crowned rocky spires of granite, deep canyon mazes, and a vastness to which the sky seemed endless. Were they up to it? So far, the frontier had been men's country and fit for only a certain breed of men. "Think they'll make it?" I ventured.

George could only shrug and smile. "God willing; some will."

I motioned toward the black-robed man. "What's he up to?" I asked with a wry smile.

George only smiled.

Commanding words interrupted us. "Let's not stand here hungry, young men. I've got breakfast heating up," said Running Waters. "Tend the ponies, wash that dust off, and we can talk while you eat." She paused. "Does your dog need feeding?" Of a sudden, she became awestruck upon realizing that Zeb was a wolf.

"He'll catch his own grub," I said with a calm confidence, as though I was used to Zeb fending for himself.

It struck me as I looked at the sun high overhead that we were rather late for breakfast. Running Waters was whipping up some grub especially for us. George joined us, as we hustled to take care of the horses and wash up.

We could smell the delicious aromas given off by the breakfast feast. Afore long we were headed back to the cabin. Zeb took a position near the porch, keeping tabs on Bear and whatever the black-robed man was up to.

As we followed George through the cabin door,

Prairie Flower handed us each a cup of coffee. Coffee was like liquid gold on the western frontier, and few brewed it better that Running Waters. It's flavor danced on the tongue. She undoubtedly added something, but that ingredient was anyone's guess.

I glanced at Spirit Talker as we sat at the table and pulled up our chairs. He couldn't take his eyes from Topsannah. Prairie Flower had filled out in a womanly way just a tad, since our departure last year. That wasn't lost on my Comanche brother. I could almost hear his heart beating from across the table.

"Where are the longhorns, Jack?" asked George, as he joined us at the table. Prairie Flower quickly refilled his cup.

"Other side of Fort Laramie," I responded. "Have roughly five hundred head. You think the Army will buy a few?"

"Likely. Indian agency, too. Thomas Triss missed y'all last year. The Army got a new commander and shored up the garrison a bit, but are hard-pressed to field experienced patrols and meet old treaty terms. The folks camped around the fort seem more restless every time I get over that way. Praise the Lord, I don't think they have it in them to cause trouble. Any warriors among them have lost their fighting spirit."

"Any new homesteads that might buy beeves?"

"Couple. Poor as church mice though. You won't be getting top dollar," lamented George.

"And the wagon train?" I asked.

"The folks by the river are having doubts. No surprise, as they endured a terrible attack. Otaktay and his Oglala Lakota warriors got their attention. A couple of them have talked about settling nearby, but they're scared of more attacks. Can't say as I blame them, but, even joining the larger train headed this way, they might yet face Shoshone and Cheyenne war parties. The Indians aren't exactly happy these days."

"Is sad for the *numunuu*," said Spirit Talker. He well knew that the people that resisted the onslaught of settlers would eventually lose their lands. The people, the *numunuu*, needed to assimilate with the White man's culture and religion. Theirs was a losing cause. "*Numunuu* must change, must accept *tosas*," he said, then paused and glanced at George. "And *tu taiboo*," he added with a smile and glance at George. "God is good. Love Black, Red, and White." He had reached the conclusion that all races must join together as a people, as a nation. Accomplishing that was where the going got rough.

"Mukwooru strong *sunipu*," offered Prairie Flower, admiringly recognizing the strong medicine delivered in Spirit Talker's words.

I couldn't tell whether Spirit Talker was more taken with what Prairie Flower had said or that she had spoken to him. I was starting to figure that I needed to give Spirit Talker and Prairie Flower some time to themselves. While I yearned to get back to the herd and begin to sell beeves, I knew that I'd have to accommodate staying at least another day or two here at George's ranch. I hurried to complete the delicious eggs, bacon, and cornbread Running Waters had served up.

George recognized the unspoken body language between the two Comanche. About the time I was swallowing a last bite of breakfast, he looked me square in the eyes and cocked his head slightly toward Spirit Talker and Prairie Flower. "Jack, let's go introduce you to the folks at yonder wagon train. Tell you what I know about the preacher man on the way over."

We eased on out to the barn and saddled up a couple

of horses. I gave Big Red a rest, though he seemed itching to be ridden. We headed toward the wagons with Zeb as escort.

As we rode, George offered up a brief assessment. "I haven't yet figured the preacher's agenda. His name is Leon Rollo. He's fully frustrated the wagon boss. Mr. Kenny says that the devil's horns are holding up the man's halo. For his part, the preacher makes quite a big show of his faith which sets the ladies all atwitter. There might be something to the wagon boss's thinking. The preacher was nearly killed in the Lakota attack. A warrior counted coup but failed to finish him. The fool may even be thinking he's immortal."

"I have a feeling that you want me to see whether I can figure him out."

"Pretty much" smiled George.

We quickly found ourselves coming upon the closest of the prairie schooners. I did a quick scan and judged the encampment to be in good order. The wagons looked clean and the livestock well cared for. There was still an arrow or two stuck in the sides of a couple of wagons. I deduced that they must still be there as crude reminders to remain cautious as the settlers journeyed on.

John Kenny saw us coming and walked out to greet us. "Welcome. You must be Mr. O'Toole. I'm John Kenny."

George had apparently told Kenny about us. We slipped from our saddles and shook hands.

"Reckoned you ought to get acquainted, Mr. Kenny. Jack here might be able to help with yonder problem," George said with a nod to the preacher.

"Much obliged at that," said Kenny somewhat ruefully. He suddenly drew back. "What the...?" he reacted upon seeing Zeb.

I smiled. "This is Zeb. He's with me, Mr. Kenny. He's no danger to you, so long as you offer no threat to me." I tried to appear relaxed. "You folks determined to reach Oregon, Mr. Kenny?" I asked matter-of-factly.

Kenny cast a guarded eye toward Zeb and took a deep breath. "That's what they paid me for," responded Kenny. "Tough folks. Determined. Did danged well fighting off the Lakota, though we lost a few."

"Any inclined to settle hereabouts?" I asked.

Kenny gave me a look, as though he was being threatened.

"Just asking," I added.

"Gonna take them west, Mr. O'Toole. Not looking to put unwelcome thinking in their heads."

I quickly reckoned that Kenny had what some called control issues. "Looks like you keep good order, Mr. Kenny. I hope you find a train to join up with. I expect you know that more wagons will discourage the Indians from attacking," I counseled by way of changing the subject. "I think I'll mosey over to your preacher and get acquainted."

"His name is Leon Rollo," offered Kenny.

George smiled. "I'll meet you back at the cabin, Jack."

"Good to have made your acquaintance, Mr. Kenny," I said, as I climbed back in the saddle and headed toward the still-praying preacher man.

Zeb gave Kenny a hard look and followed me.

———

"MR. ROLLO?" I said upon riding up to the man. "Leon Rollo?"

He slowly, even ceremoniously, opened his eyes under

a broad-brimmed black hat and turned his head toward me. "Do I know thee, my son?"

"I think not, Mr. Rollo. My name is Jack O'Toole. I'm a friend of George Freeman," I said by way of introduction. I slipped from my saddle and stood a half-dozen or so feet away.

"O'Toole? Irish, eh," he uttered off-handedly. "You normally interrupt a man at prayer, son?"

"My apologies, Mr. Rollo," I said at his unexpected response. My mind raced as to how to deal with the man. My initial reaction to him was that his halo fit a bit tight. "I'm sure the good Lord will forgive me."

He flinched at my response. He didn't seem to expect me invoking reference to God. "You a believing man, son?" he asked.

"Christ is my Lord and Savior as we set, Mr. Rollo."

The black-robed preacher slowly stood from his kneeling position. I noticed the bandage peeking out from under his hat. "Hear tell a Lakota warrior near sent you to the Promised Land," I said with a nod toward the bandage.

"The Lord protected me; protected us all, son."

"Most of you, as I understand it," I added.

"Killed the sinners," he intoned. "There were sinners among the folks on the wagon train." He was not exactly showing condolences for those that passed on.

I wanted to admonish him for making judgments, but held my tongue. There was nothing to be gained by creating conflict. "Why are you headed west, Mr. Rollo?"

I sensed that he wasn't inclined to say why, but he sighed resignedly. "I'm going to convert the heathen Indians to Christ," he said.

"How do you figure to do that?" I asked. I had a feeling that not many folks responded to him with so obvious a question. Most would likely have been a tad intimidated.

"Why...why preaching God's word to them," he responded.

Rollo seemed uncomfortable answering questions. I reckoned that he likely hadn't been questioned enough. "What if they'd prefer taking your scalp rather than listening to your preaching?" I'd asked a bold question and got a hard look in response. "They have their own religion, preacher. I expect you know that," I added.

"Heathens! Heathens!" he declared.

I tried not to show my umbrage at his declarations. He was fashioning his own death sentence. "I expect you know that the Lakota warrior that counted coup and swiped your head with his war club won't be happy until he takes your scalp?" I counseled as calmly as I could manage. "From what Mr. Kenny described, it likely was Otaktay, a chief whose name means Kills Many."

"I'll bring him to the Lord," asserted Rollo. His eyes sought to penetrate me with the passion of his mission.

Through it all, I sensed an insincerity, even a false bravado, behind his eyes. I shook my head. There seemed to be no persuading this man from the vanity of his professed calling, if in fact his was a genuine pursuit of delivering God's message. I figured it was time to flush him out a bit. "You haven't met my friend, Spirit Talker. He's a Comanche warrior; son of a famous chief. I saved his life. We became friends, then brothers, as we traveled together. He learned of what he saw as the strong medicine of my faith in God. He was even baptized last year in the waters of the North Platte River over yonder. I never had to preach to him. He realized the strength and love of the Father, Son, and Holy Spirit on his own."

"What's your point?" retorted Rollo. He obviously

didn't understand. His eyes darted from me to Zeb. "What's with the dog?" he finally asked.

"Zeb is a wolf. He's God sent," I assured him.

Rollo gave me a strange look, as though I was imbued with some sort of heavenly spirit.

With the crazed look in the preacher's eyes, I decided to change my tactics a tad. "So why do you hide behind the wagons and the skirts of the ladies, preacher? Why don't you find a Lakota or Cheyenne encampment and go preach to them?" I must admit, those were rough questions, but I was intent on outing Rollo from his holier-than-thou posture.

His words in response revealed much of his true self. "You...you...heathen yourself, boy! Wolf boy!" he declared.

I shook my head and mounted up.

He glared back at me.

Zeb growled at him.

Rollo shrank back a bit.

"Nice meeting you, Mr. Rollo. I wish you the best with your mission," I said with a smile. I turned Big Red, and we headed off to George's cabin.

———

GEORGE WAS WAITING on the porch and stood as I rode up. "How'd your little chat with the preacher go, Jack?"

I couldn't hold back a slight grin. "Your intuition nailed him, George. He's a short walk to an early grave at the hands of Indians, if he delivers on what he claims is his mission. Otaktay would love to have the preacher's scalp dangling from his lance. But I suspect the preacher will continue to leech off the wagon train for so long as they'll let him."

George chuckled. "Figured," he said. "Better wash up. Dinner will be ready soon."

"We'll leave first thing. Reckon to sell what beeves we can at Fort Laramie, then bring the rest of the herd here."

"I hear the Indian agent is back from his travels," George mused. "Despite Mr. Triss's political troubles and a few questions about his honesty, he's enjoyed a mostly peaceful situation on the upper reaches of the North Platte. He even organized a small police force of Lakota warriors to help ensure orderly distribution of annuity goods, head off tribal predations against emigrants, and help reduce intertribal warfare."

"I appreciate the information," I said in absorbing George's advice. My thoughts returned to the trail drive. "A couple of the drovers may stay to help until winter. Most will be heading back with me." Through all I had just said, I had the feeling that George was not giving me his full attention. "Work for you, George?"

"Er...sure," he said distractedly. He motioned off to the corral where Spirit Talker and Prairie Flower were gazing dreamily out at the distant mountains. "There's going to be a wedding afore y'all head back to Texas, Jack," he observed.

I looked over at the corral. "Seems like," I said. At that, I reached into my saddlebag. "Almost forgot about this, my friend." I fished out the New Testament he'd given me before our return journey to Texas last year and handed it to him. The lead ball was still embedded in its pages.

"This stopped a bullet!" George said with amazement.

"Yep. Had it in my shirt pocket. Sort of slammed home just how strong God's will is. Nothing like a near-death-experience to strengthen one's faith, George. As Spirit Talker says, strong *sunipu*." I smiled. "Keep that on your fireplace mantle. It'll be a constant reminder of the Lord's work."

George simply shook his head. "God bless us all, Jack," he said and led the way inside the cabin.

————

JUST BEFORE SUNRISE, Spirit Talker and I found ourselves headed back to the herd. Time was a-wasting, and there were beeves to sell. With five days of rest and grazing on the lush grasses sprouted up along the North Platte, the longhorns were fattening up just a tad. While weight didn't count for anything at present, it didn't hurt that they appear healthy. I could visualize soldiers thoroughly enjoying chowing down on delicious steaks and ribs.

We skirted wide of Fort Laramie again. What we could see from a distance was not especially impressive. The fort had not changed much from last year. I'd be pleased to sell them a couple of dozen head.

I had come to the realization that most of this herd would be to stock George's ranch and a those of a couple of new spreads dotting the region. I had no illusions about the Indians substituting longhorns for buffalo. They were reluctant. The buffalo met more of their needs, as they used every piece of the beast from horns to hides from meat to fat.

I was especially interested in finally meeting the Indian Agent Thomas Twiss. He'd been away, when we passed through last year. I had learned a tad about him since then. Turns out that, during his time at West Point, Twiss had tutored younger cadets including Jefferson

Davis, the current Secretary of War under President Franklin Pierce. In 1855, Pierce nominated Twiss to serve as agent of the Upper Platte in the Office of Indian Affairs. In August 1855, Twiss arrived at Fort Laramie. Around that time swirled all sorts of hostilities. General William Harney's expedition to punish the Sioux for killing Lieutenant William Grattan and his command back in 1854 created a general state of war. The conflict culminated in the destruction of Little Thunder's Brule Lakota village at a place called Ash Hollow in western Nebraska Territory in early September 1855. Now, two years later, Twiss maintained a tenuous hold on relations with the local tribes.

I learned that Twiss had come into conflict with Fort Laramie commander William Hoffman and with General Harney. The agent had vehemently opposed Harney leading treaty negotiations given his history with the tribes. Harney even ordered Twiss to be arrested and removed from office, but it turned out that the general did not have authority over Twiss. The Secretary of Interior endorsed Twiss continuing in office and determining actions related to treaties and trade. It was all about politics and not the welfare of the Indians.

I had mixed feelings about the agent, though reckoned to withhold judgment until I met the man. In 1856, Twiss had identified peaceful villages south of the South Platte and Laramie Rivers. He held a council with headmen of the Oglala Lakota and by early October was convinced that the Brulés and Oglalas had no part in conflicts during the past year. He apparently thought it important to isolate the tribes away from Fort Laramie given the recent hostilities, and so it was that he advised the establishment of missions and schools be a priority. Given what I knew of Otaktay's exploits and what I had heard from George, Triss obviously hadn't been talking with wagon trains and traders who'd come under attack.

I felt that my opportunity for selling beeves lay more with Twiss than with the Army. George shared with me that Twiss had found that certain traders were a significant source of corruption in the conduct of Indian affairs. Consequently, he established a system of trading permits and set up strict trading rules. Those rules caused great umbrage among the traders who then went about attacking his integrity. The traders charged that he had traded annuity goods (blankets, knives, sugar, etc.) to the Indians in exchange for buffalo hides, horses and even a young Oglala woman.

Thus, it was that I looked forward to meeting Twiss firsthand and making my own assessment. I also knew that Twiss had married a member of the Spleen Band of the Oglala Lakota. His wife was named Wanikiyewin, meaning "Savior of her People," and she was the daughter of Standing Elk. Given my marriage to Blue Flower, Twiss and I had marriage to Indian wives in common.

FIFTEEN

FORT LARAMIE

SPIRIT TALKER and I felt uplifted upon seeing our herd grazing peacefully before us. I spotted Collins, and we headed his way.

"Bout time y'all got back," he chided.

"Thanks for the warm welcome," I said with a laugh.

"Mostly peaceful while y'all were gone. Couple Injuns stood off a piece an' watched us. Seemed curious 'bout the critters with the extra-long horns."

"Our visit with George Freeman was worthwhile. Beeves we don't sell to the Army or the Indian agent will graze at his ranch. There was a small wagon train there, too. They'd been attacked; lost a couple of wagons. They were waiting to join the next wagons heading west. Didn't see any Indians."

"The men are hot to reach the fort, Jack. Twas all I could do to keep'em a couple of 'em from wanderin' off," Collins warned. "Expect we can head'em out, when yer ready."

I laughed. "Not like there's a bawdy house or drinking spirits around the fort, Sam."

Collins nodded. "Guess it's 'bout seein' folks other than themselves."

"There's a good-sized meadow near the fort along the Laramie River. We can graze the beeves there while you, Spirit Talker, and me see the officer-in-charge and the Indian agent."

It seemed that the time had finally arrived to find out exactly how worthwhile this first trail drive would be. I was especially interested as to whether Lieutenant Johnson was still at the fort and was very hopeful of meeting Thomas Triss.

There was no point in delaying. Collins and the drovers quickly had the herd ready to move. It was but a half-day task to move our longhorns to within hailing distance of the fort. I felt blessed that the beeves hadn't lost their trail drive habit. Full bellies and slaked thirsts contributed to an easy final push to our cattle venture destination.

———

IT HAD TAKEN the better part of the day to move our herd to the fort. We settled the longhorns in for the evening, and I decided that we would visit Fort Laramie first thing in the morning.

Our night guard was out sharing the mostly dulcet strains of cattle lullabies, when a man bearing a lantern rode up slowly toward our campfire. "Hail the camp," he called out. "I'm from yonder fort. I come in peace."

"Welcome," I called out. "Come on in." I would call what I was looking at an apparition of sorts. A man of medium build and wearing his long hair in braids down the sides of his head led his horse into our camp. He was White but had an Indian flair about him. Of course, I mostly took to buckskins and moccasins myself so shouldn't have been surprised. I saw that an Indian-style saddle graced the back of the man's horse.

The man ground hitched his horse and walked forward with hand extended to me. "My name is Thomas Triss. I done heard you been lookin' fer me."

I shook his hand. "I'm Jack O'Toole, boss of this outfit," I said. "Spirit Talker here is my brother and our scout. The gent yonder is Sam Collins, my head drover." I handed Triss a cup of hot coffee.

He sipped and made as to savor the taste. "You brew a fine cup of coffee," he observed with a nod toward Juan. Triss didn't even flinch upon seeing Zeb.

I saw Juan smile. He must have added another of his secret ingredients to the coffee pot. No telling what that might have been.

"Pleased you could stop by, Mr. Triss. We reckoned to come visit you in the morning, but it's good to get acquainted in advance of business." I felt it important to make clear why we were at Fort Laramie with five hundred head of cattle.

"Figured as such," he responded. "Saw you movin' yer herd in a bit earlier. I'm fixin' to move my quarters and the Upper Platte Agency in a month or so to Deer Creek. It's a nod to my Lakota wife to be closer to her family and for the agency to be near peaceful bands," he shared. "I'll introduce you to my Lakota interpreter Joseph Bissonette. He handles trading operations."

"My friend George Freeman sends greetings," I said by way of letting Triss know that I had connections in the region. "George is giving shelter to a small wagon train that suffered from a recent Lakota attack. I suspect an acquaintance of mine was responsible. I assume you've met Otaktay?"

"Kills Many?" Triss said with a grimace. "He's a nasty devil. It's all chiefs can do to keep he an' his friend Mato under control. A young buck named Tasunke Witko...er, translates to Crazy Horse...tries to keep Otaktay out of trouble. The way I see it, immigration and settlement is likely to spell the final solution for the Plains Indians unless our government makes big changes. The tribes need to be shown the way to succeed in a White man's world. The tough part is in doing it in a way that respects them," said Triss, ending with a slight sigh.

Spirit Talker stepped forward. "Many of my Comanche brothers struggle to find peace."

Triss was momentarily taken aback at Spirit Talker's command of English. By appearance, my Comanche brother looked every bit the part of a typical plains Indian, a heathen savage to many. He found himself staring at the scars imprinted on Spirit Talker's face and dropped to the mountain lion necklace with its cross. He squinted and asked, "You a Christian?"

"Jack save me from mountain lion. I learn strong *sunipu* of God."

"*Sunipu?*" asked Triss.

"Comanche word for medicine, for spirit powers," I said by way of definition.

Triss turned to me. By now, the bearskin had been tanned and was spread over my saddle near Juan's wagon. He saw that and the wolf-skin vest I was wearing to ward off the early summer chill of the Wyoming mountain country. He simply nodded thoughtfully. I reckoned that in combination with Zeb, he recognized that I must hold some strong medicine. "I heard about Walks With Wolves. You have strong medicine, Jack. The tribes respect and fear you."

If I were to guess, he seemed impressed by our trappings. Our youth apparently had no effect on him. We did tend to grow up right fast on the frontier. "Spirit Talker and I have journeyed together for many moons. I married his sister Blue Flower. He and Blue Flower are son and daughter to Buffalo Hump, mighty chief of the Penateka Comanche."

Triss nodded again. "I must say that you must be mighty determined. You a God-fearing man, too?"

I smiled at that. "Reckon God watched over us and our beeves all the way from little old Bandera down Texas way. We drove our way through storms, fires, floods, and Indians. Now, we're praying that folks up here around the North Platte will buy our longhorns."

Triss scratched his chin thoughtfully. "Come see me in the morning. I'm still at the fort. I'll let the Army know you'll be visiting, too." He took a last gulp of coffee. "Yep, good coffee. My compliments to your cookie," he added, as he nodded to Collins, Spirit Talker, and me. He mounted up, took a glance at Zeb, and departed.

I turned to Collins. "Seems a fair enough soul," I commented.

"We'll see," said Collins. "Talkin' money changes folks."

Collins was right, as I reluctantly had to admit. Dealing with the Army and the Indian agency depended on what sort of budget they'd been issued. I didn't figure to make the sort of profit that cattle drives to California had made, but sure hoped for something reasonable. I realistically hoped for ten dollars a head. Eastern markets were fetching twice that, but I was breaking new ground here in Wyoming. Whatever I managed to sell the beeves for, I knew that August Klappenbach back in Bandera had no highfalutin profit expectations. We were all quite aware of the risks in carving a path to new opportunity.

Simply covering the cost of the enterprise would be a most-welcome outcome. As I was pondering all of this, I felt a shiver run up my spine. I dared not forget that we were still in mostly hostile Indian country. It occurred to me that with Spirit Talker and me gone for a couple of days, there was no one in camp experienced at scouting for Indian danger. I turned to Spirit Talker. "Feels like the Cheyenne might be getting their courage back."

He nodded agreement. "I feel too. I look around."

"You take north and east, I'll take south and west."

Collins watched as we rubbed our faces and bodies with charcoal from the campfire. With a full moon, we didn't need any moonlight reflection on our skin giving us away. We took our bow and arrows and our knives. Guns were inappropriate to this little endeavor. "Good hunting," Collins said, wishing us his best as we faded from his sight.

Zeb was on high alert and padded along behind us.

————

I MOVED with a silent stride on the soft earth, keeping as low a profile as possible. My aim was to find out who was watching us and how many. If it was Cheyenne lurking close by, they'd be unlikely to bother us at night. It would be pretty bold of them to do any attacking so close to the fort. Still, I hoped to be able to figure their intentions. It would take a lot on their part to gather the strength they felt they would need to overcome my *sunipu*. If they knew about my wolf companion, they'd be doubly troubled.

I spent at least a couple of hours moving like a shadow through trees and grasses. Nothing. Perhaps, Spirit Talker was having better luck.

Zeb and I finally headed back to the encampment. I was bone tired. It'd be all I could muster to stay awake for Spirit Talker's return. I didn't have to wait long. About the time I laid out my bedroll, I heard the soft padding of his moccasins enter our camp. I briefly thought on how but months ago, I wouldn't have heard any such sound. Guess I was becoming one with the frontier.

Spirit Talker handed me a Cheyenne war club.

I tried not to act surprised. I hefted the club. "Nice balance," I observed matter-of-factly. I saw no fresh scalp.

"Cheyenne meet *Taa Narumi*," he said with a hint of a grin. "He Cheyenne scout. Watching us. No war party. Fear Walks With Wolves strong *sunipu*. Keep Cheyenne away."

I nodded gratefully. "Let's catch some sleep. We'll go to Fort Laramie at sunrise."

———

AS THE SUN crested the eastern horizon, Spirit Talker, Collins, and I found ourselves saddled up and beginning a slow ride to Fort Laramie. We rode past pretty much the same folks encamped outside the fort as I'd seen last year. I suspect many were a tad leaner for want of sufficient food. They stared at us in silence as we passed. To be perfectly honest, it gave me a creepy feeling. What had led these people to such a condition? To exist on scraps from the fort was hardly an existence.

The guard at the gate must have expected us, as he swung it open with no challenge. His eyes widened, as he caught sight of Zeb following close behind. Triss must have given the alert. Sure enough, I saw he and the fort commander standing near what looked to be a headquarters. It was fairly impressive, though desperately in need of care. The fort was a sprawling assemblage of adobe, stone, frame, and lime concrete structures. From what I'd been told, Fort Laramie was named after a trapper named Jacques La Ramee, as though that mattered at the moment. But this was today, and, despite recently adding a hospital, the fort seemed to have outlived its glory years. After the Grattan massacre of 1854, the fort was lightly garrisoned and stood more as a symbol to reinforce terms of the Treaty of Fort Laramie signed back in 1851.

Triss waved us over, as we entered the parade ground. It didn't take us long to close the distance. "Welcome to Fort Laramie. It's my pleasure to introduce Major William Hoffman," he said with a tone that gave just a hint of hostility toward the officer.

Both Triss and Hoffman had been absent, when we passed through last year. I wondered what the major had been told about our cattle venture. We dismounted and all shook hands, though the major deferred shaking Spirit Talker's hand. He clasped his hands in front of his chest as a peace sign instead.

"Pleasure to meet, sir. My name is Jack O'Toole. My companions are Sam Collins and my friend Spirit Talker."

With introductions completed, Hoffman excused himself. "I will defer Army business to Lieutenant Johnson, gentlemen. It's a pleasure to meet you." He cast a snide down-the-nose look at Zeb, as if he was trying to discount him in his own mind as a wolf. Wolves were not known to be domesticated pets.

Had the major realized that Zeb was far from domesticated or that his connection with my experiences, he likely would have been far more respectful. Clearly, Major Hoffman was as yet unaware of my warrior name.

Triss shook his head. Once Hoffman was out of earshot, he whispered, "He's all right. Just not a welcoming sort of man." He motioned to a couple of chairs outside the headquarters building. "Let's set a spell and chat 'bout them cattle, Jack." He motioned Joseph Bissonette to join us.

Bissonette shook our hands, including Spirit Talker. He was quite taken with Zeb and showed nary an ounce of fear. "You bring fine cattle," offered the trader with a slight French accent.

"Finest stock in Texas," I stated unequivocally.

Bissonette got down to business. "You seek what? Five dollars a head?"

I suppressed the urge to laugh. I looked at Collins who was trying not to roll his eyes. These moments were what the trail drive had been all about. Five dollars a head was an insulting offer, and Bissonette knew it. I looked at Zeb. His hackles were up slightly, so I seized what I reckoned to be an opportunity. "What do you think, Zeb?" As if on cue, he growled. Anyone say that wolves were intelligent? "They're paying twenty dollars or better back east and better than fifty in California, Mr. Bissonette."

Bissonette's face revealed just a hint of uncertainty. He accommodated my Comanche warrior friend far more easily than a wolf.

"Don't let Zeb bother you, Mr. Bissonette. Perhaps, Mr. Triss failed to tell you that the Indians call me Walks With Wolves." I let that sink in. "I'm thinking that sixteen dollars a head would be fair but only if you take at least two dozen."

Triss and Bissonette exchanged glances. There was an almost imperceptible nod between them.

Having learned to read faces during my brief travels, I knew I had them where I wanted them.

It took the better part of an hour to sell two dozen head to the Indian agency. Bissonette finally offered fifteen dollars a head. We arrived at an understanding that Triss could purchase more from the stock we would be delivering to George's ranch. I still had nearly five hundred head to dispose of. I felt pretty good to get the fifteen dollars a head up here on the sparsely settled Wyoming frontier.

"Been a pleasure doin' business with yuh, Jack. I'll be on my way," Triss said, then paused. "We're buildin' a cabin up at Deer Creek. Be movin' the agency right soon." He shook my hand friendly like and departed just as Lieutenant Cort Johnson strode up.

"The major said you were looking for me, Mr. O'Toole," he said with an outstretched hand. "Good to see you again."

I must say, the morning's business seemed to be passing like a whirlwind. I had a yearning for a cup of coffee and a chance to relax. I shook the lieutenant's hand and felt relieved when he invited me inside. "Glad to be back, Lieutenant," I said with a measure of relief.

Spirit Talker and Collins followed me inside the cramped office. Zeb sat just outside fixing a stare at the corporal on duty that surely gave the poor soldier the jitters. Despite the tight quarters, the four of us managed to squeeze in. The stagnant air was quite palpable, thick enough to cut with a knife...or cavalry sword.

Johnson motioned me to a seat across from a rather decrepit but still serviceable old oak desk. "Care for some coffee?"

I smiled with a nod. "Much obliged." Johnson had not forgotten his Texas roots. The lieutenant poured the heavy black brew into a tin cup and handed it to me rather gingerly given how hot it was. I took a much-needed sip, ignoring the near-scalding heat.

The lieutenant nodded toward Spirit Talker and Collins. "Help yourselves," he chuckled. "I'm not figuring to burn my fingers serving everybody."

They managed to avoid tripping over themselves to enjoy the coffee.

Johnson waited, patiently sipping his own coffee. With all cups filled, he leaned forward with arms on the desk. "How was the drive from Texas?" he asked with true interest.

"Aside from Indians, flooded rivers, a prairie fire, and storms, can't say as it was much trouble, Lieutenant." I understated.

"Well, you made it here. I'm impressed, Mr. O'Toole."

"Thanks kindly," I responded. "And somehow the North Platte country begs for less formality, Lieutenant. Please call me Jack...or Walks With Wolves, if you're feeling adventurous." That brought guarded smiles from Spirit Talker and Collins.

"Walks With Wolves? I saw your wolf friend. I must believe there's a great story behind that moniker, Jack."

"Happy to share it with you after our business," I said invitingly.

"Oh, that. I understand from Mr. Triss that you've managed to drive a fine herd of longhorns up this way and are looking to sell them," he stated with a smile, as he'd surely already seen our herd of longhorns grazing near the fort. "Oh, and call me lieutenant here at the fort, and Cort elsewhere," he said with a wry smile.

I nodded. "Mr. Triss already purchased a couple of

dozen. After y'all have bought a few head for your beef-starved troopers, we reckon to let the rest of them fatten up at George Freeman's ranch."

The lieutenant grinned. "I was impressed with your optimism when y'all passed through last year, Jack. Good to know that you haven't changed. I expect you'd charge the fires of Hell with a bucket of water," he said with a laugh.

I appreciated his touch of good old Texas humor. "You'll have to come visit us at George's spread, after we get our beeves situated."

"Thirty head," he offered up. The lieutenant didn't even wait for me to ask for the sale. "I can give you twenty dollars a head."

I gulped involuntarily. Twenty dollars was far more than I'd expected. "The major good with that?" I asked.

"He authorized eighteen, but I'll tell him you drove a hard bargain," he responded with a chuckle.

I glanced over at Collins. "Sam Collins here will cut the best from the herd for you, Lieutenant. As I said, we'll be settling the herd in at George's ranch. He'll be distributing a few of them to other spreads in the region. Figure it's time for Wyoming to seriously get into the cattle business."

The lieutenant smiled. "Not sure it'll ever be like Texas, Jack. Though, I recall y'all have the Comancheria to deal with," he said with a deferential glance at Spirit Talker, then continued, "and we have the Oglala and Sihasapas Lakota and the Cheyenne up these parts. It's as though civilization steadily reaches out to conquer savagery."

"And the savagery resides with both sides, doesn't it, Lieutenant?"

"Pretty much," he replied. "You won't hear it officially, but we know that the treaties aren't worth the paper they're written on. The folks in Washington don't have a clue about the Indian culture, but eastern money and adventurously hopeful Whites determined to begin new lives seem always to carve precious morsels away from the Indian birthright."

I found that the lieutenant's words revealed a deep and quite unexpected perceptiveness and sensitivity that tended to raise him in my personal esteem. "Tell that to Otaktay, Lieutenant."

He shook his head resignedly.

"Do come visit us at George's ranch. Bring Major Hoffman, if you like," I said. I looked over at Spirit Talker. "Just might be having a wedding right soon, Lieutenant."

"Actually, I will personally deliver the six hundred dollars day after tomorrow, Jack. I'll do the courtesy of inviting Major Hoffman, but I doubt that he'll join me. He's a stickler for maintain discipline here at the fort. I figure to have a dozen troopers accompany me. As you know, there are very real threats lurking around the North Platte these days," he said, then looked out the tiny window of the office. "I hear tell there's a wagon train heading our way. Its nearly here. Supposedly, twenty-five wagons. Maybe, we'll give them an escort."

I didn't share my own very real fears of having to deal further with Otaktay's Lakota or the Cheyenne or figure to mention the wounded wagon train waiting at George's ranch. "We'll look forward to your visit, Lieutenant. I'll be pleased to share my story of friendship with Spirit Talker and then the wolf that I consider a gift from God."

The lieutenant's expression revealed that I'd stirred his curiosity, but he quickly reverted to business. "The sergeant will show your drovers where we'll be keeping the beeves."

We shook hands, and I led the way from Lieutenant Johnson's stuffy cubby-hole office. It felt good to once again breathe the fresh air.

"Sam, please cut thirty head for the fort. This place seems a tad creepy. I get the sense that something bad may yet happen here...maybe another Grattan massacre." I was likely exaggerating, but I couldn't dispel that ominous feeling. "Soon as the beeves are delivered, let's drive the herd to George's."

"How far, Jack?" asked Collins.

"It'll take a tad more than a day. If there's enough moon, we can drive through the night," I said, revealing my anxiousness to get Fort Laramie behind us. We headed back to camp, Zeb trotting along ahead, as though he knew where we were headed. He held his nose uncharacteristically high, as though something in the air bothered him. I took that as a clue that trouble lurked.

SIXTEEN

CHEYENNE & LAKOTA THREATS

THE ABUNDANCE of opportunities overwhelmed Otaktay's senses. He'd been watching the Cheyenne watching the herd of cattle. "*Tabu*," he mumbled derisively under his breath; cowards indeed. He'd seen Triss make his visit to the cattlemen last night. He was well aware of the possibilities that yet presented themselves with the small group of survivors of his attack on the wagon train. He thought on how he would relish another opportunity to kill the black-robed man. His only concern was the young *wasichus*, the White man that rode with the Comanche. Word travels speedily across the frontier, and he was already aware that the man was being called Walks With Wolves. He saw that as a pretty heady name for a lowly *wasichus*. *Tanka*, the wolf, was revered by the Lakota. It seemed undignified, unsacred to apply it to a *wasichus*. Then again, he recalled the young man's strong medicine. It was as though he was a *nagi*, a spirit that was never a man.

Otaktay backed from the top of the hill from which he surveyed the landscape reaching out below. "*Wash tay iyaya,*" he said to Mato beside him. It was good, very good. But they must leave and seek counsel. The Lakota subchief knew it would be wise to talk with Crazy Horse. It was time to teach the *wasichus* a lesson. And he desperately wanted the scalp of the black-robed man.

―――――

THE CHEYENNE WATCHED their Lakota rivals. It was as though a huge hunt was underway. In a sense, it was a comedy of surveillance staged by competing aggressors reluctant to act upon their instincts much less combine forces. This reluctance of tribes to work together would contribute to the eventual defeat of the Indians.

Apparently, my *sunipu* was holding all of them at bay for the time being. How long that might last was anyone's guess. I suspect that word about my Indian name had gotten out. The Walks With Wolves name would especially get the superstitious warriors thinking twice about attacking anywhere I was near. Some undoubtedly were now aware that a wolf accompanied me.

I had to believe that the Cheyenne and Lakota were salivating at the prospect of attacking the large wagon train approaching from the east. A large wagon train would tend by design to discourage attacks by smaller bands of warrior. However, the tribes were disposed to be as patient as the overconfidence of their younger warriors permitted. They would seek opportunities with favorable odds in terms of terrain and number of warriors. Meanwhile, they could use small war parties to harass and generally make life uncomfortable for travelers. Attack was more a matter of when and how often than if.

———

I COULD TELL that our drovers were getting restless. That tended to worry me, as it would tend for them to be less alert to the very real threats surrounding us. By now, the folks with the small wagon train that George had taken in were recovered and anxiously awaiting the arrival of the larger train. Preacher Rollo still made his daily devotional kneeling on the banks of the North Platte as though awaiting a heathen he could convert. The wagon boss John Kenny likely wished a savage would remove Rollo from his sight.

I admit to being amused at how adding better than four hundred longhorns to George's pastures had given the appearance of cluttering the place up a might. I'm sure that the lurking Cheyenne and Lakota were shaking their heads in consternation over the wealth of prey on display before them. There was also that remuda of horses that sorely tempted the tribes.

It had become habit out here to do our utmost in being aware of our surroundings. Danger silently lurked like a prowling cat with penetrating eyes and twitching tail. I sat comfortably astride Big Red roughly a half mile from the ranch barn and scanned the landscape around me. Something didn't feel quite right, and I had learned to listen to those feelings. I looked down at Zeb, and he shared my concern. My scan caught movement in the wood line off to my west. Whomever or whatever it was disappeared upon my turning and taking a more concentrated look. I decided to investigate for better or worse, though it was likely worse around these parts.

Big Red's ears went on full alert as we approached the spot along the tree line and Zeb went on ahead. We had to negotiate our way through a dozen or so longhorns grazing between us and a grove of cottonwood. That interrupted my concentration enough that I nearly missed someone or something moving quickly away deeper into the forest. I urged Big Red to a fast lope. He snorted and obeyed, though with nostrils flared and ears still at attention. He was talking to me, if I was up to listening.

I finally reached the end of the pasture and peered into the trees ahead of me. Naturally, I saw nothing...at first. I slid from the saddle and began looking for sign.

A motion far off among the trees caught my eye, but it disappeared as quickly as it flew through my peripheral vision. About now, I wished Spirit Talker was with me. I soon enough found evidence that what was now my prey was human. Moccasin impressions! I ground hitched Big Red.

My curiosity and abiding faith caused me to throw caution to the winds and pursue whoever had been watching me. Walks With Wolves was now on the prowl with a wolf as company.

My eyes caught movement ahead and the barest glimpse of feathers. Moccasins and feathers pointed to an Indian; likely a warrior given his stealth. He wasn't quite stealthy enough to avoid discovery. Was that on purpose? Was he Lakota or Cheyenne or another tribe? I took a half-dozen steps toward the spot I had seen the feathers, when I brought myself to an abrupt halt. I breathed gently and slowly retraced my steps back to Big Red. I had nearly fallen into an old Indian ruse. I came to the realization that it was highly likely that I was being drawn into an ambush.

I climbed into the saddle and skedaddled back to the cabin. I had a sense that Big Red was relieved to be leaving the scene. I should have listened to him in the first place. Zeb looked at me before reluctantly following. As I thought on it, the Indians would figure to be a lot bolder about attacking if the strong *sunipu* of Walks With Wolves was eliminated.

I stopped about a hundred yards or so from the cabin and turned to look back on from whence I'd come. Sure enough, a couple of dozen of what appeared to be Cheyenne warriors were casting frustrated looks and threateningly waving lances my way. Soon enough, they turned and rode angrily off.

I couldn't hold back a bit of a grin. I said a little prayer of thanks.

————

UNBEKNOWN TO ME, the Cheyenne hadn't been the only ones planning trouble this day. My near-entanglement with the Cheyenne had been watched with derision by Otaktay. However, Tasunke Witko was now with him. Crazy Horse was young, but his counsel was already valued among his band of Oglala Lakota. To cross with him was to cross with his father, a highly respected warrior.

Crazy Horse carefully surveyed the scene before him. Wagons, oxen, cattle, horses, and settlers might have caused a weaker man to succumb to anger born of frustration with it all. He turned to Otaktay and nodded. The Lakota knew that a large wagon train was less than a half day from this place on the northernmost bend of the North Platte River. With nearly a hundred warriors, he judged that an attack now would have a higher likelihood of success. If they waited, the defenders would be far too strong.

The warriors had hunted buffalo, but these longhorns

were a curiosity. The Lakota looked forward to tasting the meat from some of these beasts. Crazy Horse ignored the cattle and gazed beyond toward the wagons sitting to the northeast of the ranch cabin. Otaktay had told him of his attack on those wagons. The horses he had stolen had eased most of Crazy Horse's misgivings about further attacks. Crazy Horse calculated that the wagons would be far more vulnerable than the fortress-like cabin. "*Katá wasichus*," he said to kill the Whites with a sweeping motion of his hand toward the semi-circle of prairie schooners.

Otaktay was overjoyed at the decision. He was confident that the black-robed man would be among the settlers. "*Katá wasichus*," he repeated. He was determined to not miss again.

With that, the Lakota moved cautiously and mostly-camouflaged just within the tree line along the north bank of the river until they were opposite the wagons.

Otaktay's eyes grew wide. There was the black-robed man kneeling and chanting just across the river from him. The warrior turned his eyes skyward in thanks to the great spirit. He turned to his Lakota brothers and pointed to himself and then to the preacher. This kill would be his alone. "*Katá wasichus*," he murmured under his breath.

The folks among the wagons were innocently going about their daily business, repairing clothing, caring for livestock, cooking, and otherwise busying themselves with the rigors of the trail. They looked forward to the comparative safety of joining the larger wagon train. A young women rinsing clothes at the river edge was the first to see the coming danger. It was too late; far too late. She stood, cried out a fearful warning, and made a feeble panicked attempt to flee the riverbank. The

Lakota were already more than halfway across the North Platte and splashing through the frigid waters at full gallop. The woman became the early victim of a Lakota warclub.

Otaktay veered to his right and charged toward the black-robed man. A blood-curdling shout spewed from his lips, as he raised his warclub. He was not going to miss this time.

Rollo looked up and started to wave his Bible at the charging specter. "God is..." he managed. It was too late, as Otaktay's war club struck a fatal bone-crushing blow.

Gunfire was now erupting from among the wagons. Otaktay charged toward them waving Rollo's scalp high over his head. "*Katá wasichus!*" he hollered. Death to the White men!

———

I WAS JUST ABOUT to take a sip of coffee and tell Spirit Talker and George of my earlier encounter with the Cheyenne, when the sound of distant gunfire nearly caused me to spill what remained in my cup.

We took a quick but cautious look out the window. We could see little but hear a lot. We slammed the window shutter closed and looked knowingly at each other. As though by reflex, we grabbed our guns and headed toward the barn. Time was of the essence.

Collins, Shorty, and the rest of the drovers were in the barn repairing tack and other chores. They too had heard the initial eruption of gunfire and were stirring to action as we entered the barn.

"Lakota attacking the wagons!" I shouted while grabbing my tack and heading for the corral to saddle Big Red. There was a mad scramble of men and horses, as we saddled up and were soon galloping at break-neck speed toward the attack.

We had covered half the distance and while I haven't a clue as to what caused me to do it, I suddenly pulled up. Upon realizing what I'd done, everyone else also pulled up. They looked back at me quizzically. "This is suicide!" I hollered. I pointed to the raging battle. The wagons were surrounded by raging Lakota warriors pouring arrows and even bullets into the circle. We'd be unlikely to survive any attempt to ride through the attackers and join the defenders.

Just then, a stray bullet whizzed past my head. This was utter insanity. The defenders were outnumbered at least four to one, and we wouldn't improve the odds a lick.

Two of the prairie schooners had already caught fire and a third had been pulled over on its side. Even at a distance, we could see a couple of riderless Lakota ponies, but there were at least a half-dozen killed or wounded defenders. I looked to my left and made out what was apparently Rollo's lifeless body lying near the river. I didn't have time to appreciate the irony of the preacher's prophetic end.

––––––––

AS I DEBATED the safety of George's fortress-like cabin versus the near-defenseless wagons arrayed before us, a bugle call reached my ears. Otaktay had made a terrible misjudgment. The wagon train had proceeded from Fort Laramie a bit faster than anticipated. Worse for the Lakota, they were unaware that two dozen troopers under Lieutenant Johnson's command were accompanying the wagons. Their point man had heard the far-off battle, reported to the lieutenant, and were now charging headlong to the defense of the remainder of the wagon train.

A strategy found its way into my momentarily addled mind. There were eight of us here on the opposite side of the wagons from the charging troopers. I realized that we could attack the Lakota in a sort of pincer movement. We could cut off any retreat to their west and force them back across the North Platte. A retreat across the river would make the savages especially vulnerable.

It was risky. It was likely utterly insane. I said a quick prayer for God's protection. We all exchanged glances. "Come on, let's save them!" I declared, drew my gun, and spurred Big Red to a full gallop.

Spirit Talker released his own crazed war whoops, and they tended to raise our fighting juices. He began releasing arrows about as fast I could fire my Colt.

Confused looks crossed the frightfully painted faces of the Lakota as the attack placed them in deadly cross-fire. Otaktay looked first at the charging troopers and then over his shoulder at me and my small but mighty force, gave a command, and motioned his warriors to head back across the river.

I saw one warrior in particular lag back for a moment as if taking full stock of the situation. He wore a single feather, and he was naked save for breechcloth and moccasins. It recognized him as Crazy Horse. He caught my eyes, nodded recognition, and joined the retreat. I held hope that he had grown greater respect for Walks With Wolves and that would make the Oglala Lakota just a tad more reluctant to attack again any time soon. In a fleeting thought, I wondered whether I might ever reach him about God and his love, grace, and power.

As the gunfire died down and most of the Lakota

hostiles had retreated across the North Platte, we began to take stock of the situation. I reckoned that our attack from the opposite side from the troopers had sealed our victory. As we rode cautiously toward the wagons, I counted at least a dozen warriors dead or dying, but the scene was punctuated by the mournful wails from the wagons. Not a single trooper and none of my men had even been wounded. Our counterattack had been brief and effective. All of us were accounted for. The folks in the wagon train were not so lucky. Aside from the young woman at the river and Rollo, at least another half-dozen were dead or wounded. One of the defenders was quite badly wounded and unlikely to survive.

Spirit Talker looked over at me. "Strong *sunipu*, Jack," he said as his eyes surveyed the awful scene before us.

I wanted to say that God was good, but had he been good to the wagon train defenders? We had survived and likely staved off a far worse outcome for the folks milling about the ruins of the remaining prairie schooners. Was this God's justice? His compassion? I had to believe that it was. We had just overcome an attack steeped in the evils of anger, lust, and pride couched in the conjured image of protecting an archaic way of life that was being inexorably replaced.

"Thank God for you and the troopers, Mr. O'Toole," said a grateful John Kenny just as Lieutenant Johnson and three of his troopers rode up to us.

We shrugged. It had seemed like the thing to do.

"You and your little army turned the tide, Jack. That was quick thinking," the lieutenant said with a casual but meaningful salute. "We'd better get back to the train. They'll be arriving in a couple of hours, and I don't want to tempt the Lakota any further."

I doubted that the lieutenant honestly expected

further problems with the hostiles, but I understood that he likely didn't see a need for his troopers hovering near the aftermath of the attack. "Do as you will, Lieutenant," I responded resignedly.

"I'll leave a half-dozen troopers to help here," he added upon seeing my unease. "Sergeant Stiles will be in charge."

I saluted smartly, then turned to George, Spirit Talker, and the rest of what the lieutenant had called my little army. "Let's help ease these folks' pain," I said as I dismounted.

Kenny led the way back among the wagons.

I looked over my shoulder toward the cabin and saw Running Waters and Prairie Flower in a wagon already headed our way with bandages, poultices, and their caring womanly hearts. The settlers in the wagons would begin to once again heal from an Indian attack.

Spirit Talker nudged me and pointed across the river. Otaktay sat astride his pony with his hands clasped in front of his chest in a sign of peace. "Kills Many wants to talk," my Comanche brother observed.

I nodded. When an Indian makes a sign for peace, they usually honor it. Our past experience with Indian trickery had been unusual.

"Sam, do what you can here. Spirit Talker and I are heading across the river to parley with the Lakota."

Collins's gaze shifted to the lone Lakota warrior on the other side of the North Platte. "Do try to keep your scalps," he said with a grin.

SEVENTEEN
PARLEY

SPIRIT TALKER and I paused at the south bank of the North Platte and looked knowingly at each other. Despite the distances and hours apart on the trail drive, we had gotten such that we could read each other's minds. The issue of trust coursed through both of our heads. Could this peace overture by Otaktay be relied upon. I glanced over at Zeb. "You coming?"

I felt as though God was guiding and protecting me, but was ever-more-convinced that part of the strength He had imparted was wrapped up in the wolf spirit. In any case, I was not going to attribute the wolves to the religious animism of the Indians. Despite the warm weather, I donned the wolf skin vest. The stronger my *sunipu* the better. Being accompanied by a real live wolf was like icing on my spiritual cake.

George rode up. "I must live with these warriors lurking around. Mind if I join you?"

We nodded in unison.

Spirit Talker watched my more confident body language. "Walks With Wolves strong *sunipu*," he observed as though reinforcing what I was trying so hard to achieve.

Just then, Crazy Horse trotted out from the tree line and pulled up behind Otaktay. I reckoned that Crazy Horse was a thinker and the more honorable of the two warriors. I sensed that Tasunke Witko would one day be a great leader of the Lakota nation. Spirit Talker, George, and I clasped hands before our chests, as we faced the fearsome warriors beckoning us. Would they dare attack? Were warriors hidden in the woods ready to rid their world of Jack O'Toole?

I looked at Spirit Talker and George, took a deep breath, and nodded my head toward the two warriors. We cautiously urged our mounts into the river. I felt as though we were riding to some sort of destiny. Ours? Theirs? I stroked the cross hanging from the center of my bear claw necklace as though seeking even greater strength. Zeb followed, sensing the *sunipu* lingering in the air.

Our river crossing seemed to take far longer than it actually did. We sat tall and confident in our saddles and were soon face-to-face with the two powerful Lakota warriors.

"*Wowahwa, Máni Tanka,*" greeted Otaktay.

I gathered he was opening the conversation with a greeting. I glanced at Spirit Talker for a translation, but he shrugged. I figured "tanka" was similar to the Comanche word for wolf, so Máni Tanka must be acknowledging my newfound Indian name, Walks With Wolves. "Greetings. Otaktay," I responded in English.

"*Máni Tanka wasaki,*" Otaktay responded with a fist to his chest and then motioning to me.

I gathered that he was telling me that I had strong medicine.

"Treaty not good. Oglala Lakota…want peace," he said, suddenly switching to a halting use of English. "*Wasichus* stop."

Stop the growing westward migration of the Whites? How could I assure him that the old treaty terms would ever be met? More and more settlers would continue their journeys westward along the Oregon Trail and other trails. I had even heard rumblings of building a railroad to the west. The iron horse would soon lend its inexorable force to the westward migrations. Settlers would be homesteading. The traditions of the Lakota would soon be swallowed up in the inexorable onslaught of a stronger civilization. The buffalo would disappear and starvation would kill those Indians who were spared White man's diseases. The Indian would only survive by adopting the White man's culture. I shook my head. "Máni Tanka cannot stop," I said.

Otaktay looked over at Crazy Horse, then at Spirit Talker. "What of Comanche?" he asked.

Spirit Talker stared grim-faced at the Lakota warrior. "Penateka Comanche fight Whites. Plenty die."

"You?" pressed Otaktay.

Crazy Horse pointed to Spirit Talker's mountain lion claw necklace with its carved cross and gave a questioning look.

"Mukwooru Christian. Love God," Spirit Talker responded, pointing to himself and then skyward.

"*Wakan tanka, wamaka nagi?*" pressed Crazy Horse as he asked of the Indian gods and the animal spirits.

Spirit Talker gazed off toward the mountains to the west and sighed. "God for all people, all animals," he stated and signed with a tone of finality. "Strong *sunipu*," he added.

Otaktay shifted uncomfortably on his pony. His eyes

riveted in on me. "Walks With Wolves Christian?" he blurted with incredulity. His eyes wandered to the big male wolf beside Big Red. Zeb's icy-blue eyes must have penetrated the very soul of the Lakota chief, as Otaktay blinked. This was very strong medicine.

I couldn't miss Otaktay's reaction. "Strong medicine, strong *sunipu*," I assured him.

Otaktay nodded. It was now quite clear that he held my medicine in great respect. There would be no foul play lest the gods wreak havoc upon the Lakota. He turned deferentially to Crazy Horse.

Crazy Horse's gaze shifted to George. "Black man Christian?"

"God is love and forgiveness for all people," responded George reflexively.

Crazy Horse and Kills Many looked at each other.

"*Wowahwa*," said Otaktay with a sense of finality. "Lakota...George at peace." It was an overture of reconciliation, a truce of sorts.

The two Lakota warriors nodded respectfully at Spirit Talker. "*Wowahwa*," said Crazy Horse.

"*Wowahwa*," repeated Spirit Talker.

I felt a sort of irony in how my young Comanche warrior friend, the very name of whose tribe translated to enemy, invoked peace with the Lakota.

Otaktay turned toward me. "*Máni Tanka*," he said. "*Sunkmanitu tanka*." Apparently, we were to be friends. Knowing the deep admiration the Plains Indians held for the wolf, I was honored to be so recognized and accepted. Apparently, my actions were having a positive effect on Otaktay, Crazy Horse, and the Oglala Lakota.

"*Sunkmanitu tanka*," I repeated.

With that, both Crazy Horse and Kills Many made the sign for peace, abruptly turned their ponies, and rode off.

We barely had time to return the peace sign. We all looked at each other.

"I think that went well," I suggested.

Spirit Talker nodded agreement. "Is beginning," he intoned with a sense of hope for the future.

"Guess we can breathe a bit easier," contributed George. "Only have to worry about the Northern Cheyenne and other hostiles," he said with a wry expression. "Those Blackfeet are still near, too," he added.

"Got to have strong faith, George. You know that God ultimately wins," I reassured him. "He's got some sort of plan for us." I took a parting glance at Otaktay and Crazy Horse, turned Big Red, and began to cross back over the river with Zeb trailing along. "Let's see how the wagon train folks are doing," I said off-handedly to Spirit Talker and George. The settlers had been through two terrible attacks. I wondered whether their constitutions were up to enduring further travails. They were down to three serviceable prairie schooners. Would they give up on Oregon and settle here near the North Platte or give up altogether and return to Independence? Returning through the hostile lands they'd already traversed was not a likely choice. In any case, the larger wagon train would soon arrive and perhaps give them renewed hope.

As we reached the south bank, I motioned over to where Rollo's body still lay. The three of us rode on over to where the dead preacher laid and slid from our saddles. I took a final gander at the Lakota, as they disappeared into the forest, and then turned my attention back to the now bloodied and decidedly lifeless form of Rollo laid out arms and legs akimbo in the lush grasses on the bank of the river. Such was often the contrast of life and death on the frontier.

George shook his head. "Pity. Seemed that he wasn't listening to God; just himself."

I hung my head for a moment and nodded in agreement. "We'll bury him as befitting a man of God," I said. "It's not up to us to judge him. God will surely forgive his sins." Guess I was in a forgiving sort of way. Maybe the parley with the Lakota had injected me with newfound optimism and strengthened my faith in God's strong *sunipu*. Zeb came alongside and nuzzled me, as though reinforcing my thoughts.

Big Red wasn't exactly excited by the task at hand as we wrapped a blanket around Rollo and draped his body over my saddle. After a few nickers and a show of prancing, my mighty steed finally calmed.

George identified an area near the wagons where we would respectfully bury the dead. It was a beautiful place overlooking the rushing waters of the river. We walked to the spot, grabbed shovels, and began to dig a grave for the preacher. Within moments, a couple of the settlers eased on over with the bodies of loved ones carried reverently behind them. We'd be doing a bit more digging.

"What about the savages?" John Kenny appeared from the semi-circle of wagons followed by a tearful woman who apparently felt sorry for the savages.

Spirit Talker spoke up before I could respond. "Leave them. Lakota will come back tonight for their dead."

Kenny shook his head. "Seems un-Christian."

"They not Christians," responded Spirit Talker grimly. "Take dead to their spirits."

"What if the savages attack tonight?" Kenny asked.

"We parleyed with their leaders, Mr. Kenny. We're confident that they won't attack again any time soon.

They believe that what they call our medicine is far too strong."

There was a silence as we finished digging five shallow graves in the soft soil.

"Heathens," said Kenny under his breath as he thought about the moldering bodies of the dead Lakota lying on the prairie.

The woman with Kenny looked to be with child and wore no wedding band. She seemed especially saddened by Rollo's death. I couldn't help but wonder whether the slick-talking preacher was sowing oats as well as his message. Well, I couldn't worry myself about it. We had a funeral to get on with.

I decided we shouldn't dwell on the afterlife of the Lakota warriors or possibility of another attack, so changed the subject...sort of. "Mr. Kenny, how about gathering the folks around the graves. Mr. Freeman will say a few words of comfort to convey the souls of loved ones to Heaven."

As everyone circled the new cemetery, George delivered as fine a eulogy as had ever graced the North Platte country. He was even respectful of the preacher, despite his misgivings about Rollo's faith. Men stood solemnly with hats in hand, Hank Johnson shuffled his feet more than usual, and a few tears were shed, especially from the ladies.

The wagon train folks had barely recovered from the shock of the first attack, when this tragedy fell upon them. Their wounded psyches would not quickly recover. I wondered whether any would choose not to join the large wagon train that would soon arrive. It seemed unlikely that they would backtrack on the trail. Going back to Independence was out of the question. That would be a far-too-vulnerable undertaking. I reckoned they just might fall under the spell of the beauty of the landscape here along the North Platte River near Fort Laramie. If I didn't love the hills and prairies around Rising Cross Ranch, I'd likely be tempted. George and Running Waters would make good neighbors.

I sat back in a chair on George's porch and watched the sunset. The distant mountains were a purple contrasted against the majestic crimson sky. Yep, this was a good life. Zeb lay beside me and lazily looked up at me as if to agree. Who would have ever imagined that I would find myself in Wyoming with a wolf as a companion? I mean; I'd just turned seventeen years old.

———

THE SLOW-MOVING procession of ox-pulled prairie schooners arrived at George's spread on the morning following the Lakota attack. The settlers in the wagon train had heard the distant gunfire and gathered stories afterward from Lieutenant Johnson's troopers.

I was admittedly anxious to receive the six hundred dollars the lieutenant was escorting. Collins hadn't yet shared the news with the men. By my tally, we had nearly a thousand dollars, and there was still most of the herd to sell primarily to area ranchers seeking to raise herds of their own. I'd at least be able to pay our drovers and our cookie Juan.

I also saw the wagon train arrival as a signal that the time had drawn near to head back to Texas. I still held high hopes of being at Blue Flower's bedside for the birth of our first child. I had settled with our drovers, sold the wagon to a nearby rancher, and committed to most of us joining together for the return journey. We figured that six of us traveling together would prove less inviting to any Indians considering taking our scalps. There'd be a lot of hostile ground to cover. A couple of the drovers were already talking about moving up near Fort Laramie and even further to the Montana Territory. There remained but one more event before we departed: the wedding of Spirit Talker and Prairie Flower.

Prayerfully, our parley with the Oglala Lakota would enable peace here on the North Platte for a while at least.

Of the three remaining wagons from the attacked wagon train, only one chose to join the larger train headed west. The other two decided that the North Platte country suited them just fine. They would carve a life from this raw but majestically beautiful frontier. The folks had already approached me about purchasing some of our cattle, and I'd soon sold a dozen more head.

John Kenny was a tad lost. Thanks to the Lakota, he no longer had a wagon train to lead. I caught up with him at the corral fence.

"Where are you headed, Mr. Kenny?" I asked.

"Not quite sure," he responded. He was dressed in a dirty cotton shirt and fringed buckskin pants outside well-worn boots, while a Colt revolver rested in his waistband. His wide-brimmed hat featured a couple of bullet holes. A dark-brown beard and mustache framed a soulful expression this evening.

"Think you might catch on with those folks headed west?"

"Already talked with the wagon master," Kenny said thoughtfully, as though wondering what he should say. "Our styles don't mesh none. An' I won't be dancin' with them that I led this far. Least they didn't ask fer their money back," he confessed.

"We're headed back to Texas in a couple of days. You're welcome to join us."

He smiled. "Mighty grateful, Mr. O'Toole," he offered up. "Actually, I'm figurin' to join up with that young filly with the bun in her oven. She could sure use a man 'bout now, an' she's takin' a cotton to me since Rollo passed."

I smiled inwardly. My senses about the preacher had just been confirmed. "Sounds like you're settling in these parts, Mr. Kenny. Good fortune to you."

Kenny gave me a long thoughtful look. "Yer amazing Mr. Walks With Wolves. I hope an' pray yuh taught them Injuns a lesson they won't soon ferget."

I was rightly taken aback by the compliment. "I just follow God's will, Mr. Kenny."

"Well, God has sure blessed yuh," he observed.

I nodded. "You folks will be in good company around here. Mr. Freeman is a man of strong faith and a solid citizen, and the Indian agent Triss has managed to keep most of the tribes at peace. The garrison at Fort Laramie should help, too." Zeb walked over and nuzzled me. It was time to hit the hay. Tomorrow was to bring a big celebration.

"Amazing," stated Kenny flatly with an eye on the wolf at my side. He shook his head admiringly, then ambled away toward the remaining wagon from the train he'd led. "See you tomorrow at the wedding, Mr. O'Toole."

Zeb watched Kenny leave. He knew when someone was talking about him. It tended to confirm to me that he was indeed a gift from God.

"Let's go, Zeb," I urged.

He arose and trotted in front of me toward the barn. I admired his gait as his handsome furry form paraded before me. He was sure handsome as wolves go. God sure could fashion wonders of beauty with his creatures.

EIGHTEEN
WEDDING

DROP-DEAD GORGEOUS. That was the only way to describe a day of crisp clear air and bright blue cloudless skies against a backdrop of verdant forest.

The cabin was temporarily closed to us males. We wound up sleeping in the barn or accepting the generous lodging invites from the wagon train. Apparently, Running Waters was intent on following a traditional White folks custom of the groom not seeing the bride in her wedding finery before the ceremony.

The wedding ceremony itself was driven by somewhat unusual circumstances given that Prairie Flower had no parents to accept any dowry of horses or other valuables in exchange for her hand in marriage. In fact, I was curious as to what Spirit Talker had in mind. Traditional Comanche or Christian ceremony or both?

Spirit Talker had acquired a canvas from one of the wrecked prairie schooners and fashioned a hut well off to the west of the wagon circle. It would serve as the equivalent of the teepee that Blue Flower and I had shared on our wedding night. Unbeknownst to me, he had already conspired with George to hold a brief ceremony.

The folks from the recently arrived wagon train were invited. This meant that George and Running Waters were hosting nigh unto a hundred guests for the affair. It was figuring to be quite a shindig.

———

I GUESS I was what civilized folks at weddings would call the best man. I wore my best buckskins, including the moccasin boots Blue Flower had made for me. We were still on the frontier, so I did wear a holster with my Colt Navy prominently on display along with what was being called a Bowie Knife after the famed defender of the Alamo in the Texas War for Independence. It sat in a bead-decorated fringed sheath on my backside.

Folks began moseying in from the wagon train long about mid-morning. George had built a small gazebo that Running Waters decorated with flowers.

Spirit Talker uncharacteristically fidgeted around. It was totally out of character for him to be the least bit nervous. He looked handsome in white beaded buckskins and beaded moccasin boots. The bone breastplate he wore was decorated with the downy breast feathers of an eagle. His hair was split into two long braids. Even the scars from the mountain lion attack a couple of years served to enhance his handsome appearance as a true warrior of the frontier. He looked at me, "*Kuhmabai,* Jack," he said. Indeed, he was about to be married.

About this time, Shorty stepped up with harmonica in hand. He actually began to play a wedding march.

The door to the cabin opened, and Running Waters emerged ahead of the bride. Prairie Flower was, in a word, radiant. Running Waters had outdone herself in dressing the young Comanche woman for the occasion. With head held high, she glided ever-so-gracefully to join Spirit Talker awaiting her beside George at the gazebo.

George was no preacher, but he had a solid grip on God's words. He gave a signal to Shorty to stop the music. "We are gathered to today to join Mukwooru and Topsannah in holy matrimony." He intoned, even using the Comanche inflections for the given names of the groom and bride. George looked lovingly at the two. "Today, we celebrate the union of two spirits gathered in Christ's name. We celebrate love. These two shall be as one, drawing life from each other. Love brings life, and so we gather here in His name to join these two souls in marriage." George took a deep breath and looked out among those gathered. A few were looking as though they yearned to sink their teeth into the feast that had been prepared.

Running Waters nodded toward George to hustle up the ceremony. "Y'all now bear witness, for where we gather in His name there is always love. Mukwooru and Topsannah join hands." He had to physically place their hands together as they stood as though frozen in space. "What God has brought together, let no man tear asunder. In God's name, I now pronounce you husband and wife." A great sigh of joy went up from those gathered. George exhaled. He looked at Spirit Talker. "You may kiss the bride," he urged.

Awkwardly, Spirit Talker turned to Prairie Flower. They gazed into each other's eyes for what seemed to be an eternity. Discomfort at the prospect of a public display of affection would be an understatement.

I put my hand on the back of Spirit Talker's shoulder and gave him a gentle push.

He glanced back at me then turned to Prairie Flower as though resigned to the task at hand. Apparently, they had never kissed.

George rolled his eyes. This was unexpected, even between this pair of Comanche teens.

Prairie Flower waited expectantly. Running Waters had coached her for this. She seized the moment and planted a kiss full on Spirit Talker's lips. The gathered guests went wild with applause.

Spirit Talker blushed at first with just a hint of panic in his expression. He looked down at Prairie Flower's expectant lips and planted a kiss for the ages.

Again, the guests went wild.

"Let's eat!" urged George.

Shorty began playing his harmonica and a man from the wagon train joined in with a fiddle. The party was underway.

I looked off at the wedding hut that Spirit Talker had prepared. After seeing the two kiss, I felt sure this would be a joyful night for them. I laughed to myself, then turned my thoughts longingly to Blue Flower back in Texas. I sure looked forward to returning home.

I WAS THOROUGHLY ENJOYING CHOWING down on the feast Running Waters and Prairie Flower had prepared with Juan's help, when a man from the recently arrived wagon train sidled up to me. Zeb gave a nearly silent growl, but the man didn't flinch. Of course, Zeb was telling me to be wary.

"Damn savages invoking the good Lord to bless their heathen lives," he intoned.

I could now smell alcohol on his breath.

I pulled myself up to my full height. I was at least a head taller and likely had a few pounds of muscle more than this excuse for manhood. "Spirit Talker is a Comanche by birth and Christian by choice, mister."

The man took a step back and belched. "Still a heathen," he insisted.

"You come here and enjoy a wedding feast and insult my friend. I take deep offense at that."

Zeb growled.

"You a Injun' lover?!" He glanced down at Zeb and took another step back. But he was too drunk to care about a snarling wolf. He set himself and began to throw a punch. His fist never got above waist level.

Before Zeb could attack, my own fist caught him flush on the jaw. There was a cracking sound, and he fell like a sack of rocks. An involuntary shudder coursed its way through my body. I was rapidly learning that violence had a natural tendency to be sudden and occur with little or no forethought or warning. One moment there's a peaceful tension and the next an explosion of mayhem. On the frontier, the biblical concept of turning the other cheek didn't set well. We are seized by the moment and called upon to protect ourselves.

Zeb whined with disappointment.

George came running over along with Sam Collins and Hank Johnson. "What's going on, Jack?"

"Let's get this cultural relic out of sight, men. He just finished insulting our newly wedded friends. He needs to go think on that a bit," I said with a smile. There was justice to be had, even out here on the lawless American prairie.

Zeb relaxed, settling on his belly beside me. He cocked his head up toward me. I felt his blue eyes gazing approvingly at me, though I sensed his regret at not having the chance to take a chunk from the man's leg.

Kenny walked over. "I know that fella, Mr. O'Toole. Name's Bart Toliver. He's part of that wagon train, but pure trouble. Heard he killed a man back in Kansas. Not the first time. He's a nasty soul."

I appreciated Kenny's warning. It was likely just as well that we'd be departing for Texas soon. There was no telling what burrs resided in Toliver's saddle, and I wasn't of a mind to hang around and deal with it.

NINETEEN

SOUTHWARD BOUND

"WIPE AWAY THAT GRIN, MY FRIEND," I cajoled Spirit Talker. Apparently, he was still in the throes of wedded bliss. There was serious business to be tended to; namely, heading home.

He stood before me with Prairie Flower by his side.

I finally sunk in that we were about to have a female companion on our journey southward. This was a dynamic that I hadn't considered. There would be Sam Collins, Shorty McBride, Hank Johnson, and Juan Perez traveling with us. That meant at least a half-dozen loaded packhorses, a remuda of another half-dozen cayuses, plus our primary mounts. It would present a worthy target for enterprising Indian war parties.

With Spirit Talker riding point, it would be up to us to ensure Prairie Flower's safety. I wasn't sure whether she had the aggressive mettle that my beloved Blue Flower had been known to display. I suspected that it was highly likely that we would find out. Could Prairie Flower aim a rifle and dispose of a charging savage?

George strolled over and broke my train of thought. "Y'all had best be moving out soon, Jack. Kenny says that Toliver fellow is spewing all sorts of vile threats of revenge for you embarrassing him."

I grinned. Toliver had embarrassed himself. I would nevertheless need to be on guard. The fool might take it upon himself to follow us. Worse, his ilk likely attracted others to share in his grudge. "I hear you, George. Still, we dare not head out until we are fully packed. My Comanche friend is...what's the word?" My thought trailed off as I grappled to describe Spirit Talker's condition.

"Pathetic," said George, finishing my sentence with a laugh.

I gazed out toward where the big wagon train was preparing to continue its westward Oregon Trail passage. I prayed that Toliver might dredge up enough common sense to stay with the long line of prairie schooners.

"I don't trust the man, Jack," counseled George. He no longer laughed. "I'd bet he will abandon the wagon train, find a couple of fellow human castaways, and try to pick up your trail. With seven of you and nearly two dozen horses, that won't be especially difficult. He'll eventually work himself into enough of a foolhardy drunk to ambush y'all."

"Hrumph," I asserted. "Lakota, Cheyenne, Arapaho, Kiowa, Comanche, and now an angry White man."

George's pearly-white teeth glistened brightly with his broad smile. "Seems about the size of it." He chuckled.

Spirit Talker had been standing idly by listening. "Prairie Flower tough, Jack," he said, trying to reassure me. He nodded off to where she was packing their belongings for the journey ahead.

I turned my head to look at the landscape to our south. "It'll take about six weeks of hard riding to reach Rising Cross, brother," I observed. While we drive cattle with an ox-pulled wagon at ten to fifteen miles a day, we would cover more like twenty-five miles a day on horseback. Implied was that his new wife must be up to it.

Spirit Talker nodded.

"Zeb, let's finish packing," I said by way of ending the conversation. My four-legged friend looked quizzically at me, then followed me to the barn.

"*Isa* bring strong *sunipu*, Jack," said Spirit Talker, as he ambled off to help Prairie Flower.

I didn't look back. My mind was filling with thoughts of returning to Blue Flower's loving arms and, hopefully, being at her side for the birth of our first child. I struggled to shake off the image. First, me and my "little army" had a thousand miles to cover.

———

A BIT of misty rain hung in the air, as we mounted up for the first day of our travels. We would soon be southward bound.

Running Waters had sent us off with a generous breakfast of eggs, bacon, muffins, and her special coffee. I still wondered what her secret ingredient might be that gave the brew such a rich flavor. Perhaps I didn't need to know. No telling what herbs were blended into the coffee grounds.

I had assigned tasks to each member of our party. Spirit Talker rode point, Collins rode rear guard, McBride cared for the remuda and rode behind Prairie Flower and Johnson was positioned just in front of her. Juan minded the packhorses. I was to be—pardon the pun—a sort of jack-of-all-trades, helping where needed. Just as we had with the trail drive, we would change roles now and then to keep us from getting lackadaisical and careless. In addition to predatory wildlife and Indians, I was now aware of the likes of Toliver and other lawbreakers that roamed the frontier.

As we said our goodbyes, I took a long look at where the wagon train had been the evening before. It was gone. I hoped Toliver went with them. Before urging Big Red forward, I scanned the countryside for sign of Lakota or Cheyenne. They were surely watching us. Last, I looked at Spirit Talker. "Ready?" I asked.

He sat proudly erect on his pony and exchanged a loving gaze with Prairie Flower. "Ready," he said purposefully.

I looked over at George. "Thanks again, my friend," I added, recognizing that it was inadequate to truly expressing my gratitude

The big Black man was near tears at our departure. His arms held Running Waters at his side. Her belly gave ample proof that their first child would soon be born. Despite the fact that his household would soon blossom with a new family member, George's expression revealed a loneliness at the contrast his life was about to take. Dozens of friends and strangers passed through his ranch over the past several weeks.. His morning gaze over the next few months would be taking in four hundred grazing longhorns, a few horses, and the occasional passing wagon train.

The frontier would inexorably fill with people, the ultimate destiny that would tame the surrounding forests, mountains, and rivers. Wagon ruts and railroad tracks would soon cover over the trails carved by moccasins and unshod ponies.

George and Running Waters waved until we were out of sight.

TWENTY

DRUMS ON THE PRAIRIE

ALREADY TWO DAYS into our southward journey, we were mostly retracing the route we had taken for our trail drive. It was hard to miss, as the weather had yet to wipe away the thousands of hoofprints and myriad landscape alterations created by hundreds of longhorns thundering through. Collins was already talking about another drive but wasn't sure there'd be enough buyers up around the North Platte. He'd begun to talk up the Kansas railheads and the more substantial market for beef, hides, and tallow. The drive to Kansas would be through flatter countryside with generally fewer hostiles to contend with. We could likely fetch top dollar, too. I had to agree that he made sense.

The market up around Fort Laramie would take time to develop. The longhorns we delivered would stimulate ranching, but herds of marketable size would take time to build. The beeves would also have to make it through what could be right-brutal winters.

As we rode along cogitating on these realities of the cattle business, I felt that tell-tale chill that I would feel when something wasn't right. I glanced down at Zeb. He sensed something, too, as his hackles were up just a tad. "You feel it too, Zeb?" I said as though expecting him to answer me in whatever language wolves spoke. Zeb had fast become my early warning system. Perhaps, that was why God had placed him in my life.

My senses were soon validated as Spirit Talker rode toward me at a fast trot. Something ahead of us had caught his attention, and it likely was not good news.

"Much sign, Jack. Big war party," he figured.

"Not friendly?" I asked, despite knowing the likely answer.

Spirit Talker paused and looked over at Prairie Flower. Our contingent had bunched up when I stopped, which brought my Comanche friend's wife within earshot. Everyone was now within earshot.

I looked behind me and sighed. We were bunched together, a strategically vulnerable condition.

Collins caught my look of concern and signaled to Shorty, Johnson, and Juan to spread out and stay alert.

"Not see, Jack. Just plenty sign. Maybe Cheyenne. Maybe Arapaho," said Spirit Talker.

I felt a wave of resignation sweep through me. Would our travels always involve fighting to survive, to reach our destination in one piece. "Seems like whoever is out there hasn't found their fighting spirit yet," I observed.

"Maybe hear of Walks With Wolves. Fear strong *sunipu*," Spirit Talker reminded me. He smiled reassuringly at Prairie Flower.

Zeb reinforced Spirit Talker's sentiments with a couple of guttural barks.

Spirit Talker's observation about strong *sunipu* made sense. I wondered how long it might be before some shaman convinced warriors that they were invincible against the medicine of Walks With Wolves? I looked around. Everyone in our little army, as Lieutenant Johnson had called us, was on high alert. "We won't make camp tonight. They will expect us to stop."

The idea of traveling on through the night by the faint light of the stars was not hugely popular, but made strategic sense to men now seasoned by virtue of experiencing this part of the frontier. Survival could depend on keeping enemies off balance.

The sun was dropping in the west, reflecting its glow on passing clouds as contrasted to the purplish haze of the distant mountains.

We headed our cayuses back on a southward track, each of us isolated with our own thoughts in the gathering darkness. Spirit Talker and I had likely survived more challenges than most men far tougher and more experienced than ourselves. I held to my strong faith that God was watching over us. We had escaped the clasping, grasping claws that spelled certain death and the deadly weapons of savages bent on our destruction. By all I could figure, God had chosen us to not die out here on the vast yet beautiful harshness of the frontier. Why had we been spared from fates that had taken physically stronger men? Was God so fickle as to choose us? How did Zeb play into my life drama? Why did this wolf seek me out for help and not some other human? The Indians sure were fearful of my canine friend. They thought twice about any reckoning with Walks With Wolves. Big *sunipu* indeed.

My mind turned to other thoughts, other questions. Would we make it home in time for me to share the birth of my first child? I gazed up at the stars; took in the sliver of crescent moon that barely shed light on the trail ahead. I reckoned that far too soon the darkness would be lit up by the lights of towns and cities. The dust of horses and wagon wheels and cattle and plows would dirty the crystal-clear air and make breathing ever more difficult. The melodic sounds of the sparrow and haunting call of the coyotes would be drowned by the ring of the blacksmith's hammer, the hunter's rifle, or the chatter of settlers. I wasn't so anxious to experience this inevitable march of so-called civilization, but God had me on His path. This path wasn't to be of my choosing, though I likely had some say in the matter. I gazed down at Zeb striding beside me, his crystal-blue eyes seeming to glow in the night lights. God brought him to me for a purpose. So far, so good.

———

WE WERE drop-dead exhausted as we found a reasonably defensible place to camp following our forced night ride aimed at eluding any lurking hostiles. We decided to cold camp; that is, not build a fire that might give away our location.

Spirit Talker and Prairie Flower bedded down apart from the rest of us. We understood and steered clear to afford them as much privacy as the open hills and prairies allowed.

Privacy? Likely, the most challenging occurrence on the trail was when nature called. For men, it was a simple stop and drop near the trail, but for Prairie Flower a level of privateness was in order. Even Spirit Talker knew better than to gape at his wife doing her business off in the tall grass or behind a shrub or tree. I chuckled under my breath at the thought of him on guard and fidgeting nervously and uncharacteristically all the while.

We bedded down for the night, five days into our

return journey. So far, so good. We'd managed to pretty much fend off the creeping threat of those twin perils: apathy and carelessness.

————

THREE MORE DAYS PASSED UNEVENTFULLY. By my reckoning, we were pushing close to thirty miles a day. Men and beasts were holding up right well, so far as I could tell. We'd pretty much exhausted the grub that George and Running Waters blessed us with before we left his ranch, so hunting for fresh meat fell to me. I must admit that it was a pleasant addition for us to have Prairie Flower add herbs and fresh vegetation to our evening meals. She even concocted one of the best pemmican mixes I had ever tasted. Having a capable woman along seemed to be working out to be a fine idea. I did wonder how she might handle a gun or bow and arrow? Comanche women weren't trained in those sorts of things.

We enjoyed fresh venison with a soup cooked up by Prairie Flower and turned in for the night. Juan seemed to appreciate the young Comanche woman pitching in with cooking and cleanup. It made his job much easier.

I stood first sentry duty this night, positioned near a cottonwood where we'd tethered our small remuda of horses. Silence surrounded me save for an occasional snort or chortle from one of the sleeping men. Zeb sat beside me on high alert. I found the profound silence unusually disconcerting. Even the coyotes were quiet and no owl hoots were to be heard. Then it came to me. Far off in the distance and faintly echoing off the hills and ravines surrounding us was the sound of drums. I envisioned some medicine man working every incantation he knew to pump up the juices of bravery in a band of hostiles. We were in Arapaho country or maybe Southern Cheyenne. Who might be brave enough to take on Walks With Wolves? More importantly, would God be protecting me once again? "Beware of *Máni Tanka,* you heathen savages," coursed through my mortal soul.

I didn't especially like disturbing Spirit Talker and prayed that he and Prairie Flower had gone straight to sleep, as I approached their bedroll. Much to my surprise, the bedroll was empty. Zeb already had his nose in working order and was glancing knowingly over his shoulder for me to follow.

I heard the tell-tale sound of an owl. Spirit Talker was good, but he was human. I returned the hoot and waited.

Spirit Talker and Prairie Flower appeared as if by magic from the darkness. They were but a couple of yards away, when I saw them. I might have missed them at that but for Zeb's nose nudging me.

"Arapaho," whispered Spirit Talker. "Hear of strong *sunipu* of Walks With Wolves but no believe. Shaman tell them no can die." He calmly nocked an arrow into his bowstring. Something or someone was lurking out there in the nearly pitch-blackness.

We had experienced this before. I wondered how long it might be before the Redmen would figure out that God wasn't going to truck with some hostile savage taking the life of Jack O'Toole.

Zeb let loose a low growl as if to punctuate my thinking. Of a sudden, he charged off into the darkness.

An ungodly cry of pain rent the darkness.

Spirit Talker motioned Prairie Flower to stay put as he and I moved toward the sound.

An Arapaho scout was grimacing in pain as Zeb's jaws clamped hard on his forearm. The savage had just pulled his knife from its scabbard and raised it to strike, when the arrow from Spirit Talker's bow found its way through the warrior's throat. His eyes bulged for but a moment. He tried to cry out, but the arrow had choked off any sound. Quick as a mountain lion, I finished him with a thrust of my knife.

Zeb let go of his grip on the savage's arm.

"Way to go, Zeb," I whispered, hoping he understood my kudos.

Spirit Talker instinctively pulled his own knife, then sighed and put it away. He'd sworn off taking scalps.

The Arapaho band would eventually wonder what became of their scout. Then again, we assumed there was only one.

Spirit Talker and I retraced our steps back to Prairie Flower who anxiously awaited our return. There had been no sound of a struggle and that was likely a tad disconcerting for her. Little wonder that we appreciated the concerned then joyous expressions that crossed her face when we arrived.

"We must leave here now, this night," I ventured to my Comanche brother.

He nodded.

We silently made our way back to camp and began waking up the men. Instead of extinguishing the dying embers of our cooking fire, I piled several pieces of wood and set it to flaring up a good bit. I wanted the Arapaho to think we were still encamped. By the time they figured to attack, we'd be long gone.

The drums continued their rhythmic beating. I smiled inwardly at our ruse. It did my young heart good to employ a bit of what the Comanche called *kaahaniitu*, or deception.

———

SPIRIT TALKER and I shared the story of our scrape with the Arapaho scout a couple of times with the men, as we negotiated the twisted ravines and arroyos of the terrain of northwestern Kansas Territory. It did stoke a renewed sense of caution and watchfulness among our little army as we traveled.

TWENTY-ONE

TRAPPER COMEUPPANCE

BY MY RECKONING at seven days in, we'd likely covered nigh unto two hundred miles through some pretty rough terrain. The day had broken with clear air and plenty of warm bright sunlight. Spirit Talker took his usual position riding point, but found himself a bit farther ahead than usual.

Zeb lumbered along just in front of me at the head of our main column. I say that Zeb lumbered by way of describing the unique way that wolves moved with head down and haunches raised, especially when on high alert. It made for an imposing sight. Zeb was giving off signs of foreboding. I sensed that something was in the air; something that had triggered his behavior.

Roughly a couple of miles into the day's ride, I looked ahead to see that Spirit Talker had reined in and was motioning us to stop and be silent. I slid from Big Red's back, ground hitched him, and silently closed the fifty yards or so to Spirit Talker's position with Zeb at my heels. "What is it?" I whispered.

"White men. Trappers," he said.

"How many?"

Spirit Talker held up three fingers. "Many furs," he added, still whispering.

"Seems we're downwind," I observed. "Think they're friendly?"

My Comanche brother shrugged.

"They camped or on the move?" I murmured. If they were actively trapping, then encampment likely meant they had established a base camp and were setting traps for small fur-bearing mammals or killing larger prey like bears, mountain lions, or deer as opportunities arose. I thought on how this was 1857, and trapping had pretty much disappeared as a line of work. These trappers would likely be what many would call throwbacks to an earlier time.

Spirit Talker signaled that they were encamped.

I glanced down at Zeb. His hackles were up. I quickly surmised that something about these trappers was posing a big aggravation of some sort to the core spirit of my *isa* companion. By the by, I figured Zeb to be a companion rather than a pet, owing to the independent nature of the wolf outside the pack. I respected that independence in Zeb. But what was it that had him riled?

"I expect we need to figure their intentions," I suggested more than overtly directed. "I think they have Zeb bothered, so something likely isn't right."

I motioned for the rest of our number to join Spirit Talker and me, putting my fingers to my lips to signal silence.

The men dismounted and joined us, their faces covered with a thin-veil of curiosity as to why we had halted.

Still whispering, I explained the situation. As I talked, a realization hit me. The combination of three trappers, our location, and Zeb's reaction raised my own hackles. The South Platte River was behind us, and we were yet north of the Arikarees River. This was near where Zeb had led me to the remains of his mate. Could these be the same trappers? It had only been a month since I had connected with Zeb to swipe the lone female wolf pelt from their stash of plews. I paused unexpectedly, and I guess a strange expression swept across my face.

"What is it?" asked Collins.

"Just a hunch," I whispered. "These may be the trappers that killed Zeb's mate."

Shorty cocked his head. "No way, Jack," he said a bit too loudly for my comfort.

"Keep it down, Shorty. Out here, friend or foe can be hard to figure, and we don't know these men. The beaver are pretty much played out these days, so I'm not sure what they might be up to." I was still thinking of them as throwbacks to another era, sort of like that mountain man Bear Grandy that Spirit Talker and I had encountered last year. "Spirit Talker, Sam, and I will investigate. The rest of you stay here and stay silent. We're downwind, but we don't want to spook the trappers until we figure their intentions."

Everyone nodded agreement.

"How far?" I asked Spirit Talker.

"Not far," he responded a tad too vaguely for my liking, but understandable given the terrain.

We proceeded on foot, leading our mounts. We purposely kept our weapons at the ready but not displayed in any threatening manner. I checked the load in my Colt revolver and held my Sharps carbine in the crook of my arm. I purposely left my bow and quiver of arrows hung on Big Red's saddle.

I decided that an overly quiet approach to the trapper's camp might lead them to suspect that we were up to no good, so we made no attempt to hide the sounds of our movement. I was surprised that Zeb seemed distracted, but we procedded on.

"Hail the camp!" I called out.

No response.

"Hail the camp!" I called out again.

We cautiously approached into a small clearing beyond a stand of cottonwoods. Empty. The campsite was empty. Pack mules were tethered, and bedrolls lay about along with a couple of broken clay jugs that gave off the strong smell of fire water mixed with the stale stench of sweat. A couple of bound packs of plews lay near the mules; surprising given that the beaver had pretty much played out twenty years ago. There were a few buffalo skulls, so the trio had apparently turned to what was referred to as bone picking to raise money to buy supplies. Some celebrating had been going on. They were likely drunk. When? Why? And where were the trappers?

Zeb sniffed around excitedly.

Then, it struck me like a charging longhorn bull. There were no weapons. Had the trappers gone off to hunt?

Collins appeared confused. "Somethin' ain't right," he observed.

Spirit Talker pointed toward a set of footprints leaving the campsite and headed toward where our little army was hunkered down awaiting our return.

Zeb seemed to contemplate the scene for a moment, took a look at me with head cocked slightly, and then sprinted off after the trappers.

I followed with Spirit Talker and Collins falling in behind.

We hadn't run far, when a shot rang out ahead of us.

"Dang, Zeke!" came a shout from an angry trapper. Apparently, a long gun had been accidentally fired by one of the drunken sots. The trappers now must have realized that they had been discovered.

We sort of had them surrounded.

Shorty, Juan, and Johnson heard the shot and scrambled instinctively to set a defensive perimeter. Prairie Flower slid from her saddle and shielded herself behind her horse.

The trappers hollered at each other. "Ah seen her fust, Slim. She fine Injun squaw, an' she be mine!" There was little doubting the blind-drunk trappers' intentions despite being outnumbered.

As I crested a hill, I could see the three ahead of me. My eyes bugged out at what I saw. They were not only drunk, but their gray beards and long silvered locks told me that they were old men. They were indeed throwbacks to a time when mountain men ruled the frontier.

"Stop!" I hollered.

Just then, Zeb struck. He had a death grip on the throat of one of the men. The others were apparently far too inebriated to help their friend. Blood seemed to fly everywhere, as Zeb sought to kill the trapper.

I ran toward the combatants as fast as my legs could carry me.

One of the trappers was unsteadily trying to aim his flintlock at Zeb. He'd more than likely strike his fellow trapper.

"Get...it...off me," gurgled the trapper as blood flowed freely from his throat.

I finally reached the trappers. "Stand back!" I commanded the two sotted trappers.

Spirit Talker and Collins took the trappers' long guns.

There was virtually nothing I could do to pull Zeb from his prey.

Zeb finally back off.

I gazed down at the trapper, as life ebbed from him. There was such finality in death. There was no telling how many scrapes with death the trapper had endured during his lifetime, but this was his last.

Zeb eased over to me quite purposefully and sat with his crystal-blue eyes glaring at the dying trapper. Blood yet dripped from his jaws.

"What the...?" blurted one of the trappers. "Thet wolf done kilt Zeke!"

"Kill the critter," spouted the other trapper.

"Touch a hair of him, and y'all will live to regret it!" I stated unequivocally.

The drunken trappers stopped and looked at each other. Their shoulders slouched in resignation; in acceptance of defeat. The one named Slim wobbled and dropped to his knees with tears in his eyes. "Kept his har all these years...an' now...a wolf..." he slurred with a tongue numbed by liquor.

As Spirit Talker held their long rifles, Collins deftly relieved the trappers of their knives. There was no point in the men being tempted any further.

I knelt beside the dying trapper. It appeared as though his final choking breaths weren't far off, as his breathing was labored.

Zeb watched intently, occasionally whimpering and emitting a low growl. It was becoming clear to me that he'd targeted this particular trapper.

I turned to Slim. "Did Zeke happen to kill a wolf a few weeks back?" I ventured.

Through his drunken haze and still on his knees, the trapper looked up at me and blinked. He went to shake away the haze that clouded his brain, but the sudden motion pained him. Such were the beginnings of what folks called a hangover, the aftermath of heavy liquor consumption. He nodded gently so as to not shake the jumble of brain inside his skull. "How'd y'all know?" he asked.

"You still have the wolf's pelt?"

"Nope. It was…" he said as the realization struck him. "Did you?"

He need not have asked.

Zeb had taken revenge on the man who had killed his mate. There was no forgiveness among apex predators of the wilderness.

It had been a grisly act to have witnessed, yet I found myself impressed at Zeb's apparent reasoning. The Indians were right in attributing intelligence to the wolf. I now wondered whether Zeb, with his mate's death avenged, would stay with me. He nuzzled my leg. Guess that was the answer to my question.

Shorty, Juan, and Johnson now joined us with our horses in tow and Prairie Flower trailing behind. She ran over to Spirit Talker who protectively wrapped his arm around her.

Zeke gave up his final breath.

"You two know any next of kin?" I asked.

"You know of any, Asa?" asked Slim.

"Ne'er talked none of any," responded Asa. Asa shook his head. "Thutty yars keepin' ar scalps…" he observed ruefully.

Juan took a shovel from one of our packhorses.

"No…no thank ye," said Slim. "Promised tuh plant Zeke up on the Yellerstone. We'll take his bones with us."

Despite the circumstances, I found myself harboring a

certain admiration to this trio of legacies of another time. "Sorry for your friend," I offered. "Mind if we pray for his eternal soul?"

"Twern't no God-fearin' man," responded Asa. He pondered silently for a moment and shrugged. "Guess a prayer to the Maker wouldn't hurt none."

With that, we doffed our hats and bowed our heads. I thought for a moment and tried to think as our friend George might, then the appropriate words flowed. "Lord almighty, we gather here to ask forgiveness for Zeke of any past sins and that you accept his soul into your heavenly presence. May his soul forever be at peace. God bless and keep him." I paused. "Amen," I said with gentle finality.

"Shorty, Hank...please help these men carry Zeke's body back to their camp." Unsaid was that the two drunken trappers were in no condition to be carrying anything. "Unload their guns and return them along with the knives." It seemed sad to me that after so many years trapping together, these men lost one of their number to a foolish impulsive act compounded by liquor. I'd heard stories of how the mountain men used to hold annual rendezvous to trade furs and conduct wild revelries featuring drinking, dancing, fighting, and taking advantage of the local Indian women. As the trapping began to play out and big companies controlled the fur trade, the rendezvous disappeared. This trio of old-timers had simply failed to adapt to change and outlived their craft. They likely drank and caroused out of boredom as much as reminiscing upon old times. Such a sad ending.

Zeb whimpered just a bit, as Shorty and Hank hefted Zeke's body and began the trek to the trappers' camp.

I reached down and stroked the wolf's broad furry head. I'd never done that before, nor had he permitted it.

He looked up and licked my hand. It seemed that our relationship had been cemented. It was a partnership of mutual respect. We were companions in flesh and spirit. I was fully convinced that Zeb was a gift from God.

Spirit Talker watched my interaction with Zeb contemplatively for a moment. "Walks With Wolves," he muttered. He turned and walked Prairie Flower back to our horses.

Relief swept over all of us, as a potentially deadly episode in our journey had ended well. I watched Shorty and Hank fade out of sight with Zeke's remains in tow. Death certainly had a finality to it. While these circumstances were decidedly different, my thoughts fell back to the deaths of my family, Blue Flower's killing of the Comanche shaman, the fallen Cheyenne at the North Platte, and more. Whether natural or violent, there was certainty in death's wake. Did the person's soul go to heaven or hell? Who decided? God's laws weren't often followed with violent deaths. Could any of those souls be saved? The questions haunted me despite my folks' giving me biblical teachings. What would come of Zeke's soul? The Cheyenne and Lakota on the North Platte?

TWENTY-TWO
AMBUSHES!

THE ARIKAREE RIVER flowed beside us, as we sought a reasonably shallow crossing place. The horses were tired from a long day's journey, and we sought to make it as easy as possible for them. Fighting currents in deeper waters was undesirable.

We rode eastward a couple of miles to a spot where the river widened and appeared to be crossable. We strung out in single file, partly because we never wanted to be bunched up and vulnerable should Indians attack. Spirit Talker had already crossed and begun seeking out a campsite. I was next in line.

A shot rang out and a slug ricocheted off my saddle horn. "What the?" I shouted as I spurred Big Red and made a mad dash for the south bank. The rest of my little army fell back to the north shore and sought cover among the cottonwoods. Zeb looked confused but followed me across the river.

Spirit Talker quickly dismounted, grabbing his bow and arrows as he found cover among the grasses.

A second shot blasted from upriver, and I heard a

bullet's whine as it passed my head. I pulled up near Spirit Talker and slid from the saddle while simultaneously grabbing my Sharps carbine.

"Where?" I asked Spirit Talker.

He pointed to a cluster of rocks and trees on a high outcropping overlooking our position and held up four fingers.

So, there was more than one bushwhacker. If the attackers were better marksmen, we'd already be dead by now. We needed to find better cover and fast. I had to hand it to whomever it was, as they had effectively divided our forces to compensate for being outnumbered.

Three more shots blasted from the ambushers' lair.

"Gonna kill yuh, Jack O'Toole!" came a cry.

The voice sounded slightly familiar, but I couldn't place it. The attackers apparently were White men near as I could figure from the one voice.

Spirit Talker and I spotted some nearby rocks that might provide us a better defensive position. We had to act quickly. "Let's go!" I said as I arose just high enough to run.

More bullets whistled past us and ricocheted off the ground and rocks.

Meanwhile, Collins and the rest of our band, our little army, had taken cover and were trying to figure out how best to provide covering fire. They were just a little out of range of the bushwhackers. Best they might do is distract them.

The bushwhackers fired a couple of shots in Collins's direction to keep them at a distance from the action.

"Who wants my hide?" I shouted out to the attackers.

"Me! Sam Toliver! You no-good, lily-livered, sucker-punching coward!" came the response.

Spirit Talker and I were shielded for now, but Toliver's

men would likely not waste time and try to outflank us. We exchanged glances. "Time for strong *sunipu*," I stated firmly and with a devious smile. I'd whipped Toliver once back at George's ranch, but this was now a life-and-death situation. I'd had enough with death, but a deadly outcome in this circumstance seemed inevitable. "You want to talk, Toliver?" I offered. I pretty much knew the answer before I asked.

Four shots were blasted in our direction from the gang's perch in response to my question.

Collins directed return fire from the north bank, but the shots fell just short.

"You ready?" I asked Spirit Talker. He smiled and nodded. I checked the loads in the carbine and my revolver. Toliver was a bully. I had learned from my early days back in Pennsylvania that most bullies were cowards at heart. And their so-called friends, the boys that accompanied them were usually even weaker. I figured to count on that.

Spirit Talker nocked an arrow and let fly in Toliver's direction. By pure luck, it stuck in a tree trunk beside Toliver's head. That was surely an attention-getter. We began to run zig-zag toward Toliver's position. I fired off a few rounds, and Spirit Talker sent off a couple of more arrows. It was surely the last thing the thugs might expect. A piercing cry filled the air from the bushwhackers' position. Apparently, we'd wounded one by sheer luck.

"Yuh got thet heathen arrow slinger with yuh!" called out Toliver. One of Spirit Talker's arrows had indeed found a human home.

I fired in the direction of the bully's voice.

There was another shout of pain.

About this time, I realized that Zeb was nowhere to

be seen. Sure as the sun rises, he'd latched onto one of Toliver's men.

"Git yer dog offa me!" hollered a bushwhacker.

"That's a wolf, and he'll tear your heart out!" I shouted back. "Give it up, Toliver. You can't win this fight."

Silence.

Spirit Talker and I continued our zig-zag sprint toward the bushwhackers' position.

A couple of more shots were fired in our general direction, but they weren't even close and sounded farther away. Toliver was retreating.

"I'll git yuh another time, O'Toole!" came the fading cry as the cowards continued their retreat.

Collins recognized that the attackers were leaving and headed the rest of ur party across the Arikaree River to reinforce us.

I quickly came upon Zeb with his jaws clamped on a bushwhacker's leg.

"Git'em offa me," pleaded the sorry excuse for a man. "The...the wolf's gonna break my leg." The man flailed about in obvious pain. He'd already received a nasty gash across his forehead from debris kicked up by a ricocheting bullet. Now, he was dealing with an angry wolf and looking up at the barrels of a half-dozen guns.

I spoke calmly to Zeb, and he reluctantly released his jaws from the injured bushwhacker's leg.

Collins moved in cautiously with a wary eye to Zeb and disarmed the man, leaving him propped against a rock and groveling in quite obvious pain.

The question now arose as to what we were going to do with Toliver's henchman? I had a hunch as to what Captain Benton might have done, and it would not have been pretty. Out on the remoter reaches of the Texas frontier lawbreakers never made it to a courtroom, and justice was delivered swiftly at the end of a rope. I pondered the situation for a moment before a solution to the dilemma at hand struck me. I winked at Spirit Talker.

He must have picked up on my thinking, because he smiled deviously and nodded.

I stood over the injured ambusher. "Take off your boots," I demanded.

"Huh?" he responded.

"Shorty...Hank...help the man out. He might be deaf," I directed with my own calculating grin.

Shorty and Hank jumped the man and swiftly removed his boots.

"Now, remove your gun belt and pants."

The bushwhacker looked at me incredulously.

"You needing more help?" I taunted.

Toliver's man obliged, reluctantly removing his gun belt and pants.

I couldn't hold back a broad smile. "Now...now your shirt and hat." I turned to Spirit Talker. "Prairie Flower might not need to see this," I suggested.

Spirit Talker obliged by leading her out of sight.

The man was soon down to the foulest, scruffiest, most bug-infested set of long johns we'd ever beheld. He truly stank to high heaven. Even Zeb had backed off and ceased any aggression toward the man. I unobtrusively moved upwind. The bushwhacker was just short of buck-naked. I glared at him as though about to ask him to peel off the offending long johns.

"N-n-no...please no," he pleaded. He sat barefoot, hatless, and likely unappealing to any human or animal he might encounter.

"You know where Toliver is headed?"

He shook his head. "Shorty, build a fire."

The man watched as the cowboy wasted no time getting flames going.

"Gonna brand him, boss?" asked Collins.

Sheer panic flashed in the bushwhacker's eyes.

I laughed. "Nope." With that, I proceeded to kick the man's clothes and even his boots and gun belt into the fire.

Once everything was sufficiently burned, I turned back to the bushwhacker. "Get up and start walking. You follow Toliver's trail. Maybe you'll catch up with him… maybe not," I felt that some degree of justice was being served. It would surely be a warning to Toliver.

We stood around and watched the man limp off until he was out of sight.

"Still plenty of daylight," I noted. "Let's water the horses and get back on the trail." I remained ever-determined to get home in time for the birth of my first child.

Collins shook his head but mounted up. He turned to Juan, Hank, and Shorty. "You heard the boss. Let's go, men."

It wasn't long before we had resumed our travels southward.

―――――

ANOTHER WEEK of travels went uneventfully. July was upon us and ready to punish us with its heat and weather that seemed to have no soul. We saw no fellow travelers or Indians and the weather was spectacularly beautiful. Game was plentiful, and our horses were holding up right well. The upside was that we were making great progress as we crossed ever-flatter prairies and sand flats; the downside was that we tended to be not so cautious as we needed to be. We were likely being watched, but Spirit Talker saw no threats and my own sense of danger wasn't stirred. Zeb remained a great companion, affectionate, protective, and self-sufficient. He was a kindred spirit. Indeed, I felt assured that he was a gift of God.

The terrain began to feature more ravines as we neared the Arkansas River. We necessarily grew more watchful. Any deep cut in the landscape posed risks of ambush, as we generally were forced to ride single file. Broader, flatter prairie lands lay ahead, and a few more days would bring us to the northern reaches of Texas. Our present southward course would take us through the huge canyon carved from the prairie. The gash in the terrain was at least a hundred miles long, and appeared as though the earth had received some great punishment. Spirit Talker told me that his *numunuu*, his people, spoke of a far larger canyon off to the west. The one we'd soon be riding through was plenty enough for me.

Thoughts roiled through my brain. I was anxious to get home to Blue Flower, and I wondered how George was making out with the herd, whether the folks that left the wagon train had settled in, and even wondered if Toliver's man had caught up with his fellow bushwhackers.

Our horses were holding up well under the rigors of travel. It sure was a lot easier with no cattle to drive. We switched mounts every couple of hours and strove to keep moving at as fast a pace as we reasonably could.

We were less than a day from the Arkansas, when Spirit Talker came galloping toward me. My heart sank just a tad, as that usually meant that some threat lurked ahead. As he drew closer, he pointed toward a stand of cottonwoods and motioned for us to head for it. I saw the reason why behind him.

Perhaps a dozen—things were moving too fast to accurately count—hostiles were bearing down on Spirit Talker's dust. Coup sticks, lances, war clubs, feathers, flying buckskins, painted faces, wild-eyed ponies, and war whoops were fast descending upon us.

Our little army raced to the small tree line, dismounted, and formed a defensive perimeter.

Spirit Talker was last to arrive. "Arapaho!" he shouted.

The attackers were upon us in what seemed like a mere heartbeat. A raging warrior swiped his coup stick across Shorty's shoulder, but the cowboy's revolver barked before the savage could come in for the kill. I saw the hostile's eyes widen with the pain and realization that a bullet had torn the life from his body.

Spirit Talker's bow was singing, as arrow after arrow found its mark. My Sharps carbine plowed a .50 caliber slug into a feather-bedecked warrior's heart.

The Arapaho had lost four warriors and more wounded in but seconds. One more dropped from his saddle as they beat a retreat.

"Hold fire!" I shouted.

The Arapaho war party gathered at what they felt must be a safe distance. Their ambush had obviously not worked out as planned. Apparently, a younger warrior anxious to prove himself had charged out at Spirit Talker and revealed their hiding place. The war party could retreat or attack and chose the latter. Now, they gathered to consider their options.

We were now dug in pretty good. Shorty, with Prairie Flower's help, had the horses under control.

I reckoned to give the Arapaho a bit more to think about. The warriors now numbered eight that I could count. A couple looked to be wounded, and there was a wounded warrior lying a hundred yards or so from our position. I felt sure the Arapaho wanted to retrieve the wounded man as well as the bodies of their dead. By my rough calculation, the hostiles were a tad better than two hundred yards out. I looked at Spirit Talker and smiled.

My Comanche brother returned an impish grin.

I lay prone and took careful aim. There was no wind, and the distance was well within the accurate range of my Sharps. An Arapaho was about to lose the feathers in his hair. I exhaled and squeezed the trigger. The report echoed from the surrounding hills but not before an Arapaho had dropped from his pony. My aim had been slightly off, and he'd essentially been partially scalped. The other warriors sat aghast. Ponies reared and pranced about nervously. They all turned their gazes toward the swirl of gunsmoke rising from the muzzle of my carbine.

Just then, Zeb stood beside the smoking barrel. It must have seemed like some sort of spirit apparition to the heathen savages.

I seized the moment to walk forward with Zeb at my side. I grasped my hands before me as a peace sign.

The now-panicky warriors conferred among themselves. One warrior finally broke from the war party and began to slowly ride toward me while mimicking my peace sign.

Spirit Talker moved beside me. We must have presented quite a sight; a White teenager, a young Comanche, and a wolf.

At about fifteen feet from us, the Arapaho warrior stopped and dismounted.

We stared at each other for what seemed like an eternity. I knew that four rifles were backing us up, and I was sure the Arapaho felt at least somewhat confident in his own backup.

He pointed to himself. "Buffalo Runner," he said and signed. He looked guardedly at Zeb.

I nodded and pointed to myself. "Walks With Wolves," I similarly signed my name.

Spirit Talker stepped up. "Mukwooru," he said.

The Arapaho instantly recognized the Comanche name. "Buffalo Hump?" he asked as much as stated.

Spirit Talker nodded.

There was a lot of strong *sunipu* standing before Buffalo Runner. In fact, it was likely overwhelming. He took a deep breath and pointed to the Arapaho bodies lying in the prairie dust behind us. He signed to collect his dead and wounded and depart in peace.

I leaned down and pretended to confer with Zeb. He whined and pawed the ground. "We travel in peace," I said. "*Isa* strong medicine."

The Arapaho warrior nodded agreement. He and Spirit Talker exchanged glances. The warrior signed that we would travel in peace.

I reached out my hand.

The Arapaho hesitated, then clasped my hand in a strong grip as though trying to feel the wolf spirit. If he felt any force at all, it was God's spirit. With that, he mounted up, took a parting glance at Zeb, and returned to his war party.

I motioned our little army to mount up and proceed onward, which we accomplished as quickly as possible before any hostile minds changed.

As we rode past them, the Arapaho turned to ride toward the scene of our brief battle to collect their dead and wounded. We all nodded respectfully. I wondered whether they realized that their days were numbered, if they failed to adapt to the White man's settling of their lands? I also wondered if the White man could ever keep a treaty promise? I thought back to the Indian agent Triss up in the North Platte country and his attempts to bring a balance of peace to the region. I hoped God would help sort it all out, but I suspected that in the mean time it would be up to folks like Spirit Talker, George Freeman, and me to carve a path to peace.

TWENTY-THREE
WEATHER OR NOT

THUNDER BOOMED LIKE A HUNDRED CANNON! Rain fell in wind-driven sheets and seeped into every nook, cranny, and crevice of our clothing. Spirit Talker and I would have shed our buckskin shirts but for the pelting nature of the downpour as occasionally mixed with small bits of ice. Collins called them hail. Even the poncho-like covers that Collins and the other cowboys wore were not impervious to the weather's wrath. Hat brims drooped accordingly. We were all a soggy mess. I tied my bandanna across my face, but it wasn't much protection.

One of the dangers with sustained heavy rains was flash flooding. The next ravine or mere indentation in the prairie could have us facing a wall of water that would wreak havoc among us. As though that wasn't enough, lightning and thunder added to the symphony of the frontier. I guess it could be said that we were lucky to not be driving a herd of cattle, as they'd surely stampede. Spirit Talker strove to lead us across higher ground and kept a keen eye out for temporary shelter.

———

THE ARKANSAS RIVER was raging as though hemorrhaging water and ready to suck the unwary into its death-dealing rapids. We sat soaked to our skins astride our horses and surveying the river for some hint of a place we might cross. Our little army was miserable, despite the rain offering a very slight respite from the heat. Zeb tried to shake the water free of his thick coat but to no avail. Seemed that a wolf or most any other animal was no better off than us humans.

Spirit Talker rode over to confer with Collins and me. He sat silently for a moment with rivulets of water cascading down his face. Neither he nor Prairie Flower wore hats, though she had tied a semi-waterproofed fabric over her head. Spirit Talker finally turned to me. He pointed west. "In hills, water narrows. Might cross," he conjectured. "Maybe Arapaho and Southern Cheyenne," he added. He then pointed to the east. "Much water. No cross for many days. Maybe trouble with Pawnee and Kiowa."

We had little choice. It could be a week or more before this section of the Arkansas River was passable.

I looked over at Collins, and he nodded. The rest of my little army looked expectantly at me. "May the Lord be with us. Upriver it is," I directed, and we turned into the wind.

We plodded along at times nearly blinded by the torrents. It took most of the remaining daylight to bring us to a place where the river afforded us a possible place to cross. There were cottonwoods on either side, just enough that we could string a couple of ropes to guide us and hopefully keep us from being swept downstream.

Spirit Talker and I volunteered to cross with rope leads in hand. We clung to our saddles as best we could, though Spirit Talker's Comanche saddle was of doubtful utility. We had little choice. The other end of the ropes were tied off to trees on the north side of the river.

If any horse had a prayer of crossing, it was Big Red. Spirit Talker brought his pony alongside and upstream, as we slowly worked our way across. Blessedly, we only slipped once, and Big Red was able to keep his balance and quickly regain his footing.

Upon reaching the south shore, we tied off the ropes to trees. Now, was the moment of truth. "Time for strong *sunipu*," I said to Spirit Talker.

"God bless us," responded my Comanche brother. With that and as miraculously on queue as possible, the rain stopped. The river's water raged madly on, but the sheets of rain were gone.

Spirit Talker and I stripped to our waists and shed our moccasins. Clinging to the ropes as guides, each of our little army crossed. Despite it being summer, the water was still chilly. The ropes became wet and slippery, but everyone managed to hang on.

Prairie Flower hesitated with a hint of fear in the way she stood watching the roiling rapids race past. Spirit Talker crossed back over to her. He tied a piece of rope to her and to the guide lines, wrapped a strong arm around her, and mostly carried her across.

Collins, Johnson, and I took turns leading the horses across one by one. We quickly found ourselves exhausted by the strong current.

At last, all that remained was Zeb. I wondered how he might have dealt with this as leader of his pack. Why too was he waiting to be the last to cross? I didn't have to wait long. He plunged into the river and managed to swim his way across, winding up roughly fifty yards downstream. Climbing onto the south bank, he shook off the excess water and came trotting up to rejoin us.

Our river adventure had cost us valuable time, but we were all safe. The sun had sunk nearly to the horizon by now, so we decided to make camp. There was no point in trying to take on the unfamiliar and decidedly rough terrain in the dark. A fire might have been nice, but there was no dry kindling readily available, and we were far too tired to be splitting wood. Besides, if there were any hostiles in the vicinity, there was no point in alerting them to our presence. If anyone had been trying to follow us, it would have been next to impossible given the rains wiping out any trail sign. We wiped down the horses and picketed them among the trees. We'd rotate a watch just to be on the safe side.

We hung most of our clothes to dry while remaining as modestly clothed as possible given the presence of a woman in camp. Dry? Did I say dry? A heavy humidity hung in the air. At best, our clothes wouldn't be soaking wet, just very damp. We were more tired than hungry. After feasting on jerky, we turned in. Hot coffee would have been great, but that was not to be.

————

A BLAZING shard of sunlight danced over my eyes. I raised my hand as a shield, and looked around. Everything was still soggy. It would be a day of drying out as we rode. Visions of chaffed legs from wet saddles coursed through my thinking, as I pulled on my still damp boots and went about awakening everyone. We still had a couple of weeks of travel ahead of us, and time was wasting.

The trail was a bit treacherous at first owing to having to negotiate occasional rocky outcroppings along the riverbank, but we soon managed to reach reasonably level terrain. I briefly considered heading in a southeasterly direction to try to save time, but Spirit Talker talked me out of it. The river was still at flood stage, but he felt it best to be near water for the horses. We would soon be enduring a dry stretch, as we approached the Texas border.

The weather was fully opposite from the rainy deluge we'd experienced the day before. Sweat began to dribble down my back, and we found ourselves wringing out bandannas and hanging them around our necks to stay cool. The air was so heavy, it was as though a steamy mist enveloped us as we plodded on.

Around midday, we reached the spot just south of where we had decided to find a safer place to ford the river. We dismounted and cared for our horses. Despite the damp air and profuse sweating, we had pretty much dried out. After filling all of our bota bags, we mounted up and resumed our southward journey. We remained ever vigilant for hostiles, though I reckoned that word would spread not to mess with the strong *sunipu* of Walks With Wolves. I wondered whether I might yet have to deal with Sam Toliver. Guess that depended on how long he figured to carry a grudge.

Zeb seemed to be growing ever-more affectionate. Not like a domesticated dog, mind you, but he let me groom him. At night, Zeb would lie beside me. I felt more like I'd been accepted as a member of his pack. Occasionally, he'd amble off to hunt for his dinner, as he refused any cooked meat or even raw meat. Guess raw meat was too much like carrion; fit for buzzards and coyotes but not for a self-respecting wolf. He even sidled up some to Spirit Talker, though he kept his distance from everyone else. Zeb had established a special bond which served to reinforce my belief that he was a gift from God. He developed a habit of nuzzling me awake each morning. Nothing like a damp nose and warm wolf breath to get your attention.

Prairie Flower had proven to be far less of a distraction then expected. She was every bit the independent, self-sufficient Comanche woman committed to serving her husband and minimizing any burdens on us. She made sure that Spirit Talker was fed and even made occasional small talk with me. She still spoke a mix of English and Comanche, so we got along right well so far as communicating. She missed her people which was understandable given all she had endured being a captive enslaved to an old woman and nearly starving. Now, she had the promise of a rich full life ahead.

As I was thinking on this, Prairie Flower came up behind me as I was stoking the cooking fire for breakfast. "Jack cook today?" she asked with a smile.

I laughed, as she and Juan had been doing virtually all the cooking on the trail. "My cooking make everyone sick," I laughed. "Where's Mukwooru?"

She blushed. "Very tired."

I need not have wondered why. "I'm glad you are happy, Prairie Flower."

With that, she stepped forward and gave me a hug. "Jack good man. Strong *sunipu*."

It nearly brought tears to my eyes. I hadn't realized the degree of positive impact I had on folks around me. With Prairie Flower, she recognized the unspoken bond between Spirit Talker and me and saw the love of God's creation that apparently radiated from me. I had no idea, and it was likely that naivete that kept me humble. There was no space in this frontier life for pridefulness. It served to further reinforce what I felt was my God-given life mission to subdue the earth and extract its potential. I turned back to her and saw Spirit Talker approaching. "Guess we better get breakfast fixed," I urged with an uncomfortable guffaw. I figured that Spirit Talker likely saw Prairie Flower hug me, but he gave no indication that it was a bother.

About this time, Zeb appeared with the remains of a rabbit dangling from his mouth.

"Only wolf eat breakfast?" said Spirit Talker with a laugh.

Juan showed up in the nick of time with the coffee pot and a skillet of venison steak strips and eggs gathered from who knows where. *"Desayuno pronto,"* he announced. Breakfast at this point couldn't come soon enough.

Except for Prairie Flower, we had been traveling together for roughly five months. The fact that we still got along so well was a testament to the mutual respect and teamwork we had developed, though I suspected that there was much more to it. Hank Johnson had clearly accepted Christ into his life and shed the specter of revenge over loss of his family that had long clouded his soul. Juan and Collins were God-fearing men, and I had to believe that Shorty just might be thanking God after his brush with the poisoned arrow. Prairie Flower had been exposed to the strong faith of George Freeman and Running Waters, and Spirit Talker had surely shared his faith with her.

The thing about America's western frontier was that faith in our creator God was both a stark contrast to and an integral part of life on the majestically beautiful yet at times frighteningly dangerous part of His creation. Floods, hostile Indians, outlaws, wild animals, fires, mankind's sins against each other and often challenging terrain gave folks like myself pause to ever remind ourselves of God's presence.

TWENTY-FOUR

HOMESTRETCH

FOR WHATEVER CRAZY REASON, we decided to push through the huge canyon carved from the northern Texas prairie. I think it was to break up the sheer monotony of the flat lands stretching for days around us. That's measuring in days, not miles. Palo Duro Canyon was a challenge, but also offered a direct route and access to water and wood for cooking fires.

Within the hallowed walls of the canyon, a traveler could feel the ghostlike presence of early Spanish explorers. Perhaps, Coronado himself journeyed through the place. Later explorers like Hernando de Alvarado passed through the canyon in search of Quivera, a city purportedly setting on vast quantities of gold and silver and shared with Alvarado by El Turko, a captive Pawnee likely trying to save his own life. El Turko later paid for his lie with his life. Comanche, Southern Cheyenne, and Kiowa eventually displaced Apache as the primary residents of Palo Duro Canyon. Thus, the canyon presented both a relief and danger.

We began setting extra watches at night, and Spirit

Talker stayed a tad closer riding point just in case we ran into an ambush.

We threw caution to the winds for our first night in the canyon, as we lit a respectable cooking fire and feasted on antelope, berries, biscuits, and coffee. The biscuits were a special treat, as Prairie Flower had found some grains and ground enough for a decent flour.

After dinner, Spirit Talker placed Prairie Flower's bedroll closer to camp in deference to any hostile threat. He then walked over to Zeb and me and motioned to walk away from prying ears.

"You have a concern?" I asked once we were a few yards from camp and out of earshot. Heavy thinking was written all over his face.

"I take Prairie Flower to my *numunuu*, to the Penateka Comanche," he said softly but firmly.

I was not surprised at his desire to return to his people, his *numunuu*. I harbored a long-held feeling that he was destined to become a great influence on the Penateka Comanche as a shaman. His challenge would be that of being a Christian while living among those whose religion was animism, the worship of animals and objects. "I reckoned that you might," I responded.

"Buffalo Hump grow old. Comanche must live in peace with Whites. Mukwooru must show way to God."

I figured that was going to be a tall order. The Comanche, like other tribes, would cling to the old ways so long as they possible could. Spirit Talker's influence would likely be in setting an example by living Christian principles, for I doubted that wholesale conversion would happen very quickly. By my reckoning, God had a plan to use Spirit Talker in some way for the ultimate good. I thought back on my pa's quoting from John in the Bible to the effect that in the final judgment light came into the world, and folks preferred it to the darkness of evil. Truth would always come to the light. I felt certain that this was the case with Spirit Talker.

"Does Prairie Flower know?"

My Comanche brother nodded. "We talk. She agree. No place for us in White man world...yet," he paused with a wry smile and winked. "Always place at Rising Cross Ranch."

He took the words straight from my mouth. "You must stay strong, my brother," I said. "Your travels may not be easy." I already envisioned that he might be facing a new shaman that had risen to that role among the Penateka Comanche. Buffalo Hump was growing old and his influence ebbed along with his physical strength.

"Jack must bring Blue Flower to village with little one."

I nodded. Seemed to me that a visit was a given. It might be a few months, as there would yet be plenty of work before me at Rising Cross Ranch. We would be preparing for the next cattle drive north, likely a couple of years off. Of course, no one could be sure what the future portended. That was God's business. I'd come to the realization that God must often laugh in the face of man's plans. He apparently had an outsized sense of humor. "How long you figure to stay with us at the ranch?" I said after what must have seemed an interminable pause.

"Me see sister's child," he responded with a smile. "Then go home."

We grasped arms in a sign of brotherhood and deep respect.

"May God ever watch over us," I said, gazing into Spirit Talker's eyes.

The scars from the mountain lion attack deepened as

he grinned broadly. "God smiles upon us, Walks With Wolves."

We both looked down to behold Zeb sitting between us. Indeed, I did walk with at least one wolf...or was he walking with me.

The supposed life debt that had brought Spirit Talker into my life after having saved him from the mountain lion had been paid in full many times over. The words of release from that debt did not have to be spoken. So far as I was concerned, God had already reconciled any debt through Christ. Nevertheless, we existed in a world of mankind's making; an often very challenging world that we had to conquer as best we could. "May He give us strength to endure," I rejoined.

"Amen," rejoined Spirit Talker.

We headed back to the camp. I think Zeb sensed that there'd been a change, as he walked a bit closer than usual beside me. I felt as though his presence was a reassurance that God would continue to watch over Spirit Talker and me.

———

PALO DURO CANYON was soon behind us. The journey through it had been uneventful. Its rough-hewn beauty made it seem as though we had trekked through hallowed ground. How many had lived, hunted, fought, and died within the layered seams and stratum of its aged red and orange walls. We knew we were ever under the watchful eyes of Indians, but none were inclined to challenge the strong *sunipu* of Walks With Wolves.

I reckoned that the journey ahead would be relatively safe. We were in pretty much friendly territory so far as any Comanche threat was concerned; though that could change faster than a prairie fire with a tail wind if one subtribe looked crossways toward another. I kept in mind that peace on the frontier was always tenuous at best.

Spirit Talker continued to ride point, keeping a watchful eye for threats and informing us of any wildlife or terrain threats. We knew there were all manner of rattlesnakes, mountain lions, wolves, coyote, bears, bobcats, and more out there licking their chops for a piece of us. The prairie would be mostly flat until we hit the gentle rolling hills near the lower portion of the Comancheria. Flat was the good news. Rivers, streams, arroyos, grasses, cacti, brush, thorns, and a very few mottes of mesquite and live oak often conspired to slow travel to a crawl. At times we walked; other times we rode. Shade was a mostly a figment of our imaginations, and heat was a given. It was a dry heat akin to being inside an oven. Then there was the sky. It was nearly always cloudless and the distant horizons made it seem that its crystalline blueness reached to infinity. Folks referred to this as big sky; and that was downright accurate.

Onward we journeyed. Would we ever reach Rising Cross Ranch? Given our riding in single file, there was little or no conversation save for when we stopped to rest. We traveled immersed in our own thoughts; our own hopes and dreams.

————

WE STAYED WELL to the east of what we would eventually learn was the llano estacado or staked plains, a geological formation that stretched for roughly two hundred fifty miles along the westernmost border of Texas. It formed the very heart of the Comancheria. To the west of the caprock lay nary a bush or tree or much of any kind or a living thing. To the east where we traveled, it stretched out before us-one uninterrupted plain featuring low-lying vegetation.

Soon the Pease River and Brazos River were behind us. They ran pretty-shallow, as mountain-fed springs ran ever-dryer.

A huge elongated hunk of pink granite rock soon loomed in the distance ahead of us. Spirit Talker never said anything about it, though he began to head us due east so as to give the more than four-hundred-foot-high edifice a wide berth. Unsurprisingly, the Indians saw the huge boulder as spirit-filled, a sacred place. I understood that there were many legends associated with the rock. It even had its own language, as it creaked and groaned with changing temperatures. Haunted? Perhaps. It was often referred to as enchanted or crying. Little wonder that the tribes felt that it was inhabited by spirits.

It wasn't long after the granite rock that we found ourselves on the north shore of the Pedernales River. Our little army easily crossed the shallow waters. We were well to the east of the most recent Penateka Comanche encampment, and I saw Spirit Talker ahead of us take a brief wistful look in that direction and whisper something to Prairie Flower. I'm sure it was reassurance.

We now sought the Pinta Trail that would lead us to the Guadalupe River and a short ride eastward to Rising Cross Ranch. A couple of easy-riding hours, and we found ourselves heading southward on the trail. My mind flooded with memories of the trials and tribulations that Spirit Talker and I had experienced in this part of the Comancheria. We now kept our eyes peeled for Captain Benton and his company of Texas Rangers in addition to local Indians. We remained ever-wary of travelers sharing the trail.

We did encounter a half-dozen Penateka Comanche hunters. After a brief conversation with Spirit Talker and a few nods toward Prairie Flower and me, they moved on with broad smiles. Apparently, they would be sharing the news of Spirit Talker's return with Buffalo Hump.

I rode up alongside Spirit Talker after the hunters moved on.

"Comanche *ana o'a hi'it,*" shared my Comanche brother with a grin. He had to talk them out of sharing a meal and smoking a pipe, as it likely would have delayed us for at least a couple of precious hours. "No say about return to village," he added with a grim look. He wanted his return to the encampment with Prairie Flower to come as a surprise to his father and did not want his stepmother conjuring up any unsavory thoughts. They knew of his baptism, but figured that the Comanche religion would dominate. He also learned that one of the older warriors was making overtures toward becoming the new shaman. As the worthy son of a famous war chief, Spirit Talker would surely be a threat to that.

———

THE FAMILIAR BANKS of the Guadalupe River soon lay before us. Home was close at hand. We were trail weary to say the least.

Juan, Shorty, and the other members of our party would spend the night at Rising Cross before moving on to Bandara. Collins was especially anxious to return to the Circle N, but knew his duty was to me and August Klappenbach. I would have little choice but to join them.

We had a couple of hundred dollars of cattle profits to share with the Bandera general store proprietor.

Assuming no further danger ahead, Spirit Talker no longer rode point. He settled in beside me and Prairie Flower urged her pony up to join us.

I led the way down the north bank and into the river. Plenty of bass frantically swam about, as we waded the horses across. I could likely have caught a couple of fish by hand. Big Red tossed his head as though anticipating home and his waiting brood of mares. I thought back on how I used to easily fill a stringer of the ravenous Texas river bass. They were so abundant...then, as though someone had snapped their fingers, my thoughts took a turn, drifting back to the day but a couple of years back; the day of the Comanche raid. I had been here fishing while the savages killed most of my family.

Spirit Talker read my face and caught the sudden shift in my spirit. "Kate and Buck will be pleased to see you," he ventured with hope of breaking me from my gloom.

I nodded, but there was no life in my eyes.

"Blue Flower waits for you," he said as though pulling an ace from a deck of cards.

I looked toward him and tried to smile. Yes, she would be waiting. My mind turned. Would I be there in time to witness the birth of my first child? Would it be a son? A daughter?

Prairie Flower moved alongside. "She waits for you, Jack," she assured me, as though she had some special vision.

I was surrounded by love and support. We couldn't turn back time and change outcomes. What was past was past. A promising future lay ahead, and God surely had a plan for us all.

Our little army rode at a quick walk along the south

bank of the Guadalupe. Everyone seemed to sense that we were nearing the end of our cattle venture. We would soon be home; just a few hours more. What could possibly go wrong?

We hadn't ridden more than a hundred yards, when the sound of horse hooves, squeak of saddle leather, and jingle of spurs came to our ears. Several riders were heading our way. Friends? Foes? We immediately fell back to form a defensive perimeter.

Texas Ranger Captain Nathan Benton pulled up his company in a cloud of dust and spattering of sweat and lather. He'd apparently been riding hard. He took a look at me, and it took a moment for whom I was to sink in. "You seen them?" he hollered.

"Howdy, Captain. Seen who?" I shouted back.

"Bunch of dang Nokoni Comanch!" he responded. "Hit the Sanders ranch couple days ago!"

The news raised my hackles and surely got Spirit Talker's attention. He had hoped there would be no further hostilities in this part of the Comancheria.

By my quick assessment, I found myself wondering why Benton was so intent on ruining his horses with the hostiles as much as a day ahead. Moreover, the Nokini camped to the north, not to the east. Could Benton be so thick-headed as to confuse Penateka with Nokoni. Then it struck me, all Indians looked alike to Benton and most any dead Indian would do. "Hold there, Captain!" I shouted back.

"Yer blocking my path, O'Toole!"

"Well, you're hellbent in the wrong direction, if you're chasing Nokoni!"

Benton's face reddened. He wasn't one to take orders, especially from what he figured to be a teenage Indian lover. He began to slide his carbine from its saddle scabbard. In his momentary distraction, he failed to note that he was looking down the muzzles of a small but highly effective arsenal.

We were outnumbered but had the drop on the Texas Rangers. None of them moved a muscle, and Benton let his carbine slip back into its leather home. There'd be no gunplay for now; not this day. "Stand down," he ordered his men, not realizing they'd never gone for their guns in the first place.

"We're tired, Captain. Delivered a herd up in Wyoming and looking to get home," I took a deep breath and pulled myself up such that my sitting tall on as big horse was quite imposing. "We don't figure you to be troubling with peaceful Comanche. If you have a beef with the Nokoni, go chase them. But sure as I'm setting right here, I'll swear to hunt you down and kill you if you harm a hair of my friend's people."

As if on cue, Zeb stepped forward and snarled directly at Benton.

Benton's eyes widened at Zeb's appearance. The Texas Ranger captain stared hard at me as though considering his next move. Should he test me?

I heard several hammers pulled back in full cock behind me. The message to Benton was getting louder and clearer. As for me, I had likely broken the law by threatening the Texas Ranger, but it didn't seem likely he was going to go down that road.

"I'll be back to visit you at Rising Cross, Mr. O'Toole," he said by way of trying to save face. His pride had been sorely wounded, and he was not about to let that pass. Neither was he ready to take us on in any pitched battle.

I smiled. "I'll look forward to it, Captain Benton."

With that, he turned his cayuse and led his men northward across the Guadalupe.

We watched them reach the opposite bank and head off toward the Nokoni region of the Comancheria. I turned to my little army. "You'd think he'd have learned by now," I observed. "Let's head home." I reckoned that at this point the Texas Rangers wouldn't dare attack the Penateka Comanche. Benton might have the law and his mission of protection to fall back on, but he wasn't so foolish as to confront me. He had to know in the depths of his prejudiced soul that I was in the right. I counted on that shred of decency.

As we rode on, I found myself lamenting the mentality that failed to treat the Redman fairly. Yes, the cultures were very different, but both sides were at fault. Pride, greed, envy, lust, and more held sway in far too many hearts. Prejudice abounded among both races. My own efforts at living a moral Godly life seemed paltry, inadequate in the great scheme of frontier life. Yet the more of us that modeled solid biblical morals, the greater the promise that the frontier might eventually thrive in peace and good fortune. We might yet realize my own dream of extracting the potential of God's bounty.

Spirit Talker drew up alongside. He smiled. "Texas Ranger *hawokatu!*" It was as close as he could come to describe Benton as crazy.

I nodded. "Not *hawokatu*, Benton is wrongheaded. He does not understand." I didn't know whether there was a Comanche word for wrongheaded.

We all rode on in silence. The sounds of Benton's Texas Rangers had long since faded away.

———

MY OLD FAVORITE fishing spot soon came into view. I recalled how a stringer of bass could be filled about as fast as you could bait a hook and drop it in the waters. I used to feel as though there was no sport in fishing. Well...life sure put an end to those speculations. I drew Big Red to a halt. We stood there for a moment, as I caressed the cross centered on my bear claw necklace and murmured a little prayer of thanks. I longed to have a fishing rod in my hands. I envisioned Blue Flower and me picnicking at a shady spot along the riverbank with our baby while I casually tossed a fishing line into the swirling waters. We laughed while the baby gurgled nonsensically.

Zeb woofed with anticipation. I think he knew that we were close to something important. The Indians seemed quite spot on in crediting wolves with special gifts. Zeb couldn't hold back.

I looked up to see a half-dozen longhorns sporting Rising Cross brands grazing in the far north pasture. Big Red whinnied and pranced a bit, as he must have caught a whiff of some of his mares not far off. If I could have caught Blue Flower's scent on the air, I might have shared Big Red's excitement.

My gaze shifted toward where I should begin to see the roofs of the cabin and barn peeking over the horizon. An involuntary shudder coursed through my body, as I realized that a column of heavy smoke was twisting skyward about where the cabin should be.

Horror swept across all of our faces.

"No!" I cried as I put spurs to Big Red and bolted for the cabin. "No!" I repeated. I pulled the Colt from my holster and prepared to engage an as yet unseen enemy. Would we be in time? Could God possibly bring tragedy on me a second time?

My little army set their horses to a gallop and joined behind me in the charge. We would not permit history to repeat itself. Thundering hooves pounded across the north pasture of Rising Cross Ranch.

The smoke ahead of us seemed to grow. A seriously fierce blaze was ahead of us. The pungent aroma of woodsmoke began to reach my nostrils. We were but a couple of hundred yards from the cabin. How many attacking warriors would we face? Would my family be alive?

EPILOGUE

THE AMERICAN WESTERN frontier was mostly unforgiving, a meeting of savagery and civilization. Imagine the perils of the trail from Texas to Wyoming (see the map on page X). Then envision the hazards encountered in driving a herd of cattle north through that wild country. Some folks said it was the very roughest part of our western frontier. What made it so? It was Lakota, Crow, Cheyenne, Pawnee, Kiowa, Shoshone, and Comanche territory for one thing. Stretching hundreds of miles northward from Texas all the way to the upper reaches of the North Platte River, the region was a virtual no-man's-land for White settlers. *Longhorns North: Jack's Great Trail Drive* offers peek into the courage, faith, endurance, and pure grit entailed in the conquest of the west. It presages the decades it would take to reap the bounty the region would eventually deliver.

Life expectancy on the frontier was nothing like today. A male Indian did well to live beyond age thirty and women could expect to live a tad less. Little wonder that older tribesmen were highly respected. Life expectancy for Whites wasn't much better. A White man on the frontier tended not to live beyond his late thirties. Notably, the brevity of life generally meant that folks had to mature sooner. By the time a man or woman reached age fifteen or sixteen, he or she was pretty much an adult in terms of others expecting him or her to carry an adult set of responsibilities.

Dangers? Anthropology-minded folks claim there were as many as thirteen tribes of Comanche from the Quahadi or "antelope eaters" in the north to the Penateka or "honey eaters" in the south. Mix in Kiowa, Apache, and Tonkawa, and settlers had their hands full. The very name Comanche loosely translates in the Ute tribal language as "enemy." Capture by the Comanche invariably led to terrible outcomes. A fearsome lot these tribes were. Notably, Penateka Comanche Chief Buffalo Hump led more than 600 warriors on a raid through the heart of Texas in August 1840, murdering Texans, looting the city of Victoria, and looting and burning Linnville on their march to the Gulf of Mexico. It was not until 1858 that Texas Ranger John Salmon "Rip" Ford led a force of 102 heavily armed Texas Rangers into the Comancheria and brought the Comanche to their knees at the Battle of Little Robe Creek on the Canadian River.

The northwest plains were peopled by many tribes but especially the Sioux, comprised of three groups: Dakota, Nakota, and Lakota. *Longhorns North: Jack's Great Trail Drive* focuses on the Lakota, in turn made up of seven subgroups: Oglalas (famed for Red Cloud and Crazy Horse), Hunkpapas (famed for Sitting Bull), Miniconjous, Oohenunpas (Two Kettles), Itazipacolas (Sans Arcs), Brulés (Burnt Thighs), and Sihasapas (Blackfeet). The Lakota history was no less combative than

Comanche or Cheyenne. For example, there was the Grattan Massacre or Cow Incident of August 19, 1854, in which the Army erroneously accused the Lakota of stealing a Mormon settler's cow and resulted in a confrontation in which the entire 30-man company was killed, including 2nd Lieutenant John Grattan. Troops under Brigadier General William Harney avenged that massacre a year later at the Battle of Ash Hollow. Most folks have heard of the Little Big Horn (called Greasy Grass by the Lakota) where troops under General George Armstrong Custer on June 25, 1876, were massacred by Sioux and their allies. Far fewer are aware of the Fetterman Massacre on December 21, 1866, also known as the Battle of the Hundred-in-the-Hands or the Battle of a Hundred Slain, during Red Cloud's War. It involved a confederation of the Lakota, Cheyenne, and Arapaho tribes and a detachment of the United States Army based at Fort Phil Kearny, Wyoming. Oglala Lakota chief Crazy Horse lured an entire 81-man detachment of troops into a trap where they were all killed. Massacres cut both ways. There was the Sand Creek Massacre of November 29, 1864, in which members of the Colorado Militia attacking a peaceful Cheyenne village, killing up to 600 men, women, and children at Sand Creek in Kiowa County. Despite the violence of the frontier, it's worthy of note that the Lakota held to a worthy set of virtues: generosity, courage, fortitude, and wisdom.

Oh, I do refer to bison as buffalo. Just for the record, bison and buffalo are quite different. Visualize the water buffalo and then the shaggy awkward bulk of the American bison. Seems that "buffalo" came into common usage in America to refer to the bison, so I've chosen to use it in my writings. Also, note that what is today's

Colorado was referred to as part of the Kansas Territory and for a brief time after 1859, as the Jefferson Territory.

In *Longhorns North: Jack's Great Trail Drive,* young Jack O'Toole drives a herd of longhorns north while facing an unforgiving land featuring savage Indians, unpredictable weather, predatory beasts, and vegetation that could literally tear flesh from bone. It is said the United States' western frontier offered new opportunities for hearty folks willing to endure its rigors. It might also be said that folks that settled certain parts of the frontier like the Yellowstone region with its Lakota tribe and the Comancheria with its Comanche tribes were not playing with a full deck. They had to be crazy.

Jack had no modern creature comforts. Invention of cell phones and social media was a century and a half into the future. Transportation? Horses and mules were the vehicles of choice. Jack had no refrigerator to preserve sweet treats. There were no flush toilets or showers. Folks mostly ate what grazed upon or grew from the land. Learning was squeezed from the few books that might be found, especially The Holy Bible. By way of example, my own great great-great-grandfather brought his collection of books from Ireland in 1851. As a serious and religious-minded pioneer, he had gathered quite an impressive library for his time. It included *The Holy Bible;* three volumes of *Lives of the Saints, Lives of Irish Saints and Martyrs*; Geoffrey Keating's *History of Ireland*; Edward Clarendon's *History of Ireland*; a *History of the Christian Church*; lectures and sermons by Father Burke titled *Instructions for Youth*; Hume's *History of England, Trials of a Mind*; Moore's *Life of Lord Edward Fitzgerald*; *Washington and His Generals*; a *Bible History*; and Cobbet's *History of the Reformation.* Sort of makes a head swim, doesn't it?

Can't say as the living of the era was luxurious unless you counted the sheer grandeur of majestic landscapes and of nights so quiet you could hear the stars twinkling. To fully appreciate the place, you simply had to love beauty of the outdoors. Fishing the meandering Guadalupe River in Texas or the chill waters of Wyoming's North Platte River, hunting deer and antelope, raising cattle and horses, and reaping the bounteous yield of the rich soil was sheer joy for a courageous visionary few. For a teen on the frontier, life could be pretty good...mostly. Otherwise, it was downright dangerous.

Thus far, Jack O'Toole has grown to manhood, conquered fears and prejudices, fought Indians and bandits, taken on prairie fires and storms, defended against wild beasts, traveled the wild country, driven cattle, and found the love of his life. As you have seen, he especially draws upon his faith and what he was taught by his parents. He has to learn to trust in instincts forged from his biblical lessons. Yes, Jack is on a frontier adventure and more.

WATCH FOR WARPATH: JACK'S FAITH IS TESTED (THE FRONTIER CHRONICLES 4)

The gripping fourth installment of *The Frontier Chronicles* plunges readers into the unforgiving wilds of the American West. As Jack O'Toole faces the most brutal challenges yet, his courage, faith, and unyielding grit are put to the ultimate test...

In 1858, the Comancheria was a deadly battleground where savage and civilized worlds collided. Jack, barely eighteen, finds himself navigating this treacherous no-man's-land alongside his Comanche ally. Together, they confront relentless threats from Comanche warriors, White settlers' growing hostility, and the escalating violence that leads to the fierce Battle of Little Robe Creek.

This riveting historical western not only chronicles Jack's survival against impossible odds but also sheds light on the complex and often untold truths of the American frontier. With each step, Jack's journey is shaped by the harsh landscape, relentless enemies, and a destiny governed by faith and fate.

Will Jack's unwavering faith guide him through the bloodshed, or will the relentless violence of the frontier consume him? Discover the powerful tale of endurance and belief in *Warpath: Jack's Faith is Tested.*

AVAILABLE NOVEMBER 2024

ACKNOWLEDGMENTS

Authoring books doesn't simply happen in a vacuum. The author provides the creative talent and crafts the stories, but there's so much more that demands acknowledgment. There are lots of folks and places that contribute to my authoring endeavors. So it is with *Longhorns North: Jack's Great Trail Drive*. The tale is set in 1857 and shares the trials and tribulations of a teen forced to meet the challenges inherent in the dangerous vastness of the western frontier; but this novel stands apart. At its core, it is also about the taming of the frontier. Step in two teen boys becoming men. The protagonist epitomizes the freedom of America's western frontier and represents a final bastion of honor in America. The tale follows Jack O'Toole's adventures in *Perilous Trails: Jack's Adventure Begins* and then *Wyoming Calls: Jack's Risky Quest*. Hopefully, readers will find *Longhorns North: Jack's Great Trail Drive* worthy of their time and emotional involvement.

I've been blessed with many friends and family who have supported my writings. My wife Carolyn's reviews and encouragement were a huge help along with very important tech support from our sons Mike and Matt. Thanks to my nephew Shawn for his faith insights. Many more friends and family have contributed support at some level to the creation and publication of *Longhorns North: Jack's Great Trail Drive* be it encouragement or advice.

Naturally, I am major grateful to the great folks at Wise Wolf Books. The team they bring to publishing is first-rate in editing, cover design, and the myriad tasks that lead to successful book sales.

It's only right to acknowledge my ancestors who were actual settlers of the south Texas frontier. In addition to inspiring me, they provided a quite helpful true-to-life framework as to the life and times on the Texas Nueces Strip. It has been appropriate to weave them into the tapestry of my western novels. Matthew Dunn (1815-1855) immigrated to Corpus Christi from County Kildare in 1845, established a homestead on Upriver Road, and served as a sutler to General Zachary Taylor's Army in the Mexican-American War. Peter Dunn (1807-1890) immigrated from Ireland in 1850 and established a blacksmith shop in Corpus Christi; John Dunn (1803-1889), my great great great grandfather, raised cattle and grew thousands of acres of cotton; Lawrence Dunn (1837-1864) fought and died with Captain Ware's Confederate cavalry; and my great great grandfather Nicholas Dunn (1835-1912) was a rancher, drover, live-stock speculator, and Comanche fighter of some repute. My cousin John Beamond "Red John" Dunn (1851-1940) served as a Texas Ranger in the 1870s under Captain Bland Chamberlain (Company H), subsequently joined a "vigilance committee," became a farmer and merchant, and curated a museum of military weapons displayed to this day in the Corpus Christi Museum of Science & History. Red John Dunn's brother Matthew Dunn also served as a Texas Ranger, and another cousin Rut Evans served as a Texas Ranger in the 1890s (Company E, Frontier Battalion, Alice, TX). My cousin Patrick Dunn was quite successful at raising longhorns on North Padre Island just east of Corpus Christi from 1883 to 1937.

John Hillard Dunn (1883-1958), whose personal narrative about his family and his own adventures drove my pursuit of my Texas family legacy, inspired my own writings, and led me to write his yet-to-be-published biography *Tough Hombre – Recollections of a True Texan*. Finally, my grandfather, Horace Charles Greathouse served as a Texas Ranger in 1920 (Company C, Austin, TX). Such real-life characters coupled with actual events have served to reinforce the historical settings for my writings.

Most of my authoring has occurred in my office as decorated to channel my inner Texan, but my creative juices have often been inspired and imagination stoked in cafés and coffee houses across America. My favorites were Hester's Café & Coffee Bar in Corpus Christi, TX; Nueces Café in Robstown, TX; Java Ranch Espresso Bar & Café in Fredericksburg, TX; PAX Coffee & Goods in Kerrville, TX; Ragged Edge Coffee House and Bantam Coffee Roasters in Gettysburg, PA; 1889 Coffee House in Helena, MT; Dunn Brothers Coffee in Rapid City, SD; Postmasters Coffee & Bakery and Brio Coffeehouse in Waynesboro, PA; Birdie's Café and American Ice Co Café in Westminster, MD; Deja Brew Coffee House, New Oxford and Deja Brew at Miney Branch, Carroll Valley, PA; and Baltimore Coffee & Tea Co., Frederick Coffee Company & Café, and Dublin Roasters in Frederick, MD. I must admit to also frequenting a few Dunkin Donuts and Starbucks around our fine nation. The décors and easy-listening music in these fine establishments combined with savory cups of coffee tended to set me in the right creative frame of mind.

Last but not least, I'm especially thankful for the many folks who have read and enjoyed my books.

I do believe it's important to acknowledge how the

old west represents the brave pioneering spirit of settlers that met the challenges and transcended mere survival to enable America to achieve exceptional growth. The settling of the American frontier west is replete with tales of leveraging freedom for individual achievement. I hope you'll agree that reliving our past—even through history-based fiction—often has the effect of pointing the way to an ever-brighter future. Might we be up to it? I hope that the inspiration I've drawn from my having walked the very earth my characters have trodden coupled with my extensive historical research will enable readers to fully experience the grit, adventure, and passion of my characters while sensing aromas of gunsmoke, trail dust, leather, and bluebonnets.

Thanks kindly to all of you and please do enjoy *Longhorns North: Jack's Great Trail Drive*.

ABOUT THE AUTHOR

Award-winning author Mark Greathouse's love for the western genre draws upon his deep family roots and love of the outdoors honed from teen years hiking the Appalachian Trail and family travels across America's frontier. Greathouse began writing full time after a successful career as a business executive and later as an entrepreneurial investor and advisor. His service as president of several business and community nonprofits led to their extraordinary growth. He holds a BA in English and MBA in marketing. Greathouse donates time and books annually to support wounded military warriors. He was a Boy Scout leader (Eagle Scout) and served on a local school board.

A member of Western Writers of America and the Wild West History Association, he also contributes articles on the history of America's west to western-themed magazines. Greathouse was recognized as a 2024 Finalist in western genre by the American Literary Book Awards for his sixth Tumbleweed Saga, *Nueces Truth: Texans Face War's Realities*.

His *Frontier Chronicles,* a series of western novels aimed at adventure-minded teens and young adults while weaving a Christian message within their fabric, are aimed at lighting fires of truth, faith, hope, and life purpose in the bellies of today's teen boys and girls. Just as seeds must be sown to reap the harvest, so the seeds of faith must be planted to raise tomorrow's men and women.

GLOSSARY

DEFINITIONS

Big Father—All-powerful Comanche deity.

Bota bag—A canteen fashioned from leather and popular among Indians, mountain men, and many travelers of the western frontier.

Life debt—A cultural phenomenon in which someone whose life is saved or spared by another becomes indebted or in some way connected to their savior.

Pemmican—Lean dried strips of meat pounded into a paste, mixed with fat and berries, and then pressed into small cakes.

Possibles bag—A leather or canvas sack carried by cowboys and containing essentials like soap, matches, bandages, extra spur, smoke makings, and playing cards

Remuda—A herd of horses frequently used on trail drives and by Plains Indians.

Shaman—Comanche medicine man.

Teepee—An enclosed conical transportable shelter constructed of long poles and buffalo hides with a vent at the top to permit smoke to escape.

COMANCHE TRANSLATIONS

Aitu—Not good

Ana o'a hi'it—Phrase for *desire to eat*

Ap—Father

Aruka—Deer

Eetu—Bow

Ekakwitsɨbaitɨ—Lightning

Ekapitu—Red

Eekạsahpana paraiboo—Army officer (soldier chief)

Hawokatu—Hollow, loose

Hoikwa—Hunt, look for prey

Isa—Wolf

Isa wasu—Poison

Kaahaniitu—deceive, cheat

Kahni—Life

Kamakuna—Loved one

Kee—No

Kobe—Wild Horse

Kohto—Build a fire

Kooitu—Die

Kutseena—Coyote

Kwakuru—Defeat someone

Nahuu—Knife

Natsuitu—Strong

Numu—Teepee

Numunuu—Referring to the members of the Comanche tribes. Literally: people.

Ohapitu—Yellow

Paa—Water

Paaka—Arrow

Peeka—Kill

Pia—Mother

Pia huutsuu—Bald eagle

Pia wa'óo—Comanche words for mountain lion, puma, or cougar.

Pihi—Heart

Puuka—Horse

Sunipu—Medicine (as in strong medicine)

Suumaru—Ten

Taa Narumi—Master/God

Tabu—Coward

Tamu—Rabbit

Tasiwoo—Buffalo

Tenahpu—Man

Tomoobi—Sky

Tosa—White man or woman

Tosaabitu—White

Tumah tuyai—After life

Tuhibitu—Black

Tumhyokenu—Believe, trust

Tu Taiboo—Black man

Umaru—Rain

Unha haksi nahniaka—Phrase for *what's your name?*

Wa'ipu—Woman

Wasápe—Bear

Wutsutsuki—Rattlesnake

LAKOTA TRANSLATIONS

Ate – Father

Ayústan – Abandon, retreat, leave

Igmuwatogla – Mountain lion

Isan – Knife

Iya Tate - Wind

Iyaya – Go, leave

Jiji – Light hair

Katá – Kill

Kize - Fight

Maka – The earth and grandmother of all things

Mato - Bear

Mini – Water

Nagi – The spirit that has never been a man

Niya – Ghost

Oyate – The people or nation

Sapa - Black

Ska - White

Scan – Sky

Sunkmanitu tanka - Wolf

Takuwe - Why

Tanka – Wolf

Tatanka – The great beast (patron of health, ceremonies, provision)

Unk – Created by Maka; embodies all evil beings

Unktehi – One who kills

Wakan tanka – God (monotheistic)

Wamaka nagi – Animal spirit

Wanbli – Eagle

Wani – Four winds (weather)

Wasake – Strong

Wash tay – Good

Wasichus – White man

Wasna – Pemmican

Wi – The sun (chief of all gods)

Wica – Complete man

Wicasa – Man (gender)

Wicasa wakan – Shaman

Winyan – Woman

Wowahwa - Peace

Zuzeca – Snake